Other
People's Weddings

Also by Noah Hawley

A Conspiracy of Tall Men

Noah Hawley

Other
People's Weddings

St. Martin's Griffin ♏ New York

www.stmartins.com

Library of Congress Cataloging-in-Publication Data

Hawley, Noah.
    Other people's weddings / Noah Hawley.
       p. cm.
   ISBN 0-312-32273-9 (hc)
   ISBN 0-312-32274-7 (pbk)
   EAN 978-0312-32274-8
   1. Wedding photography—Fiction. 2. Commitment (Psychology)—
Fiction. 3. Women photographers—Fiction. 4. Weddings—Fiction.
I. Title.

   PS3558.A8234O74 2004
   813'.54—dc22   2004040568

First St. Martin's Griffin Edition: June 2005

10 9 8 7 6 5 4 3 2 1

To my parents, inseparable to this day

Once upon a time . . .

Other
People's Weddings

1

Byron Alexander has a giant head. Seen through the wide-angle lens of my Leica it looks like a lie, a doctored photograph clipped from a supermarket tabloid: LOCAL MAN'S HEAD SWELLS, PREPARES TO BURST. He is wearing a black tuxedo, a vintage bow tie. His bride-to-be, Candy Newell, is standing beside him in front of a trickling stream, ready to commit to richer and poorer, sickness and health. Her cheeks are like shiny red apples. It is a startlingly blue August day and hot, stifling. We are shooting the formal portraits before the wedding begins, the glamour shots, the mantelpiece collection. I am using a high-speed black-and-white film and a small white bounce to light their faces. A half dozen in-laws are standing by, ready to slip into the shot, ready to tamp down their lipstick and suck in their bellies. Everyone is giddy, tense. Somewhere on the other side of the gazebo a crowd is building, row after row of relatives in formal dress praying for a breeze. I check my watch. It's important to stay on schedule, but at the same time, you've got to keep things calm.

"Okay," I say. "Just a few more of the bride and groom, and then we'll open it up."

The Alexanders and the Newells huddle together in the shade of an elm tree. They're like a stage troop on opening night, nervous, rehearsing their lines. Candy's mother can't stop blinking. Byron is smiling like a man who's suddenly found himself answering questions at a press conference on the moon.

"Try to relax," I tell him.

Lowering my camera, I squint. His head is just too big. It makes him look closer than Candy. I pause for a minute, considering my options. Beside me, my assistant Jerome loads film into a medium format camera. He's twenty-five, with good hands and a discerning eye. Jerome grew up on television shows where everyone was acerbic and cavalier, and so this is how he has become. A venal wit.

"Is it possible to sweat to death?" he says.

I gaze at Byron and think about changing lenses. This is the second wedding I've photographed today. The fourth this weekend. At ten A.M. I shot the Davidsons, Glenda and Ed, trial lawyers with normal size heads, who read passages from famous children's books and released doves into the dewy blue sky. In three hours I'm supposed to be at the First Methodist Church on Baxter Avenue to photograph the Gilhooly affair. I am a thirty-six-year-old woman who spends her days cataloguing other people's promises.

Jerome crosses over to Byron, takes a light reading. He holds the meter up to Byron's face, frowns. All that pale skin set against the deep black of the tuxedo makes it hard to find the proper setting. Jerome comes over, shows me the meter.

"Maybe a filter," he whispers, "to cut the glare."

"Let's try it," I say, smiling at the family.

Don't you worry, I'm saying.

Everything is perfect.

Byron clears his throat. He tells me they met in the city. Candy was the girl in the coffee shop. The one he couldn't let go. So he chased after her and introduced himself breathlessly. Shy, stammering.

"I was desperate," he says, putting his hand on Candy's shoulder.

"Desperate," she agrees, "but cute."

Candy lifts the train of her long, white wedding gown and smiles for the camera. This is her moment to shine and she's not about to let it go to waste. She is a beautiful woman, dark brown hair curled and piled above her blue-eyed face. Her dress is a masterpiece of seductive purity, long-sleeved, low-cut, the back open all the way down to her waist. Her skin is smooth, unblemished. Compared to Byron she has a head like the period after a word that ends in O.

"How do we look?" she wants to know.

I reach out and take her arm and gently position her in front of her fiancé. I do this so her head is closer to the lens, a little bit of forced perspective. It helps, but not enough. So I ask him to lean back a little and smile. Farther. Farther. This way at least she has a chance. This way his head is oversized, sure, but at a distance, like a hazy picture of bigfoot caught loping through the trees. This isn't just a job to me. These people aren't just a bunch of sappy rubes. No matter how the rest of their wedding goes, the ceremony, the reception, I want Byron and Candy to be able to look back at this moment and see perfection. Memories fade, but pictures last forever. What couples like Byron and Candy hire me for—and I am one of the top wedding photographers in Westchester county— is to create a myth, a fairy-tale document of true romance. The wedding they should have had. The wedding everyone should have.

"Kiss her," I say.

He leans in, eclipsing her face with his own.

Click.

Lately though, my heart hasn't been in it. I have trouble getting out of bed in the morning, trouble getting my energy up for the show. I still find them beautiful, all the weddings I shoot, but something is missing. Something has changed. These days, these slow, muggy, torpid days of late summer, it feels like love is no longer handmade. Like what was once a fragile, precision art, is now being mass produced on some kind of assembly line. Tux after tux, gown after gown. This is something I would never say out loud, certainly not to all of the brides and grooms I see, who think that what they've done is unique — to meet, fall in love, commit — when the truth is, it's everywhere you look. Like the world's oldest fad.

"Hold the bouquet higher," I say.

Candy smiles, hikes up the bust of her dress.

I raise my hand and say "Cheese." Everybody smiles.

I pull the trigger.

On the other side of the church, two hundred people in heavy formal wear have taken their seats on narrow, white folding chairs. They are an unsteady crowd that seems to undulate, swaying and dipping, as the legs of their chairs sink at unpredictable moments into the sprinkler-saturated sod.

"Okay," I say, checking my watch. "Let's get the parents in here."

Jerome moves forward to help position the family, creating a peacock spray of relatives that fans out behind the happy couple. This is the first wedding I've photographed where the bride and groom have their own Web site. The first where they've designed merchandise: Candy and Byron baseball caps, Candy and Byron coffee mugs, T-shirts that read, I WENT TO CANDY AND BYRON'S WEDDING AND ALL I GOT WAS THIS STINKING SHIRT. They're giving them away as gifts to thank people for coming.

"I thought it would be fun," Candy tells me as I snap her picture standing behind a spray of succulents. She's wearing a shade of eye shadow that is not quite blue and not quite green. Her teeth are as white as paper. She tells me she's a brand consultant for a large advertising agency.

"Give people something to remember you by," she says. "Because, I don't know about you, but all these weddings tend to blur together. Am I right?"

I tell her she has no idea. The fact is, in thirteen years I've photographed over eleven hundred weddings. That's twenty-two hundred parents, forty-four hundred grandparents, over three hundred thousand roles of film. I am the queen of the candid exposure, slipping through the crowd like a shadow, catching people at their best and worst. My neck muscles bulge from sixty thousand working hours logged with two cameras around my neck.

A single woman surrounded by togetherness.

Posing for the camera, Candy seems relaxed, confident, and I want to ask her how she does it. I want to ask her how she can be so certain that Byron is the one. Isn't she terrified? Doesn't she know how hard it is to make these things work? The questions percolate inside my head but I keep them to myself. Voicing them would be unprofessional, rude. Instead, I lift my camera and take her picture. This is my way of staying out of things, of keeping my distance. I look at people through a mirror and two sheets of glass, calculating angles, measuring light. I tell her how beautiful she looks, which she does, and what a great couple they make. And as far as I can tell it's true. They kiss easily. Their eyes lock. They have that wedding day glow.

And, as I do at every wedding, I cross my fingers and silently wish them luck.

The ceremony begins. The band strikes up, playing a wedding march written especially for Byron and Candy by a downtown composer. Part John Cage, part Celine Dion. There is a vibraphone, a bassoon. Candy's father comes over and takes her arm. Seeing her smile up at him, her eyes already filling with tears, I switch to autowind and fall into step behind them, capturing the action as it happens. I am looking for the moments between the moments, the gesture unfinished, the shy, private smile. When they reach the altar, shaded by a canopy of maple leaves, Candy reaches out to take Byron's hand. He is smiling, and she is smiling. They look exhilarated, terrified. Behind us the crowd seems to open up, readying itself, relaxing under the familiar weight of ritual.

"Ten bucks says they're divorced in a year," says Jerome.

I glare at him and point. He takes his camera and works his way east, hunting for reaction shots. I turn back to the bride and groom. They seem to glow in the summer heat, their outlines wavy, fluctuating, like a mirage. They've spent tens of thousands of dollars to show the world they're serious. Chosen the most glorious vistas, hired the most expensive caterers. They're serving monkfish and lamb tonight because they want people to understand the gravity of their choice. This union isn't some fly-by-night operation. Everything in their lives has led them to this moment. Everything that comes after will stem from this event. It is like the symbol for infinity, with the wedding fixed squarely at the point where the figure eight connects.

Where all lines cross.

The priest steps forward. He is wearing Candy and Byron cuff links; a picture of Byron on the left, Candy on the right. He is an old man, somebody's uncle or cousin.

"Dearly beloved," he says. "We are gathered here today."

I lift my Nikon and frame the three of them as Byron steps forward and takes Candy's hands. He swears that before he met Candy he was a sleepwalker. He says meeting Candy was like waking up, and now he lives in a world of constant daylight. Listening to him, Candy cries so hard her cheeks run black and spit bubbles form between her lips. In the back of the crowd I float right and shoot him over her shoulder, giving her time to pull herself together, concentrating on focus and composition, aperture and film speed.

Later, in the darkroom, I study the faces. Six weddings in one weekend. Already they're starting to run together in my mind. So many suits and dresses. So many happily-ever-afters. I crop out the faces of scowling fathers and disapproving mothers. I excise the frozen looks of doubt and regret I. zoom in on the great flowering centerpieces. Everything has to be perfect, so I highlight the looks of pride from family and friends. I print only the biggest smiles. All the pictures where the bride's boob pops out of her dress I cast aside, the photos of the groom caught making advances on members of the bridal party. There can be no mixed messages, no foreshadowing of the difficulties to come. The unfaithful urges and second thoughts. The loneliness. The boredom. Trouble with the children. Sickness, poverty, struggle, change. In the darkroom I study the happy faces looking for the secret.

Love.

I can't help myself. The allure is overwhelming: the mystique of true romance. Despite the numbers, against my better judgment, I find myself wanting to believe.

Till death do us part.

Because in this moment, the moment of matrimony, where everyone has gathered, where the priest or the rabbi or the imam or the ship's captain has raised his hand, has asked the question, and everyone leans forward in their chair, in that moment of *Do you, Will you, Could you* the future is a hot green meadow that rolls on forever. And I step up and capture it in just under one-five-hundredth of a second.

I now pronounce you man and wife.

You may kiss the bride.

2

W e've been friends just forever," says Shelly.

"Forever," Roger repeats.

He reaches over, touches her shoulder. I meet the waiter's eye, lift my empty glass, then turn back to them smiling. If love stories were candy bars I'd weigh a thousand pounds by now. A pimply, obese diabetic. I should stop listening, I know, but I can't. I'm addicted.

"Forever," I say.

"Roger used to drive me home after parties. In high school. He was always very chivalrous."

Shelly is nineteen. Roger is twenty-five. It's the first marriage for both of them, and they want everything to be just right. We are sitting in a restaurant in Hastings-on-Hudson, New York, the sleepy, little river town where I live. I'm showing them my portfolio, and just the thought of marriage, the glimpse of their own wedding in these photos is making Shelly cry.

"I've dreamed about this since I was a little girl," she says. "This moment. The flowers. The dress."

I nod encouragingly. Someone once told me that inside every act of history, every act of heroism, is an act of love. Requited, unrequited. The stories offer something intangible: hope, the promise of a new beginning. That's why on Sunday people gravitate toward the engagement announcements in the newspaper. Those and the police reports. Love and crime, the bedrock of modern living. Both are acts of transgression. What were Romeo and Juliet, after all, if not criminals? A boy and girl stealing time, breaking laws. Our own stories can feel mundane after a while, but other people's love lives are like fortune cookies, full of intrigue, mystery.

Roger is impossibly handsome; high cheek bones, blue eyes. He's a first-year associate at a big law firm. Shelly is his best friend's sister. He's been in love with her since she was fifteen.

"Not that we haven't had our ups and downs," he says.

"The whole long distance thing," she says.

"But the important thing is you made it," I say. "You're here."

They smile, squeeze each other's hand. I sip my wine.

"Have you thought about whether you'd like black-and-white or color?"

"Oh, definitely black-and-white," says Shelly. "There's something, I don't know, classier about it. Don't you think?"

I look at Roger. He is smiling benignly. For him these minor details are best left up to his fiancée and her mother. All the time these women put in, the endless hours on the phone, days spent poring over bridal magazines, drawing up lists. He learned early on that there's no point in fighting. Weddings are the biggest relationship killers out there. If you can survive the wedding, they say, the rest is a piece of cake.

"Just tell me where and when," he says, "and I'll be there."

I show them photos from the Bliestock wedding, scores of white chairs set against a jagged cliff edge, everything falling away into the ocean. During the ceremony the bride's veil flew off her head and as one we watched it sail out over the surf, growing smaller and brighter, like a seagull strafing the waves.

"What's this?" says Shelly, pointing to the floating white circle, like a second sun glaring in the sky.

I tell her the story.

"That's what I want," she says. "Something magical to happen."

I ask if they've got a band yet.

"Roger's dad plays in a ragtime band," she says.

"Great," I say, thinking, *Ragtime?*

"We're getting a DJ too," says Roger.

"People like to dance," says Shelly. "My friends."

"And do you want to take the formal pictures before or after the ceremony?" I ask.

They look at each other.

"What do most people do?" Shelly asks.

"It depends. Do you want him to see you before the wedding?"

"No. Definitely not."

"Then after," I say.

They look relieved. Another hurdle overcome. Another decision made. Only fourteen hundred left to face.

"Are you married?" Shelly asks me.

The inevitable question.

"No."

Roger checks his watch. He told us earlier that he has an important filing this afternoon and he can't stay long.

"That's a pity," says Shelly. "All those weddings, but never one for you."

I sip my wine, knowing how reassuring it is when the person selling you your car drives the same one. What Shelly wants to hear is, *Yes, I've been married for twenty-one years. It's better than money, better than sex. You can stop worrying now. Relax. Eternal happiness is just around the corner.*

"It's better not to mix your work life and your personal life," I say.

I say this because right now their love is a bubble. A delicate, fragile prayer. I could pop it for them without breaking a sweat. Tell them horror stories about pregnant brides and drunken brides, and brides so nervous they vomit. I could describe all the brides I've seen left at the altar, the brides who couldn't stop crying, the brides who fainted, falling straight backward like toppling trees. I could tell them about grooms who shake like seismic needles, grooms with laryngitis, grooms who spot old girlfriends in the crowd and make a sudden break for the exit.

I look for the love in their eyes, and when I see it, I take a picture.

Wide angle, zoom, soft flash.

I could tell them this, but what's the point? All they want is to be happy. And for their sake, for all of our sakes, I hope they are.

"Well, I think it's beautiful," says Shelly. "Two people standing up in front of God and everyone, swearing to love each other."

I smile at her. The check comes. I start packing up my stuff.

"Just make sure I have all the details by Saturday," I say.

Shelly reaches out and grabs my arm. Her pupils are huge.

"You've seen a lot of couples, right? A lot of people who do this. Do you think—I mean—Do we look . . ."

The moment hangs there. I look them over. They're so young. They have such baby faces. Roger looks at his hands. He's not someone who's comfortable emoting in front of strangers.

"Shelly," he says.

But she's focused on me, and there's so much uncertainty in her eyes, fear. She's only nineteen after all. Not even old enough to drink. I reach down and pat her hand. The truth is I have no idea what makes a good marriage. Why some people stick and others don't. You could fill a book with the things I don't know about love.

"I'm sure you're gonna be very happy together," I say.

*   *   *

Later, I pick up three sets of contact sheets from the developer, sit on a bench in the park next to the strip mall, and look them over. The Goldstein wedding, Myrna and Phil. Five pages of color negatives. On the second page there's a shot of the groom kissing the bride under the chuppah. He has his hands on her shoulders. His head is tilted to the left, and you can see as clear as day that he has an erection, even on a print the size of a postage stamp.

"Oh Phil," I say, wondering if I can airbrush that out, wondering if anyone would notice if I left it in, or whether it would sit there in the photo album, a subliminal time bomb, till one day twenty years in the future they have the album out, showing the kids, and little Leroy points and says, "Daddy, what's that?" then the whole Disney mystique of their betrothal comes unglued.

I drive home, hang my keys on the fridge. My house is a small, two-bedroom Arts and Crafts structure that slants four inches to the right. The floors, the walls. Drop a basket of cherry tomatoes, watch them roll downhill. It's eight o'clock, the magic hour, pink light streaming through the windows. I go into the bathroom, start a bath, pad naked into the kitchen, get a glass of wine and a bag of popcorn. In the tub I stare at the cracks on the ceiling and think about my mother, who willed herself into oblivion after my father died. Who was so incomplete without him she was like the open quotation mark on a quote that never ends.

Madness.

I think about Shelly, about myself at nineteen, out of control, untamable. I try to imagine marriage under those circumstances, to imagine a love strong enough to make up for all my flaws. The water is scalding, steam rising in gusts, obscuring everything. I close my eyes, slip down under the surface, feeling the heat on my face, the pressure. I lay there, breathless, almost floating, until I'm out of air, and even then I don't come up. It seems impossible. My body might as well be a shipwreck: I open my eyes. Everything is wavering, water pressing against my pupils, and lying there, lungs burning, my life flashes before my eyes, but as it passes I realize it's not my life. It's other people's milestones. It's other people's joy. I emerge gasping, sit rattled, dripping.

Later, I stand in front of the mirror, steam obscuring my reflection. I put my palm against the glass, wipe myself into focus. *There you are*, I think. *What's left of you.* Because I'm thinner than I used to be. My legs are skinny, my arms. In the last year I've lost a full cup size. Standing there, I touch my body to make sure it still exists. My hair is a black rope hanging wetly between my shoulder blades. I have my father's height and my mother's eyes. I hate my knees. My teeth are straight on top, crooked on the bottom. Men have always complimented my ass, my eyes, my lips, which is what men do, cataloguing the parts they like, throwing the rest away.

Steam swirls in the bathroom and the patch I've wiped begins to fog again. I start to disappear. Just before I'm completely gone I lean forward and kiss my reflection on the lips, feeling the cool damp glass on my mouth. It is a quick kiss and afterward I feel silly for doing it, but in the moment it feels kind. Like kissing a long lost friend, like making up after a fight.

A kiss for luck.

At ten o'clock my sister calls. She wants to talk about her boyfriend.

"I'm off duty," I say. "The doctor isn't in."

"Hah-hah," she says. "Always with the jokes. This is serious. I think he's cheating on me."

"How can you tell?"

"His underwear is—"

"I don't—"

"Crusty."

"Lisa," I say.

"In the front."

"No. Stop."

"I think he's having an affair with the girl at the copy shop."

I take the phone from my ear, still dizzy from the tub, feeling like the straight man in a comedy troupe, the gullible sidekick.

"Why?"

"Because lately he's been making a lot of copies."

A breeze comes over me. I consider hanging up, unplugging the phone, going to bed. But Lisa's the only family I have left, so I say:

"He's a graphic designer. That's his . . ."

I hear the click of her lighter as she lights a cigarette, the quick exhale. This is Lisa's M.O., to find a man of questionable character and then investigate him, steam open his mail, eavesdrop on his phone calls, tail him if necessary. She is the Philip Marlowe of the dating world, always looking for evidence of some greater conspiracy.

"I don't know what I'm getting so upset about," she says. "It's not like I love him."

"Then why are you doing this?"

"Because who wants to be alone? I figure I stick this out till something better comes along."

I take the phone out onto the porch and sit on the swing. The air is chilly, but I prefer talking outside, the anonymity of it. In the darkness, fireflies blink in time with the sounds of a distant car alarm.

"You're not a role model for anyone," I tell her.

"Christ, who ever said I was? Not that you're one to talk."

I don't argue with her, and she rants for ten more minutes without taking a breath, cataloguing David's misdeeds. The long trips to the Laundromat, the early morning "meetings." I'm used to it by now, letting people talk. It comes with the territory. You lift a camera, ask for honesty, and you get more than your share. People will tell you their whole life story if you exhibit the least bit of interest.

"What about you?" says Lisa, finally winded. "Any boys on the horizon?"

I play with the phone cord, watch a pack of kids on bikes race by in the moonlight. The cards in the spokes of their wheels make a sound like zippers.

"At my age you have to call them men," I say.

She inhales a plume of smoke, lets it out.

"But that doesn't mean they are," she tells me.

3

People do a lot of terrible things in the name of personal growth."

Eric is sitting at his kitchen table. He lives in a condominium on the south side of town, a bachelor pad with framed posters of Vargas girls on the walls and eleven kinds of cereal in the cupboards. It's next to the freeway, across from the hospital, over a bar. I have my Leica out and I'm taking pictures—of the furnishings, the decor, of Eric.

He sits there uncomfortably, not knowing what to do with his hands. I ask him about the divorce.

"She said I was holding her back," he says. "That we were supposed to be growing together, but instead we were growing apart."

I focus on his eyes. There is a smell in the air, a mixture of marijuana and spaghetti sauce. The carpet is wall-to-wall brown. There's a big screen TV in the living room, a La-Z-Boy chair. A

Fender Stratocaster leans against the stereo, unclipped strings jutting from its head like porcupine quills. Looking at the scene through my viewfinder I wonder, *Why do men always revert to adolescence after their wives leave?*

Eric says he was surprised to hear from me last week. I tell him I'm just following up. That I want to know what happened. And not just to him. Where are all the people I've seen married? What happened to all those vows? These are questions that came to me at breakfast one morning, dangling variables, like a thousand rolls of undeveloped film. So I started making phone calls. And a lot of the couples were still together, still happy, with children and puppies and manicured hedges. They too, seemed surprised to hear from me, fumbling to place the name, voices suspicious as if I were calling to sell them a time-share. But when I explained, when I told them I was their wedding photographer, that I wanted to know how they were, how it was working out, they seemed really touched. And when I offered to come by and take a follow-up photo at no extra cost, they jumped at the opportunity. They were tickled by the romance of it.

At home I went through all my old ledgers and bills. The Johnsons, the Bradleys, the Hughes. Sandy Berman who wore pink taffeta and Stanley Gaddis who got married in a wetsuit. But sometimes when I called, the number had been disconnected. Sometimes the bride was listed under her maiden name again and the groom had left town. Sometimes it took weeks to track them down, and when I did, they didn't want to talk to me, didn't want to be reminded. But I'm persistent. I kept calling.

"Don't you think your divorce is just as important as your wedding?" I'd say. "Don't you want to show that you've survived it, that you're still standing?"

Not everyone agrees to be photographed, but some do, and so for the last few months I've been traveling the state, taking pictures of estranged couples, separated couples.

I am a wedding photographer.

Photographing divorce.

Eric sits at his oval kitchen table. The overhead light is tungsten and will give the pictures a jaded, yellow glow. His hair falls over his collar, into his eyes. He stares at the lens with defiance. Jeannine walked out on him after seven years of marriage, he tells me. She lives in Tucson now, selling software. Eric works for a local car stereo installation outfit. He is thirty-five years old.

"Old enough to know better," he says. "Old enough not to make the same mistake twice."

I ask him if he still has his wedding pictures around. He rummages through the closet, brings out a worn leather album. We sit on the sofa looking at photographs. Jeannine was his college sweetheart. They got married when they were twenty-six. Looking at the pictures I am reminded of myself when I was younger. I think about the year these were taken: 1991. Wedding photography was just a sideline for me then. A way to pay the bills. I had dreams of being a real photographer, traveling the world, dreams of gallery shows and European collectors. At every wedding I worked, I cried when the couples said "I do," cried at the beauty of their love, their faith and commitment. The pictures I took have a candied, haloed quality to them, like the pictures you might take of angels or prophets, worshipfully, from low angles.

Eric puts his hand on my leg. He tells me he's been so lonely. No one wants to date a thirty-five-year-old car stereo installer.

"You're so pretty," he says.

"Eric," I say.

He cocks his head, trying to meet my eyes, moves his hand up onto my thigh. He's not a bad-looking guy. There is a certain wide-eyed, wounded quality to him that I respond to. A feral hunger. I sit there mute, motionless, trying to figure out what to say, what to do. The problem is, I don't know what I want. When you've been single long enough, the rules you've made for yourself stop making sense, all the hard-fought rationales you invented in your youth. The words lose their meaning. No casual sex, but why again? What am I waiting for? Because sometimes I just want to feel connected, grounded. Not to be the kind of person who feels alone even when surrounded by other people. In those moments, I worry that life is like a big game of musical chairs where the goal is not to be left standing alone when the music stops. Then I think, maybe the music stopped a long time ago and I didn't notice. I freeze, cock my head, listening.

Eric moves closer. He probably hasn't had this kind of attention in a while. Someone asking him questions, taking his picture, showing interest. I want to tell him he's not the only one. That he's the third divorced man to put the moves on me this month. I want to tell him that sometimes the women try to sleep with me too. A glass of wine, touching my hair. I'm a connection to a happier time. Maybe they think that by conquering me they can get back some of that happiness. Fight off some of that fear.

Or maybe they just wanna get laid.

He leans over, kisses my neck. I close my eyes. It would be so easy to give in to it. To be the bandage, the balm. He kisses my cheek, my ear. I push him away, stand, trying to pull myself together. He sits there looking injured.

"Don't you ever get lonely?" he wants to know.

I fiddle with the aperture dial on my camera, focusing on the floor.

"This isn't about me," I say.

I say this because my own heartbreak is uninteresting to me. It's a rock I push around, a dead body handcuffed to my wrist. I choose not to acknowledge it. Not to empower it. I prefer silence.

He leans back, rests his head against the wall, and stares at the ceiling for a long time. I lift my camera. Light spills through the curtains, casting one side of his face in brightness, the other in shadow. Looking at him framed by narrow black borders I feel safer. Hidden.

"Sometimes," he says. "I don't even feel part of the world. I walk around, and it's like I'm invisible. I try to talk to people, strangers, and they don't seem to hear me. I talk louder, but that just makes it worse. Eventually, I'll push someone, you know, shove 'em, just to get them to see me."

I focus on his silhouette, a slice of sun across his belly. I can't let myself get drawn in by him. Can't afford to fool myself into thinking he could help, could make everything better.

"I see you," I say.

Click.

He reaches out to try and touch me again. I step back.

"Where's the bathroom?" I ask.

He offers to show me. Something in his voice tells me it's next to the bedroom.

"Never mind," I tell him. "I'll find it."

When I come out he's rolling a joint. He lights it, inhales, offers it to me. I shake my head, start to pack my bags. Through the open window I can hear the sound of traffic rolling by on the interstate. The sound of loneliness, of hundreds of people's lives passing you by.

"I never thought it would be like this," he says.

"No one ever does," I tell him.

4

Then there was the couple who got married in Yonkers. The bride wore ecru. When it was time to cut the cake the groom said, "I'm not in a cake cutting mood." Later he went to find his wife to tell her he was ready. And she said, "I cut it without you." They lasted eleven months.

I photographed Stacey and Tim's wedding in color. They got married at Temple Emmanuel in 1995. He wore a tuxedo with tails and had three groomsmen. The bridesmaids wore lavender dresses that made their arms look flabby. The couple spent months writing their own vows. At the wedding, a parade of friends stood and read poems comparing their union to a flower. The band played "Brick House (She's a)" and "Play That Funky Music White Boy." Three years later Stacey had a miscarriage. For five months she stopped bathing, stopped getting out of bed. Tim started going for long drives at night and closing his eyes in the face of oncoming traffic. Now he lives in a rented duplex in Revere, and she's married to a landscape architect. And looking back they tell themselves that people change. Their priorities. Who they are. What they want.

Three towns over, Jennifer was convinced that Tony would change, but the only thing that changed after they got married was that he started wearing pants a lot less. He'd come home from work and strip down to his boxers, take a box of Wheat Thins out of the cupboard, open up a beer. He watched TV in his underwear. He ate dinner in his underwear. It got to the point where Jennifer had to bribe him with sex to get him to put his clothes *on*. They never went to the opera. They never ate at fancy restaurants. Meanwhile, she was taking classes, reading books, trying to better herself. You can see where this is going. Everyone could. It was like a slow-motion train wreck. Day after day her patience stretched thinner, like the waistband of his boxer shorts, until one day she went to her mother's house and never came home. And nine months later, they were divorced, and the whole thing seemed like a dream, a detour, like *Did that just happen?* Because sometimes in life you find yourself on a strange road in a strange town suffering from shock, from some kind of posttraumatic stress disorder, and you ask yourself, *How did I get here?*

How did I get here?

Recently, I've become skittish about romance. Gun shy, you could say. *Who me?* is the first thought that comes to mind when a man's eyes linger, when a probing look is given, an awkward first line. I find myself avoiding tight spaces, staying out of corners and doorways. Whenever I enter a room, I look for the exits. Door, door, window. It's a slippery slope. You meet a boy, go out on a date. The first kiss comes, and suddenly the ground is slanting, falling away like those stairs that turn into a ramp in vampire movies. And before you know it, you're in a relationship with this total stranger. And there he is smiling at you over breakfast, kissing you with his morning breath, gasping his orgasms into your ear. Practically speaking, love makes me sweat. At night, under the covers, both our bodies kicking out all those BTUs. By three A.M., it's like an oven in there, and I fidget and kick, my pillow soaked through, the silhouette of my body bleeding into the sheets like the chalk outline of a murder victim scratched onto the sidewalk.

Didn't it used to be easier? I wonder. Easier just to be happy. To meet someone, date, feel good about yourself? Or maybe that's the problem. Maybe it's too easy. Too easy to get involved, too easy to fall into what? Love? What feels like love at least or lust or like. And then it fades, for you, for him, or someone cheats, or someone gets bored, or turns out to be callous, needy, insane, and you're back on the street, washing away the chalk outline, taking a deep breath, preparing to start all over again.

At night I sit in the darkroom and study the pictures. All those smiling couples. All that happiness, that joy, that promise. How is it possible that they've done it? Figured it out. How is it possible that they're not afraid? That she doesn't sweat like a heifer every time he sleeps over. That she doesn't hang up on him, then change her phone number at the first sign of trouble. How can this woman commit to more than just a long weekend? Maybe love can work. Maybe men and women are meant to be together.

But then I make a few phone calls. I tally up the results, and suddenly it doesn't seem so clear-cut anymore. Fifty percent. Fifty percent of marriages end in divorce. You might as well flip a coin, spin a bottle. That's what you're doing anyway. Gambling. Taking your life in your hands. Because people change, or they don't change enough. Because novelty turns to routine and routine to boredom. Because people's eyes wander. Because no matter what you say, you can always change your mind later.

And so Kevin had an affair. Linda and Ted grew apart. Jeannine felt like Eric was holding her back. Ferdinand traveled too much. Debbie drank vodka at lunch. Heywood had anxiety attacks. Phil stopped making the effort. Melanie let her body go after the baby was born. Ned succumbed to nostalgia. Frank turned out to be violent. Tanya realized she was gay. Lester got bored. Sarah and Chris tried having an open relationship, then spent a lot of time in therapy, then had a baby to bring them closer together, then separated, then got back together, then fought constantly and separated again. And in the end, the divorce was a relief, like the thunderhead that breaks the storm and suddenly the air is cooler and you can think clearly again.

Because in the end a picture is just a picture. A frozen moment in time. But people have to go on with their lives, have to live every moment, connecting the future to the past.

In the pictures I take the couples will always be married.

In real life the future's not so clear.

5

The support group meets once a week in the basement of the unitarian church. There are doughnuts and coffee. People wear name tags. Everyone looks sickly in the fluorescent glare. I use a filter to compensate, but not too much. I like the mystique of desperation that cold green light can give a profile — the harsh, unflattering reality, the circles under the eyes. Because these people aren't sleeping. Because they don't eat enough, or they eat too much. Because lost people should look lost, not glamorous the way Hollywood would have us believe. I exaggerate their discomfort by shooting them head on, using a telephoto lens. The corners of the room distort, the dirty cellar windows. Upstairs they worship God in nontraditional ways. Down here people tunnel up toward the light.

Howard looks at the ceiling. He says, "I guess forever doesn't last as long as it used to."

Morgan lights a cigarette, yawns smoke. She is an investment banker. Her husband divorced her because he said she worked too much. He'd thought about it and decided he wanted a wife who would stay home, pop out the kids. Since he left, she's slept with seventeen men, most without protection. She details her orgasms the way some men talk about hunting trips—the warm beer, the hours spent hiding in duck blinds, cramped, predatory, waiting in ambush. When she talks, I can almost imagine the heads mounted to her wall, the notches on the bedpost.

I drift the fringes, shooting the confessional atmosphere, the group hugs, pausing only to change rolls. Afterward, I ask new members to sign waivers. I tell them the pictures will be exhibited in galleries or maybe collected into a book. I assure them I'm not a journalist, that this isn't about exposing their failures, but cataloguing their rebirth. Art, in other words.

Today Sarah says "No," she's not going to say a word until they hear from me. Until I give them something. Otherwise, it's like I'm just lurking in the shadows, judging them.

"Come on," she says, "tell us about *you*. Let us help *you*."

I shrink backward, raising my camera.

"I don't think that's such a good idea," I say. "There's a journalistic distance that's necessary in these endeavors. A level of scientific detachment."

I say this, and I don't know what it means. It's just words coming out of my mouth.

"Bullshit," says Sam. "Spill."

I stand there dumbly. I consider telling them I'm terrified of speaking in front of groups, of saying personal things to strangers. How it makes me uncomfortable to be the center of attention. That and a thousand other phobias I'm ready to claim if push comes to shove. Instead, I fidget with my camera, looking at the floor.

Finally, Abigail breaks the silence. Thank God for the narcissists.

"My mother just told me about her first divorce," Abigail tells us. "It was 1958. She married a painter. And it became, you know, clear really quickly that he wasn't the one. Not right. So she took the bus to Texas and over the border. 1958. She's maybe nineteen at the time, doesn't speak a word of Spanish. But she found a Mexican court and filed for divorce. Can you imagine? And she gets up in front of the judge, and he looks over her petition, stamps it. And as she turns to go he stops her and says, 'Better luck next time.'"

Better luck next time.

I move slowly, repositioning myself, not wanting to redraw attention. Sam takes a handkerchief from his pocket, blows his nose. I lift my camera, focus. When you're taking someone's picture, you look for the unguarded moments. You hunt for a real expression, for honesty. No poses, no phony token smiles. We've all been trained to mug for the camera, to put on our best face. Often I pretend to capture those moments. I line up my shot. The subject makes themselves picture friendly. Crinkling eyes. Corners of the mouth turned up. Coy glance.

I open my mouth. "Click," I say.

The smile falls away, the mask. Some measure of truth returns to the face.

This is when I strike.

Natalie says, "You have to work on a marriage. I know that now."

Her eyes are red-rimmed, boggy. She is still in the manic phase, the I-can-beat-this phase. *I can keep it together.* Her husband left six weeks ago, and since then she's been a dynamo of human efficiency, every spare moment filled, every waking second. Her refrigerator is anchored with lists. Things to do. Her apartment is immaculate. Her underwear is folded down to business card proportions. She treats her grief as a problem of logic. "I just need some time," she says. "A vacation. Maybe a little fling. Before you know it—good as new."

She is sitting in a ghetto of chain-smoking women. Anorexic, middle-aged ladies who may be addicted to speed. They go bar-hopping together on Friday nights, put on their makeup and their fuck-me shoes, and hit the clubs. From across the room, packs of men check them out. With their expensive handbags and their push-up bras, they look like a million bucks, Like the exception to the rule about women you pick up in bars. But close up, there is an air of desperation about them. They laugh too loudly, drink too fast. They have their eyebrows waxed weekly, nails done. They do forty minutes a day on the StairMaster. Their bikini areas are as hairless as the sun. The men buy them drinks, looking for some-thing fast. They think women over forty should be grateful for any-thing. By midnight, they are back at her place, fumbling in the dark. The men rarely last until morning. They vanish in the night like a fever breaking. And all that's left is the smell of sex in the air, a wet spot on the sheets, a used condom floating in the toilet.

I crouch and frame Natalie against a giant wooden crucifix and I think, *What about the sin of abandonment, the sin of falling out of love, the sin of not putting the toilet seat down, of growing apart, the sin of drinking too much, of bickering over every little thing? What about the sin of a thousand cold shoulders?*

Harvey comes up to me during the coffee break.

"Tell me about your father," he says.

I look at him, the second chin, the comb-over.

"What?" I say.

He hikes up his pants, pours himself a cup of watery coffee.

"That's what it always comes down to for you ladies, isn't it? *Daddy didn't love me, or he loved me too much, or there was no daddy.*"

"I think you have me confused with somebody else," I say. "I'm the—"

"Photographer," he says. "I know. God forbid you should open up in here. God forbid you should act like part of the group. What I'm saying is, you wouldn't have come if everything was hunky-dory. If life was just so la-di-da. You'd be off living your happy life with your happy family instead of here with us freaks."

He raises his eyebrows, as if to say, *Am I right?* I shoot him from the hip, angling the camera up toward his face. When I get the print back, the white Styrofoam cup will loom in the foreground, Harvey's doughnut-hole head leering at me off camera in the distance, in shadow.

"You're not listening," I tell him. "This is about uncovering something hidden, something powerful and real in our tragedies. It has nothing to do with my life."

"Right," he says, and winks.

I take my coffee and retreat to the other side of the room. I think about a photograph I keep in my living room. A picture of my parents lying on an old horse blanket in the middle of an open field. It's a snapshot taken before I was born, the Kodak print browning, sunflowers turning green. Before marriage, before children, back when everything was new. One of my first projects when I decided to become a photographer was to recreate all the old family snapshots. To restage them. I was in college at the time and I went to the drama department, put up a notice. I recruited two actors of my parents' shape and size, found an old horse blanket at a thrift store, drove down to an open field. I had the snapshot in my camera bag for reference. The actors changed into their costumes — beaded sixties vests and ash-blackened blue jeans. They lay on the ground. I coaxed them to the relax, look at each other. I wanted to recreate the moment so I could understand it.

"Look at him, his eyes," I told my actress. "You love him. You met him ten days ago, but already you know. He smokes hand-rolled cigarettes. He wants to be a poet. When you kiss, his mustache tickles your lips."

I took pictures of actors pretending to be my parents, because even then I wasn't so sure. Even then I needed help believing. I took pictures of actors pretending to be my parents, because it's our parents who first teach us about love. They're our first model of understanding. And now, fifteen years later, I look around at all these abandoned people kvetching to the ether and wonder how many of them have children. What kind of model are they making for their kids? What jaded impression of love?

I fade left toward the exit, zooming in on fresh faces. The uninitiated. The newcomers, who always sit by the door, looking nervous, tentative. They don't like to admit that this is what their lives have come down to, opening up to strangers in subterranean settings. In my pictures, they always look like rookies, fresh meat jumping from low-flying helicopters at the front lines of foreign wars. The old timers eye them hungrily, eager for new stories of disillusionment and heartbreak. Eager to offer advice, to disseminate clichés. *Just take it one day at a time. It was probably for the best. You're better off without him.* During the coffee break, male veterans approach the freshman women, handing out phone numbers, offering words of consolation, understanding. "Maybe we should get a drink later," they say. "Talk it over."

Click.

Their photographs hang from clotheslines covering my apartment, drying. I eat breakfast with them every morning, drink coffee looking up at their faces. In pictures there are no words, no stories. Just expressions. Gestures. All their cleverly constructed logic, the lies, their rationales about how they're really fine, how *This is the best thing that ever happened to me*, all that disappears, and what's left is their emotion.

For better or worse.

"This time I want to be the one who chooses," says Marjorie, and everybody nods. I zoom in on her eyes, adjust my focus, capture the moment of doubt that follows the moment of strength, and I think:

Don't we all.

6

The Haverfields are married on Sunday, Julia and Ted. He's an investment banker. She teaches preschool. I wear a simple black dress, arrive two hours early. My hair is pulled back. I'm wearing makeup, but not too much. The point is to blend in, not to draw attention. To look good, but not great. Brides get jittery when they see women at their wedding who've gone all out, who have dressed to impress. That's why there are bridesmaid dresses. I've learned this lesson the hard way, suffered the poison glare of brides who hate me for being tall, for being thin, for turning heads on their wedding day. Now I wear dresses that are a little too long to be sexy. I hang cameras over my breasts and frown professionally. In this business, you have to be sensitive to your clients' needs.

Jerome is standing in the parking lot, waiting for me. I have two camera bags in the trunk. He hauls them out onto the lawn of the church, lights a cigarette. I squint up at the sky. It's overcast, but the weatherman says no rain. I go through my stuff, choose my lenses, load two rolls of Agfa black-and-white four hundred speed film, mount my flashes.

"I was thinking we'd use long lenses today," I tell him. "Flatten the backgrounds a little."

Jerome puts on his jacket, pulls at his tie. He's never been comfortable in a suit. He flicks his finished cigarette into the road.

"I like that dress on you," he says.

I put my cameras back in the bag.

"Save it for the client," I tell him.

He stares at me for a moment, one eyebrow raised.

"You're right," he says. "It looks awful. What was I thinking?"

The groom comes over with his brother, the best man. I catch them checking out my legs. Ted says that everyone is gathering behind the church. We wander back together.

"How's Julia?" I ask.

"Nervous," says Ted. "She threw up once already."

He says they're expecting over three hundred people. I start counting my friends, family. Do I even know three hundred people?

The rest of the family is waiting restlessly. Portly men in tuxedos, matronly women in formal dresses. The wind has kicked up and people are clutching their hairdos. Ted gives me the quick introduction. Father of the bride, father of the groom, the four mothers (two natural and two step), the three surviving grandparents, a handful of cousins, the best friends (two for her, one for him), two brothers (his), two sisters (hers), four step-siblings (of undetermined relation).

I say, "Where's the bride?"

Her stepmother says she's in the bathroom.

The groom's father says, "I know exactly how she feels."

I eye the surroundings. A sloping lawn, a tiny pond, a weeping willow tree. I point toward the pond, away from the cemetery.

"Let's shoot down here," I say.

Jerome carries the equipment down the hill, sets up the tripod, starts pulling cameras. The bride emerges, pale under her makeup, smiling, dazed, like the survivor of a shipwreck rescued after fourteen days on the high seas. Her mother hands her the bouquet. She takes her fiancé's hand. Now that the moment is upon them, they look spooked, frozen, as if their bodies aren't really theirs, as if they just woke up in them this morning, the bodies of strangers. I pull them aside.

"Okay," I say. "I want you to forget everything. How the caterer didn't show up on time. How the florist brought calla lilies instead of trumpet lilies. Forget that your parents don't get along, that your mother can't believe your father had the nerve to bring his new girlfriend, that your brothers haven't spoken in eight years. Forget how many people are coming. Forget everything except each other. Do you hear me? The game is over and you won. You found each other. You love each other. You do love each other, don't you?"

Staring into each other's eyes, they smile.

"Yes," she says.

"Yes," he says.

"Good, then let everything else go and just be happy. No one can hurt you now. You've found love. You're invulnerable."

I tell them all this and I want it to be true. For them, for me, for all of us. If only there were a star I could wish on, a wishbone I could break. If only there were a scientist who, late one night in his chaotic laboratory, could discover the cure for not-so-happily-ever-after.

I pose them by the pond, the weeping willow tree. I take pictures of them together, then the bride alone. She tells me she starved herself for four months so she could fit into her dress, a tight, white, Vera Wang gown with ten-inch cuffs. She tells me her entire pre-school class is here, a mob of four-year-olds ready to storm the church. I push the hair from her eyes, step back. Overhead the sun emerges from the clouds and, caught in a sudden rail of light, she smiles.

Click.

You can tell a lot about a couple by the way they interact in public. How comfortable they are touching, kissing. The patience they have for each other. Ted and Julia seem pretty evenly matched. She isn't grabbing him, and he isn't pulling away. They reach for each other at the same time, lovingly, with just a hint of panic. Sunlight shimmers on the pond. I tell Ted to step in. He puts his hands awkwardly around her waist.

"Just relax," I tell them.

Ted plasters a smile to his face. I tell him to think about the place they first met. The smile becomes a little more genuine. Julia steps backward and stumbles. Ted catches her. I take their picture.

By two o'clock the church is filled. The groom's side, the bride's. Rows of family, friends, coworkers. Rows of nieces and nephews, bosses and former bosses, high school chums, college roommates, people they haven't spoken to in years, relatives they didn't even know they had. I float to the front of the church, take a few group shots. In the back Jerome has the tripod set up and he shoots without a flash, letting the exposure run long, letting the light from the stained glass windows saturate the film, letting the settling-in motion of the crowd blur across the frame.

In the back row a man is watching me. I take his picture. He smiles, shakes his head.

"What's so funny?" I say.

"There are two dozen four-year-olds running amok in the rectory," he says.

I nod. Later I will get a picture of Julia surrounded by children, children climbing her, pulling at her hands.

The man is maybe late thirties, handsome, wearing a dark suit. His hair is brown, just starting to gray.

"You look familiar," I say. "Have we met?"

"I don't think so."

I scan the crowd for shots, catch the groom moving in silhouette past the blue-and-red window figure of St. Paul.

"Bride or groom?" I say.

"Pardon?"

I look at him.

"Which side are you on?"

He shrugs.

"Neither," he says.

"What do you mean? Who invited you?"

He looks around, then raises his finger to his lips in the universal sign for silence.

I stare at him.

"Are you saying you don't know them? Either of them? Bride or groom?"

He smiles. His eyes are hazel. There is a small scar running through his left eyebrow.

"Is that bad?"

Despite myself I smile. There's something about his face, how relaxed he is, something about his sunny, blue-green eyes.

"Let me get this straight," I say. "You're crashing the wedding."

He's wearing a muted, patterned tie, a crisp white shirt. His face is freshly shaved.

" 'Crash' is such an ugly word," he says. "I prefer to think of it as an oversight. They were so busy preparing they forgot to meet me, forgot to be friends, forgot to send the invitation."

Behind us the ushers close the doors. I turn to look at them, turn back.

"Whatever you want to call it," I say, trying to sound official, trying to scare him, "the fact is, you're not supposed to be here."

He nods.

"You caught me," he says.

Again the smile.

"Now the question is, are you gonna turn me in?"

I look around the hall. The priest is moving toward the podium. A man is sitting down at the organ. The groom takes his place. At the front of the church, Jerome waves to me, beckoning.

I turn back, hold the man's eye for a moment, feeling his challenge like an electric light, and something else, a thawing, a strange, unsettling movement somewhere in the frozen tundra of my heart. It scares the shit out me.

"Live in fear," I say, and walk away, hurrying down to the front, my heart racing in my chest.

After the ceremony I wander back calmly, broadcasting my indifference, but he's gone. I stand for a moment staring at the spot where he sat, feeling . . . disappointed, and at the same time disturbed by my disappointment, by the tiny bulb that's blossomed inside me, unwanted, life-threatening, pushed up through the cold cement of my heart like a weed.

Stop it.

Put it out of your mind.

Jerome comes over, sees the look on my face.

"What?" he says.

I shake my head.

"Let's pack up," I tell him.

He takes the camera from me, puts it in the bag. Watching him, I think about the man's eyes, his smile. I feel dizzy suddenly, anxious. *Snap out of it*, I tell myself. It isn't like me. I don't get fluttery about men, like some hysterical thirteen-year-old girl. I am the brick wall. The wrecking ball. To calm myself, I think about the shots I've taken. The bride and her father, arm in arm. The preschool ring bearers decorated with ribbons and bows. I think about the words "fairy tale" and "storybook," and how capital "L" Love has a vaulted, fantastical quality that runs so counter to the repetition of daily life. I think about how love stories are always about beginnings. First glances, first kisses, the crisis, and the crisis overcome. Love stories end on wedding days, they don't begin on them. And maybe this is the problem, maybe we have so much divorce because no one knows how to persevere. There are no role models. How did Cinderella cope once it became clear that the prince was never going to talk about his feelings? How did she keep the romance alive after their lives had turned into a never ending sea of dentist appointments and soccer games? How did Prince Charming readjust his expectations after gravity took hold of Sleeping Beauty, after her breasts fell and her waist expanded, and she started looking more like Sleeping Ugly, Sleeping Wrinkle, Sleeping Mustache?

Everybody acts like the future is so far away, when really every moment that passes is the future. A minute from now, an hour, a day.

I pack my equipment and think about the wedding crasher, his smile, how it made me feel. A spark, a spike in the EKG, a sign of life returning.

They say love is for the young, but sometimes I wonder if it isn't too delicate a process to be wasted on them. Maybe love can only be appreciated by someone older, someone with a sense of history, a longer attention span, someone who understands how fragile everything is, how easily things are lost. Or maybe I'm just rationalizing. Trying to console myself, to convince myself that things are for the best. My life. How it turned out.

Maybe I'm just trying to make up for the fact that, though I go to a hundred weddings a year, I'm always the one packing my things at the end and going home alone.

1

Okay.
Now a confession.
People always ask if I'm married. And I look at them and say "No."
But I was.
For just over a year, I was a bride. I slept in a bed next to my husband. I wore two rings on my left ring finger, changed my last name. I had a joint checking account, joint savings. We did, Jim and I. We lived in a little house, shared drawers in the same dresser. I was the first person he saw in the morning, the last person he saw at night. We had married friends, went to parties where wives joked about their husbands' inadequacies and children ran amok. I became one of those married people who argue about parking and make love with the TV on.

And for the most part I was happy. The weddings I photographed became celebrations thrown for long lost friends. *Welcome home*, I'd think, focusing. It affirmed something I'd always suspected: Being married is like joining a secret society. You share knowing glances, hold the door for each other as you enter all the clubhouses and meeting halls. Fancy restaurants, specialty markets, all those backyard barbecues. Once you're part of the club, you have to learn the rules. Where to shop for bedding, how to choose wine. There's a smugness to married life, a sense of victory. This is why married people tend to gather in clusters. You get together and express pity for all your single friends. Because now that you're married, you realize that single people can't be trusted. They represent a world of uncertainty, of isolation and loss. When you're married you want to socialize with others of your kind. People who reinforce the rightness of your choice, who can coach you through the steps toward home ownership, parenthood, republicanism.

I was the artistic wife, not quite homemaker, not quite bread-winner. I used to take Polaroids of myself and hide them for Jim to find. Pictures of the things he loved. Newspapers tied with string, foggy windows, an unmade bed. He'd get up every morning, put on his wool suit, and head off into the city. He'd call me at three o'clock, give me his ETA, say "I was thinking we could do that pasta thing for dinner," or "Let's rent a movie, order some Chinese." In the summer, we could go weeks without seeing each other, because he worked weekdays and I worked weekends. We'd pass each other at night like the sheepdog and the coyote in those old Bugs Bunny cartoons. Off duty, on.

Until I met Jim, I'd always been a loner, isolated, capable. But somewhere around month six of our marriage something odd happened. I stopped being me, one person. And became one of two. I became we, became us. And I realized that marriage is the perfect preparation for motherhood, because you have to stop thinking in terms of *What do I want?* and start thinking in terms of *What do we want?* It struck me as biologically ingenious. To be seduced into

being part of a team, and to be happy because of it. Before that I'd
always been proud of my self-sufficiency. Being married was like
letting go of a habit I thought I needed but had been hobbling me
all along. And knowing this, feeling comfortable in my new iden-
tity, I wondered could kids be far behind?

Growing up, marriage had never been that important to me. I
wasn't one of those girls who fantasizes, who dreams all white
dreams about princes on horseback and glamorous ceremonies.
Given what happened with my parents, it seemed crazy to hunger
for that kind of oblivion. For a long time, I was against the whole
conceit of marriage. I was an independent woman who didn't need
a man, didn't want one, didn't want the house in the suburbs or
children. I would succeed on my own terms or not at all. And yet
when I met Jim, when we'd dated for a year, and he got down on
one knee, I said "Yes. Of course." Because by this point I'd seen so
many weddings, been a part of so many processionals, it felt natural,
welcome. And I realized that all those weddings were just a rehearsal for my own. I was the stage manager who fills in for the
missing actor. The usher who's seen the show so many times she
knows the lines by heart.

I'd had the place picked out for months before I even met Jim.
An orange grove an hour north of the city where I'd shot the Fitz-
patrick wedding. A sprawling orchard next to a trickling stream.
Planning it was a breeze. I knew all the tricks, used the almanac
to play the percentages, finding the one September day on which
it hadn't rained in twenty-three years. I called in favors. The caterer
owed me. The florist. I was like a Green Beret planning a camping
trip. I knew all the pitfalls, the hidden costs and last minute hurdles.
I knew how to keep things small, the perfect excuses to give distant
relatives to keep them away. I knew where to get the best cake for
the least amount of money, how to stock the bar. I'd heard a thousand denominational services, had determined the perfect length
for the ceremony (eighteen minutes), the perfect music (Mozart),
the perfect balance of personal detail and sermon.

When the morning came, Jim and I sat on the porch of our house and took a self-portrait, wearing our pajamas, hair a mess, sleep still in our eyes, cups of coffee clutched in our soon-to-be married hands. We were implacable, relaxed. But the moment I put on the dress at the wedding hall, everything changed. I started to panic. An unnamed sense of terror took hold of me. I broke out in a cold sweat. My mind raced. Gasping for air, I pushed out of the dressing room past my sister, knocking an usher to the floor. I stumbled down the hall and into the room where Jim was waiting in his tuxedo with a baseball glove on one hand, tossing a ball back and forth with his brother.

"Out," I said.

His brother took one look at me and split. Jim studied me quietly, trying to gather all the facts before he spoke. I started pacing. I kept trying to talk, to get the words out. Jim watched me warily, like you watch a rabid animal that's wandered into your living room.

"I can't . . ." I said.

"I'm not sure . . ." I said.

"Laurie," he said.

I turned. He was holding his brother's mitt out to me.

"What?" I said.

"Put it on."

Put it on? A baseball glove? Now? When everything was falling apart? When I was dying? Literally dying. The old me. The single me. Suffocated. Crushed. Because only in death can there be re-birth. Only in giving up can you go on. Here I was losing my mind, spiraling down into an abyss of insecurity and doubt and he wanted to play ball?

I put the glove on. He tossed me the ball. I caught it.

"Now you throw it to me," he said.

"I know how to do it," I snapped and threw it back. He caught it, threw it to me. I caught it, threw it to him. And after a few minutes something odd happened. I started to relax. I focused on the ball, the glove, the act of throwing. I let myself settle into the comfort of repetition, the satisfying routine of toss and grab. And this is how his brother found us ten minutes later, a man and woman playing catch. Synchronized. Inseparable.

"It's time," he said.

I took off my mitt, laid it on the table. I was calmer now. My hands weren't shaking. I could breathe. This was the final stage: acceptance. I started for the door.

"Laurie," said Jim again, as I stepped out into the hall.

I turned and looked at him, at this man I'd soon be standing next to, declaring my forevers, this man I adored, who saw me so clearly, who knew who I was, what I needed.

"I love you," he said.

I pulled the veil down over my face. Had anyone every found a better match? A kinder, more wonderful mate?

"Will you marry me?" I said.

Fourteen months later, we filed for divorce.

8

On Monday, I pack a camera bag and drive over to divorce court. Judge Woolery has given me permission to shoot in his court-room. He's a short, hook-nosed man with a horseshoe of hair who wears monogrammed shirts. The courtroom itself is a small, win-dowless room with battered furniture and a plastic flag on the wall. I put my camera bag behind the clerk's desk and try to make myself inconspicuous. When couples come in for their cases I ask them to sign waivers. It's amazing how many people do. Even in the middle of the worst fight of their lives, even with lawyers present. I think about the story of the photographer who found a suburban house he wanted to photograph. He left a note for the occupant, saying "I want to create a perfect mulch circle in your backyard and photograph it." He left his phone number and that night when he got home there was a message from the woman saying "Do what you have to do."

Do what you have to do.

So he went back the next day with a crane and a truck full of mulch and built the circle, photographed it, cleaned up, left, all without ever meeting the occupant, without even talking to her. The point is, people will do amazing things if they feel like their lives can become part of a work of art. We have so little art in our lives, so few brushes with meaning.

The first case is *Anderson v. Anderson.* The husband is suing his wife for divorce, claiming irreconcilable differences. Most of the property issues have been settled, but his wife is fighting for joint custody of the dog. The judge hears testimony, looks at pictures entered into evidence of the three-year-old border collie mix. A bitch named Jenny.

" 'Y' or 'I-E,' " the court reporter wants to know.

" 'Y,' " says the wife, handing forward a certificate of training. "And I haven't seen her in three months. He won't let me."

She starts to cry. And I think, *You know you've lost all sense of proportion when you're litigating over the pets.*

The husband, on the stand, makes a sour face. He tells his wife, "You can't make up for ruining a marriage by being nice to the dog."

I mount a one-hundred-fifty millimeter zoom lens and shoot him from below, just his head, the anger in his eyes. Around me the courtroom is a haunted house. A cemetery filled with the ugly ghosts of human emotion. This is not a place built on love. It is a chamber of bitterness and acrimony, jealousy and rage. An atom smasher, where all the tenderness and promise, the vulnerability and fear, the dashed hopes, denial, negotiation, the loneliness, and desolation are thrown together at super-high speed under immense pressure, trying to split something once believed to be unsplittable. The human heart.

I sit there and watch Mr. Anderson pluck at his collar, loosen his tie. He sweats, his hands balling into fists. While across the room, shielded by lawyers, his soon-to-be ex-wife purses her lips and chews her nails. She writes notes in tight, anger-driven script and shoves them at her attorneys. Hearing the *click* of my camera, she lifts her head, shoots me pleading looks, her eyes begging, *Help me, please. You're a woman. You understand.* Under her gaze I feel exposed, smashed open. My grip on the Leica tightens. I try to look away, but I can't. Mrs. Anderson searches my face, looking for empathy, understanding. I feel frozen, paralyzed by her need. I worry that if I give her something, anything, I won't be able to stop. This is what happens when you retreat from the world. Too many years spent living alone in the wilderness, and you start running at the sound of footsteps. No matter how lonely you might be, how isolated, the idea of exposing yourself, of being vulnerable, is too much to bear. I stare silently, the camera half-raised, half-lowered. And then she lifts her hand in a kind of hopeless wave, and I turn away, focus on her husband, my heart beating fast, like an animal that's just escaped the jaws of death.

Mr. Anderson steps down. Mrs. Anderson takes the stand. She holds her pocketbook tightly to her chest, unaware of how frightened it makes her look. She is a trim, middle-aged woman trying to hold on to her dignity.

"I'm still trying to wrap my mind around it," she tells the judge. "I mean, what is this all about? Really. What does it mean?"

Both she and her husband look stunned, as if they can't believe it's come down to this. After the accusations and separation, the fights and reconciliations. After the rough and tumble makeup sex has faded to a disturbing memory. After the negotiations have failed, the arbitration. After all the pleas for understanding, for mercy, have fallen on deaf ears. To be here finally, settling matters of heartbreak as if they were just another kind of business. As if you could really make a list of your property and split it up calmly, rationally. As if you could take a house or a car or a child and say, this is mine and that's yours. As if that's even the point.

"I don't care about all this crap," she says, throwing the list into the air, pages scattering, raining down. "I just want my marriage back."

While across the room, her husband takes a sudden, powerful interest in whatever is stuck to the underside of the table. I photograph him through a hail of paperwork, from my seat beside the court reporter, pausing to change lenses, to change film. Mrs. Anderson yells over the judge's gavel, trying to provoke her husband, to get some kind of answer from him, some kind of understanding about what happened to them, how they ended up here, in this place.

Later, in the ladies' room, I step out of the stall and walk to the sink. Mrs. Anderson is standing by the door drying her hands with forced air. Seeing her, I freeze, feeling awkward, exposed.

"So," she says, "did you get what you wanted?"

For a moment I don't know what she means, because when have I ever gotten what I wanted? But then I realize she's talking about the pictures.

"I don't know," I tell her. "I won't know until I develop them."

Under the harsh glare of the fluorescent lights, she looks strung out. There are bags under her eyes, wrinkles lining her mouth. The dryer shuts off. She pats the sides of her skirt absently, looks at herself in the mirror.

"I don't know what I expected," she says. "Not this. A little respect maybe. A little loyalty."

She sighs and rubs her eyes. Standing there, I wish I had my camera. I watch her sway and think, This *is the shot*. The real her. But my bag is back in the courtroom, and even if it weren't, even if I were to take out a camera right now, it would destroy the moment. She would cover up, protect herself. This is the trouble with technology. It introduces an element of artificiality into what it means to be human. Makes us self-conscious. I have to settle for taking a picture of her in my mind. A picture of her as she pulls herself together, straightens. A picture as she shakes her head, gives me a quivering smile.

"Is it possible to die of disappointment?" she says.

Watching her leave, I am hit with a wave of self-loathing so powerful I feel nauseous. Catching my reflection in the mirror, I see myself the way the people I photograph must see me: As a parasite. A compassionless intruder reveling in their lowest moments. Standing there alone in the bathroom, I want to chase after her, to tell her it breaks my heart. The things people go through, the things they do to each other. I want to tell her I'm sorry. Sorry she had to go through this. To be airing her dirty laundry in front of strangers, to be paying lawyers by the hour to wallow in the filth of her own making, the sordid details of who hit who, who missed whose Little League games, who never had dinner ready on time, who fucked who and how often.

I start for the door, my voice catching in my throat, calling out to her, but then I stop. I let her go. What could I say that would make it better? That would bridge the gap? I stumble into the stall, turning circles, overcome by a feeling I can't name, a greedy weight dragging at my limbs, pulling me down. I feel like I'm going to throw up, but when I crouch down, nothing comes except grief. A sob escapes. I clamp my mouth shut, refusing to let it out. Refusing to fall too far. I am a woman in a courthouse restroom, bawling silently, convulsing, one hand holding a wad of toilet paper, the other covering my eyes, as if to block out all the images I've hunted for. As if to fend off the very thing I wanted most.

I wipe my face. My eyes are puffy. I feel stuck, like I'm at the bottom of a well. Afraid to come out. Afraid to move on. What's gonna save me? What's gonna set me free? I think about the man who crashed the wedding. His eyes. His smile. Like the promise of a better life. I tell myself, *Shut up.* I tell myself, *Don't be crazy. You don't need him. He can only hurt you.* I tell myself this, because for the last few months I've been teaching myself not to want. I tell myself this, because when you're trying to find balance in your life, to restore a sense of order, desire is the enemy. On all those endless nights, when you're trying to pull yourself together to keep your fragile heart from breaking all over again, dreams are an invitation to disaster.

I'm trying to be strong, to be happy with what I have. Exactly what I have. My clothes, my car, my house. This has been my strategy. If a pair of shoes wears out, I buy the same pair again. I've stopped watching television and reading magazines, because advertising is all about fostering lust, about provoking desire. I've stopped listening to the radio, because hearing songs I like, but don't own, makes me want to buy records. I go to restaurants and order steamed fish and vegetables. I deny myself flavor, because flavor leads to yearning.

I've lost twenty-five pounds in six months.

I'm getting thinner.

Disappearing.

I stand up, drop the tissue into the toilet, flush. I feel exhausted, wiped out. For some reason, I think about my mother dying of cancer in the hospital, her body whittled down to skin and bones, covered in scars from all the operations, tubes sticking out of her. How she looked at me one day and said,

"How did this happen? When did I get so old?"

Because when we're young, we never think, one day I'll get cancer or have a heart attack. One day I'll lose a leg to diabetes or have an aneurysm. One day Parkinson's will set in. When we're young, our bodies are powerful and healthy. Our bones heal fast. And it seems impossible in those moments to think that could ever change, that youth could ever fail, that decay will one day take root in our organs, our marrow.

In this same way, when our parents ask us what we want to be when we grow up we never say:

Divorced.

9

For some people, when they fall in love, the whole world disappears. They live their lives together in a kind of hypnotic bliss. Other people are nothing, just background noise. There are no other loyalties worth mentioning. No relationships of any real substance. The French have a name for it: *solitude à deux*. This is how I remember my parents. They were inseparable. Whether kissing or fighting, their focus was absolute. My sister and I were peripheral to their affair, a by-product. We weren't so much a culmination, an end to itself, as sparks thrown off from a welder's torch.

Before my father went insane, before my mother's cancer, we lived together as a family in which the focus was up instead of down. On the adults, rather than the children. If you wanted to participate, to get attention, you had to rise to their level, play on their field. It was seductive, their single-mindedness. True love is a drug that gives off fumes, a heady narcotic wafting like smoke, offering the allure of height by association. People were drawn to them. That much heat, that much friction. They were as hypnotic as fire, and there were times when watching them was like watching a house burn to the ground.

For my father, a drifter, a modern gypsy, everything was romantic, beautiful. A traffic light, the roar of the vacuum cleaner. My mother, on the other hand, believed in tragedy, in the ultimate betrayal of all things. Together they carried around a fatal glamour. My father smoked cigarettes until his fingertips were yellow. He was a poet. He spoke elliptically, in half sentences and sudden proclamations. My mother liked to throw things just to see them smash. She was bigger than life, blowsy, zaftig, a siren luring sailors to their beautiful death upon the jagged rocks. Looking back, I'm amazed that Lisa and I made it through infancy, so infatuated were my parents with each other. Luckily for us, there was always a support network. My grandmother, who lived just blocks away, would shuffle over every few days to fill the void my parents left when they ran off, when they locked themselves away. It was my grandmother who made sure we got fed, who dressed us and tucked us in.

For ten years, we lived in the shadow of my parents' drama. The weeks my father would lock himself in his study, trying to write, while she pounded on the door, threatening to leave him if he didn't open up, if he didn't come out and give her the attention she deserved. Until finally, he came smashing from the room, furious, wild-eyed, screaming at her, telling her she was killing him.

"Is that what you want?" he'd scream. "To kill me? To bury me alive? Would that make you happy?"

And she would stare at him implacably as he ranted and spat, then turn and go back to their bedroom, where she would put on her makeup and most revealing dress. She would stand in front of the mirror and brush her hair and then walk back to his study, where he had already ensconced himself again, smoking two cig-arettes at once and staring at the blank page.

"I'm going out," she'd say. "If you don't want me, I'm sure there's a dozen men at Clancy's who do."

And she would turn on her heels and clip-clop toward the front steps. And he would sit for a moment fuming, turning red, and then let out an agonizing scream and go after her, grabbing her, stopping her, dragging her into the bedroom and slamming the door.

When we were children, a constant sense of auditioning existed for my sister and me, an olympic struggle for attention. Half the time, Lisa and I would be at each other's throats, competing for every grain, every whisper, every look. Other times we worked in tandem, a well-oiled machine trying to shift the focus, to get a little light thrown our way. In the quiet moments, the new moon mo-ments, when all the angry dogs were sleeping, it was possible to break through, to tunnel our way into their affections. It was like passing through a rift in time and space, like stepping over a thresh-old into the warmth of a house that until now, we had only stared at through a frozen windowpane, like orphans on a winter sidewalk, yearning to get in. Once inside, we basked in the warm glow of their attention, like cats nuzzling, purring, giving up our bellies for love.

"What pretty girls I have," my mother would say as we took turns brushing her hair at night. "What good girls."

She had the most amazing white skin, her lipstick a fiery blood-red. Her hair was a heavy dark brown, eyes flinty and green. There was always a drink by the bed, a glass of wine, an amber nightcap. It sits in my memory, a flash of color shimmering under the bedside lamp. We were six and four, seven and five. Lisa, with her puffy cheeks and hair-trigger temper. Me, with my bangs down over my face, a thin veneer I could hide behind, a shield I could watch the world through. These moments too, I have recreated for the camera, casting my actors and furnishing my sets. The shadowy room, flushed with the glow of the moon. The two little girls in lemon yellow nightdresses fighting for possession of the hairbrush. And my father, who would come in humming, having finally worked a whole day without distraction, having filled page after page with lean lines of vengefulness and misery. He would put his hands on my mother's shoulders, bend down, kiss her forehead. Lisa and I would grab at him like beggars. What we wanted was a look, a smile, the rare moment when he would bend down and pick one of us up and turn the full brunt of his gaze upon us, hugging, tickling.

"All these beautiful women," he'd say, throwing his hand up to his chest in mock surrender. "How can one man be so lucky?"

And Lisa and I would laugh and spin like tops fueled by his attention. But already he would be turning away, back toward my mother, his hands in her hands, caressing, his face lowering, nuzzling her neck.

I see them now, frozen in my memory, and yet no matter how many pictures I take, there is no way to truly recapture these moments, these looks. This is because true love cannot be faked. Real emotion cannot be imitated. You either feel it or you don't. Which is why, halfway through making love, I push Jerome off me and lie there trying to catch my breath.

"Thanks a lot," he says.

"Sorry," I say. "I'm just . . ."

He rolls over, starts pulling on his pants. Naked, Jerome's stomach is flat, hairless. He has muscles on his arms, his chest, and back. We've been sleeping together on and off for about six weeks. He's the tourniquet I put on sometimes to stop the bleeding, the drug I take to numb the pain. Lying with him, letting him stroke my hair, I feel, at least for a few minutes, like someone who has access to pleasure, to kindness, to love.

This, in itself, is a kind of faking it.

He lights a cigarette, opens the window, sits on the sill.

"When are you gonna let me buy you a real dinner?" he says.

"I told you. No dates."

"You think I'm too young for you," he says.

"I think you're too everything for me," I tell him.

He lets the cigarette dangle between his lips.

"You don't like yourself very much, do you?" he says.

"I think I have nice hair," I say. "My penmanship is good."

"Always joking."

"It's called survival."

Jerome runs his hand through his hair. Sometimes I find notes in my camera bag, tiny haiku written just for me. He thinks it's romantic. He thinks one day I'll wake up and realize we were meant to be together. That he's The One. It breaks my heart, how naive he is, how innocent.

I've never been anything but honest with him. This isn't about love, I say. This is about sex. About blowing off steam, reducing stress. "Think of yourself as a health-care professional," I tell him. "A doctor. A nurse." This has been my strategy from the beginning: to try to separate my body from my heart, to have sex without love. That way there's no mess, no pain. I lie underneath him and sweat, trying to be scientific about things. Detached.

He studies his face in the reflection of the window.

"I'm a real catch," he says.

I pick up my robe, put it on, feeling like his mother. I want to go over and ruffle his hair, pinch his cheeks. And these feelings, coming so soon after his dick has been in my mouth, after our tongues have been exchanging spit and warmth, seem sick, wrong. I feel like going into the bathroom and locking the door, hiding. But it's not him I'd be hiding from, it's me. And the sad fact is, there's nowhere you can go to hide from yourself. I pick up his jacket, get a cigarette of my own. He lights it for me.

"You need to find a girl your own age," I tell him.

"I don't want a girl my own age," he says. "I want you."

I retreat to the other side of the room. The smoke tastes like punishment. For some reason, I think about the man from the wedding, the crasher, though why I think he would be any different is a mystery. But then the grass is always greener; the thing we don't have so much more seductive than the thing we do. All I know is the way he made me feel, that spark, a spark Jerome for all his eagerness, has never lit.

"Tell me something," he says, after it's clear I'm not going to respond.

"What?"

"I don't know. Anything. About you."

I stare at the bed, the rumpled sheets. I wonder what would happen if I dropped my cigarette onto it, what he would do. Once the flames started leaping, licking at the walls. I can picture him running into the kitchen, racing back with a fire extinguisher, biceps bulging. He's like a Boy Scout. Pure goodness and light. And standing here naked across from him makes me feel dirty, like just being with me is corrupting him.

"When I was ten years old," I tell him, "my grandmother had a stroke. My sister found her slumped over the kitchen table. She was chopping onions when the stroke hit, and there she was, lying with her eyes open, tears running down her face. Lisa started screaming. I was in the other room, folding laundry. I came running. My parents had been missing for two weeks at that point. They did that a lot, went out to dinner and never came home. So I called an ambulance, and they came and took my grandmother away. They wanted to know where my folks were. I lied and told them 'at the store.' I said they'd be home any minute. So they rushed off with my grandma and then, suddenly, the house was quiet. It was just Lisa and me. We had no money, no one to call for help. It was August, so there was no school. Just the food in the house. And I was afraid of the stove so we ate everything cold."

I stub out my cigarette, exhale.

"It was six more days before my folks came home," I say. "The house was a wreck. Lisa and I were sticky, feral. The first thing my mom said when she came in was, 'Your dad bought me a new coat. Isn't it beautiful?' "

He looks at me, and by the look on his face I can tell he thinks he's breaking through, that I'm opening up. But he doesn't get it, the point of the story. How now I don't need anybody. How now I can take care of myself.

I look at him and think, *I'm such a fool.* People who get burned don't turn to fire to heal them. They don't apply heat to their flaming wounds. People who have frostbite don't press ice packs to the affected areas. So why do I keep running out looking for love? A woman with a broken heart. Why do I think more romance is the answer?

He takes a step toward me, and I retreat. There's too much warmth in his eyes, too much intimacy and concern. With Jerome I thought it would be different. I thought I could control it. Us. Because he's so young, such a ladies' man, I thought we could keep it casual. I thought he'd be grateful to have an older woman who wanted nothing from him but the occasional roll in the hay. Dodging him now, I can see that I was wrong.

"Why do you even like me?" I say. "I'm such a bitch."

He looks at me softly, kindly.

"I've seen the pictures you take," he says. "The real you."

"Those are just pictures," I tell him.

"No. That's how you really feel," he says. "Hopeful. Vulnerable. I can see it. There's something more inside you. Something warm and yearning and good."

I look out the window. There's a crescent moon hanging above the neighbor's house.

"I take pictures of weddings," I say. "You think that's art? It's marketing."

"You don't believe that," he says.

I don't respond. I am a mountain, a canyon. Immovable. Unphasable. Outside, I can see leaves blowing, trees bending in the wind.

"Then why do you do it?" he asks, moving closer. "If you hate it so much. Why not quit?"

"Because it's my job. I need the money."

He shakes his head.

"I've seen the way you look at them," he says. "All those couples. The envy."

I don't say anything, just stare at the moon. I'm willing him to leave.

"I'm not trying to be mean," he says. "But you're like a criminal returning to the scene of the crime. A ghost haunting the house where she used to . . ."

"I think you should go," I say.

He takes his shirt off a chair, puts it on.

"Will you call me later?"

I don't respond. Eventually he gives up and goes home.

10

After he's gone, I stalk the apartment, feeling wound up, scattered. I'm angry at myself for letting him get to me. Angry at myself for sleeping with him in the first place. For thinking lust was enough. For convincing myself that I could substitute something shallow for something deep. I thought it would help, but it only makes things worse. It only makes me feel more alone.

I go into the kitchen, pull out the contact sheets from the Haverfield wedding. I'm like a madwoman, muttering to myself, robe untied, glass of whiskey in hand. I flip the pages, scouring the boxy little pictures for something. Someone. Using a magnifying glass, I hunch down over the table like a monk translating an ancient religious text. I find the picture I'm looking for on the second page, a single shot of a man in a pew. His dark suit and slightly graying hair. He looks at the camera with an air of total relaxation. This man who steals other people's happiness, who gets high on other people's love. My pulse is racing. I place the loop over the image, remembering the jolt in my stomach, my legs.

I go into the darkroom and switch on the enlarger. I place the paper in the tray, the chemicals. If you asked me what I was doing, I'd say, *How the hell should I know?* Nothing makes sense to me anymore. I just know that something has to break. Something has to change. I switch on my red light and get to work. An hour later, I have an eight-by-ten print in deep, contrasting black-and-white. Close up, his eyes are dark, the left brow slightly raised. I take the print, still wet and start pulling out boxes, stacks of work prints from weddings past. I go through them quickly. The Henderson wedding, the Ascot and Preston weddings, the Connelly and McCaw. I flip the pages, searching. It takes me five minutes to find the first one. A group shot of the bride and her family, and there in the background is my man, turned in profile, that same smile on his face.

Got you, I think.

I put the picture aside, keep digging. Ten minutes later I find a second photo. A different wedding. Here he is with a piece of cake, sitting at the bridesmaid's table, listening to the band. And here, a shot of him dancing with the mother of the bride. And here, a photo of him shaking hands with the groom at the receiving line. Again and again I find him, eleven weddings in all. Spanning the last eighteen months. This matrimonial thief, this romantic intruder.

This man I can't stop thinking about.

I line the pictures up against the wall and study them. How could I not have noticed him before? How is it he slipped by me so easily? But then, for me the weddings are a blur. So many faces, so many pictures, always rushing, always working. It's a wonder I even recognize the bride sometimes on those hot June Sundays, running from one wedding to another, dashing into gas station rest rooms to freshen my deodorant and reapply lipstick. The morning ceremony, the afternoon affair, the evening nuptials. Summer, the wedding season, like mass hysteria, like a mob rioting, everyone wanting to be special, unique.

I stand back and look at the pictures and try to figure out what it means. He goes to weddings he's not invited to. Is it sweet? Creepy?

I drink the whiskey, pour myself another.

Pick up the phone, I think. *Call Jerome. Tell him to come back. Tell him you're sorry. At least that's safe. At least there you won't get hurt.*

I picture Mrs. Anderson's tired face, the slump of her shoulders. *Is it possible to die of disappointment?*

Because the Calvinists had it right. The Taliban. The human soul is weak, vulnerable. The heart is too easily corrupted by pleasure. Desire leads to vulnerability and vulnerability leads to pain. Therefore, to give yourself pleasure is an act of masochism.

I can see that now.

I walk to the computer. I go to the Web site for the local paper, find the classifieds page. I fill out the form to place an ad.

It reads: WANTED: HOME-WRECKERS. HAVE YOU HAD AN AFFAIR WITH A MARRIED MAN OR WOMAN? MODELS WANTED FOR PHOTOGRAPHY PROJECT. ALL RESPONSES CONFIDENTIAL.

Reading it over, I think about something Jerome said. *It's not true,* I think. I'm not a ghost. A criminal. I'm just a working girl. A struggling artist trying to make ends meet.

But maybe that's why they call it *taking* pictures. Maybe that's why you talk about *shooting* a camera. Like it's a gun and I'm a hunter, and all those weddings are just big safaris. Like instead of honoring these couples, I'm trying to kill them.

Because why should they be happy when I couldn't be?

Why should they have love when I don't?

The phone rings. When I pick it up, my sister says, "This time he's gone too far."

"Who?"

"David. When I came home last night, he was on the phone,

and when he saw me, he went into the bathroom and shut the door. 'Who was that?' I said later. 'Nobody.' Who was it? He didn't want to say. I kept pestering him. Finally, he broke down, said it was his mother."

She snorts.

"Maybe it *was* his mother," I tell her.

"Whose side are you on?" she wants to know.

11

I'm at the Mukharjee wedding when I see him again. He's not hard to spot. Seventy-five Indians and him.

"Got you," I say, coming up behind him.

He turns and, seeing me, smiles.

"What gave me away this time?" he asks.

I look around at all the women in saris, the men in full-length formal wear.

"I'll give you this," I say. "You've got guts."

He takes a glass of wine from the bartender.

"No. This time I actually know someone in the wedding party."

"Who?"

He sips his drink, thinking.

"Well, I don't know him that well. We just met twenty minutes ago."

I lift my camera and take a picture of somebody's Hindu grand-father dancing to disco. Hoping I might run into him, I've broken my own rule and I'm wearing three-inch heels and a cocktail dress that accentuates my body. My lipstick is a color called Savage.

"You have no shame," I say.

"Shame is overrated," he says.

"Modesty, on the other hand," I say.

"You look great," he tells me.

I blush. I haven't blushed since high school, but here I am, turning red.

"Don't change the subject," I say.

"Oh right," he says.

I consider telling him about the evidence I have, pictures from eleven weddings, but that would make it look like I've been think-ing about him, checking up.

"So is it just weddings?" I say. "Or are you crashing bar mitzvahs too?"

"Right," he says. "Look, are we going to stand here being clever all night or do you want to dance?"

Flustered, I look around.

"I'm not supposed to . . ." I say.

But before I can finish, he's putting down his drink, lifting the cameras from around my neck.

" 'Supposed to' doesn't work on me," he says. "In case you haven't noticed."

He hands the cameras to the bartender.

"Watch these, will you?"

He takes my hand and the feel of his fingers, his warm, human skin, makes all the words in my mouth break up and blow away. He leads me onto the dance floor, my legs feeling rubbery all of a sudden, fish flipping in my belly, nerves.

On the dance floor he turns to me, puts his hand on my waist. He is an inch or so taller than I am in these heels. Six foot one and solid. Up close, his skin is smooth, a faint blue stubble hidden just under the surface of his jaw. The band plays a popular radio ballad. We start to move.

"I don't know if this is such a good idea," I say.

"Shhh," he says.

He's a good dancer, smooth. There is none of the random circling, the boxy two-step. His cheek is next to mine and I can smell his shampoo, the scent of his shaving cream, and, underneath, him. The smell of his body.

"It'd be a lot more romantic," he says, "if you'd stop fighting and let me lead."

"Sorry."

I worry that my hands are sweating, that the dress I'm wearing makes my hips look big. I wish I'd done laundry this weekend like I planned, so I wouldn't be stuck here, heart in my throat, dancing in my granny bra.

"I've been watching you the last few months," he says.

"I thought we weren't talking," I manage.

"I'm not talking," he says. "I'm whispering sweet nothings."

I try to swallow, can't.

He says, "You float around just outside the group."

"That's my job."

"No, I think you live out there. You seem comfortable."

I try to think of something to say. He pulls his head back and looks me in the eye and his eyes are blue and deep and happy and they break my heart and I think, *Run away! Run away!*

"Oh shit," he says.

"What?"

"I'm gonna dip you."

And then my back is arching and I'm falling.

I close my eyes.

Thank God, I think.

Thank God.

*   *   *

Later, I ask him his name, but he won't tell me. He says he doesn't want to rush things.

"What rush?" I say. "It's your name."

He smiles.

"Take my picture," he says.

The way he says it makes me suspicious.

"Why?"

"What do you mean 'why'? That's what you do, right? Take pictures?"

"My *job*," I say, "is to take pictures of the bride and groom and their *invited* guests."

"Ah," he says, then takes my hand.

"Come on."

"Where are we going?" I ask, as he pulls me across the room. He doesn't answer, and against my better judgment I let him lead, the heat of his hand traveling up my arm, settling in my chest. Too late I realize that we're headed toward the receiving line, toward the bride and groom, all smiles and flushed faces, and that we're cutting in front of a half dozen New Delhi relatives to get there. I start to pull him away, but he holds on tight, a smile on his face. And before I can stop him, the bride and groom are looking up at us expectantly, eyes bright.

"A beautiful wedding," he says. "Just beautiful."

Their smiles waver a little as they try to place him.

"Thank you," says the bride and looks at me questioningly. My heart is in my throat, and all I can do is smile back at her like an idiot.

"I have a confession to make though," says the man.

"Oh yes?" says the groom. "What's that?"

We are surrounded by their families, everyone looking at us expectantly. I'm digging my fingernails into his palm, willing him to shut up.

"I don't remember Ana being so beautiful," he says.

She smiles politely.

"I'm sorry," she says. "Do I know you?"

He stares at her, his smile faltering, looking like a man who's waiting for a punch line he's beginning to think won't come. My heart sinks.

"You're kidding, right?" he says, finally, and his tone, his expression is so convincing that her gaze falters. She looks at him again, embarrassed now, struggling to place him, his face.

"No, I'm really sorry."

"From Ann Arbor?" he says. "High school?"

"I don't . . ."

"Wow," he says. "This is a little embarrassing."

"Please. Maybe—I mean it's been such a hectic year."

He claps the groom on the shoulder.

"Your wife and I used to be great friends."

"Oh yes?" says the groom, struggling to maintain his courteous demeanor after greeting relatives for two hours.

"I can't believe she doesn't remember. Her mother was so excited that I was going to be able to make it."

"Oh," says the bride, a flood of relief coming over her, "my mother invited you."

He smiles, looks at me. Dumbstruck, I can only blink at him.

"Do you think that I could get a picture, just the two of us?" he asks her. "You know, for old time's sake."

She takes his arm and he stands up straight, facing me. I stare at them, flabbergasted.

"Any time," he tells me.

This snaps me out of my daze. Flustered, I raise my camera.

"Say 'cheese,' " I say.

"Cheese," says the bride.

"Cheese," says the thief.

Click.

*   *   *

"Are you crazy?" I ask, after dragging him to an empty hallway. He stands there all mock innocent, smiling that infuriating smile.

"What?" he says.

"You are," I say. "You're deranged. Disturbed."

He shrugs, fingers the leaves of a plastic plant.

"You should have just taken my picture when I asked," he says. I stare at him.

"You know what?" I say. "I've changed my mind. I don't want you to call me."

"You don't?"

"No. Give me back my number, so I can tear it up."

He thinks about this.

"You never gave me your number," he says.

"I didn't?"

"No."

I look at him for a minute, then go through my camera bag, pull out a piece of paper, a pen. I write down my phone number, not breathing, knowing that *I'm* the crazy one. The lunatic. I hand it to him. He looks it over.

"Thank you," he says.

I watch him study the piece of paper, heart in my throat, feeling out of control, overwhelmed.

"No," I say. "Give it back."

"What? Why?"

I grab for the piece of paper. He takes a step back.

"Because I'm gonna tear it up," I say. "I don't want you calling me. You could have gotten me fired."

He stares at me, trying to decide if this is a game, then puts the number in his pocket.

"Please," I say.

"No."

"I swear to God," I say. "If you don't give it back I'm gonna scream."

He reaches out, presses his fingertip to my lips. I stop talking, imagining his lips on mine, the feel of his body.

"Don't worry," he says quietly. "I'm gonna call."

My heart skips a beat. I feel dizzy. He's smiling at me again, but this time the smile is heated, a warm, open promise that threatens to melt me down to my bones.

"You are?"

"Yes."

I shake my head, thinking,

What happened to not wanting?

To hope is the devil?

"That's what I was afraid of," I say.

12

When I get home my sister is sitting on the porch.

"What's the story?" she says. "You never call. You never write."

I let us into the house, drop my camera bag by the door. She follows me into the bedroom and watches as I take off my dress and put on some sweats.

"All right," she says. "Who is he?"

"Who is who?" I say.

"You're wearing a thong. You never wear a thong. I didn't even know you owned a thong. This to me says there must be a boy. So cough up his name."

"I don't know his name," I say and go into the kitchen. She follows, her eyes narrow. My sister the detective. Now that she's found a clue, she'll never let up.

"But there is a boy," she says.

"I feel like we're back in high school," I tell her, opening the fridge and pulling out two beers.

She takes a seat at the kitchen table, starts going through a pile of photographs.

"Who are these losers?" she says.

"Those are the Goldsteins," I tell her. "Myrna and Phil. They got married at the golf club."

"Is that an erection?"

"Yup."

She holds the picture up to the light, moves closer for a better look.

"I've seen bigger. Is she sure she picked the right guy?"

"We're all just doing the best we can, Lisa," I tell her. Which is true. Just a bunch of blind little mole rats groping around in our burrows, trying to make things work.

She finishes flipping through the pictures, throws them aside.

"I'm waiting," she says.

"For what?"

"A name. Two words. First, last. I'll even take a nickname. Thor, Columbo."

"I told you, I don't know his name."

She sips her beer, looking around idly, then sees something in the living room. She stands up. From her face I can tell she's found the photos I've left up, the eleven prints tacked to the wall. My mystery man at all his crashed weddings. I follow her inside, trying to cut her off.

"What's this?" she wants to know.

"It's a long story," I tell her, and start pulling them down, shoving them into a folder.

"Is this him?"

I tear them down one by one, rushing, trying to protect myself, but she's like a cop chasing down a suspect. She knows the truth is near. She pulls the last print off the wall, retreats to a far corner.

"He's cute."

I try to get the print away from her, but she hides it behind her back.

"Are you stalking him?" she wants to know.

"No I'm not *stalking* him," I say, blushing.

"Laurie likes a boy," she teases in her most childish singsong.

"Give me that," I say.

But she won't.

We stand toe-to-toe, both of us flushed, breathing heavy. From the look on her face I can tell she's thrilled. The whole cynical thing was really making her nervous. Her zombie sister living the life of a monk.

"So tell me," she says.

I walk into the kitchen. She follows.

"How's David?" I ask.

"Don't change the subject."

I turn around. She has me cornered against the counter. From her expression I can tell I'm not going to get out of here without telling her something close to the truth, so I take a deep breath and give her the story. A man I hardly know who crashes weddings. When I'm done, she hands me his picture, picks up her beer.

"Definitely a serial killer," she says.

She sits back down at the table. Outside I can hear the sound of a garbage truck chewing up other people's trash. I think about how he folded up my phone number, put it in his pocket.

"I don't know what I'm doing anymore," I tell her.

"Who does?"

"I just know I can't take it. Being alone."

"You say that like it's a bad thing."

"And Jim . . ."

"Jim was an asshole."

"Only at the end," I say. "And that's what scares me."

"Laurie, he was always an asshole. You just couldn't see it."

I stare at her dumbstruck and wonder if it's true. If the whole thing was preventable. If I should have seen it coming a mile away. The thought is too horrible to bear.

"Maybe," I say. "But it wasn't just his fault, you know."

"We've been through this. You have to stop beating yourself up."

I sigh, rub my eyes.

"I get so sick of myself," I tell her. "I need someone else to make my life interesting again."

"You need to get laid."

I think of Jerome.

"No," I say. "It's more than that."

She takes the picture from me, studies it.

"So how are you gonna find him, his name?"

"I'm gonna ask him when he calls. I gave him my number."

"Slut."

"Tramp."

"Bitch."

I sit down across from her, put my head on the table, suddenly exhausted.

"I could find him for you, you know," she says. "Track him down."

"No."

"It'd give you a tactical advantage. The mystery man revealed. Even the terrain. Because you know like ninety percent of his allure is the whole enigma thing."

I lift my head and look at her.

"You're not gonna spy on him," I say. "Besides, I wouldn't even know where to start."

She shrugs.

"Leave that to me."

I take the picture from her, slip it under a phone book.

"No," I say.

She sits back, sighs.

"You never let me have any fun."

We sit in silence for a moment. Headlights from a passing car throw light across the wall, panning slowly, illuminating nothing.

"So how's Dave?" I ask her.

"He's planning something. I can tell."

"Like what?"

"Something sinister probably. Have an affair. Smother me in my sleep."

I reach out and touch her hand.

"I'm sorry I haven't called," I say.

She shrugs.

"Go ahead," she says. "Abandon me. I can take it."

"Nobody's abandoning you."

She holds my hand, examines my fingernails.

"I know," I say.

"Stop biting them."

"I get nervous. My life makes me nervous."

"It makes me nervous too."

"Thank you."

At the door she hugs me quickly, as if embarrassed.

"Be nice to David," I tell her.

"I am nice."

"He's a good guy. And he loves you."

"I know."

I watch her walk down the lawn and climb into her car. The sun is down and the sky has that midnight-blue hue, clouds on fire. I go inside and stare at the telephone for a little while, then head into the darkroom and print until dawn.

13

My father was hospitalized for the first time in 1979. He was thirty years old. The doctors diagnosed him with manic depression, which is a clinical way of saying what we already knew, that he was moody to the extreme. He stayed in the hospital for six months, until the spell broke, the mood passed. After he left, my mother became forgetful. She forgot to get dressed in the morning, forgot to eat. It was like half of her brain had disappeared. The half that coped with daily life, that recognized other people. She would turn around whenever I came into the room, expecting to see him, her face lighting up. But seeing me, she lost interest, turned away. When it was apparent that she wasn't going to snap out of it, my grandmother moved in, making sure Lisa and I got fed, got off to school.

On weekends, my mother would bundle us into the car and drive to the hospital, parking in the shade.

"Stay here," she'd say, rolling up the windows and locking the doors. I was nine. Lisa was seven. We'd watch her walk to the front door, disappear. Usually she was gone for half an hour, forty minutes, but once she disappeared for close to two hours. Lisa and I sat patiently for as long as we could, playing with our toys in the backseat as the sun angled its way across the sky. But then we started to fidget.

"I have to pee," Lisa said.

"Me too. Try to hold it."

We tried to fall back into play, but the spell had been broken. We began exploring the far reaches of the car, climbing into the front seat, turning the steering wheel, fingering the controls. Finally Lisa reached out and unlocked the passenger side door, then froze, waiting for punishment. When nothing happened, she pulled the handle. Fresh air poured in. We looked at each other. To speak would be to acknowledge what we were doing, our transgression. The door swung open. By now the sun had fallen behind the hospital, an old, dirty, brick building sprawled across a weedy lot. I swung my legs out of the car, taking the lead because I was older. Even then I couldn't bring myself to disobey fully. I sat there with my legs dangling for what seemed like hours before finally lowering myself to the pavement. Lisa followed, still clutching her ratty doll in her hand. The parking lot seemed huge, a sprawling expanse of cracked concrete. Slowly we approached the entrance, the foreboding stone arch.

"Mommy?" I said quietly, calling out.

Nothing.

We edged closer, step by step, until we were at the door, until there was nowhere else to go but in. Behind us the car door hung open, beckoning, promising warmth, safety.

"What do we do?" Lisa asked.

I tried to imagine what had happened, why she hadn't returned. The possibilities seemed endless. At the root of my fear was the fact that I didn't really understand what had happened to my father. I was too young to comprehend mental illness, hopitalization, and my mother was too upset to explain it, too short-tempered at all my questions, at my inability to comprehend the complexities of modern medicine. All I knew was that my father was inside this building, and my mother was in there with him.

"I have to pee," Lisa said again, her face scrunched, her legs crossing.

I nodded. I knew what I had to do. In front of us was a revolving door, the glass translucent with dirt. I stepped forward, reaching back for Lisa's hand. She grabbed on to me. I put my other hand on the glass of the door and pushed, but it didn't move.

"You have to help," I said.

Lisa moved up beside me, and the two of us put our hands on the glass. A little girl and a littler girl, pressing her upside-down doll against the dirty glass. We pushed. Nothing happened.

"Harder," I said.

We pushed, straining our little muscles. Slowly the door turned. Slowly we revolved away from daylight, away from the known world, away from safety. Slowly we turned our way inside.

The lobby was oversized and dark. There was an empty waiting area to the right, molded plastic chairs and cigarette butts crushed and scattered across the floor. A giant chandelier hung overhead, bulbs dim, casting a murky glow. In front of us was an information desk too high to see over. We heard the sound of voices echoing from unseen corners. I looked around trying to decide. What to do? Which way to go? Light spilled in from behind us, casting long shadows, filtered by the cloudy glass. I saw a sign that said REST-ROOMS. I squeezed Lisa's hand and together we walked across the lobby, moving tentatively, cowed by the knowledge that we shouldn't be here.

In the days before my father had been admitted to this place, he had dropped into a bottomless funk. For weeks, he had been flying, sleeping little, locked away in his study writing. At night he took my mother out to restaurants and nightclubs, staying out till dawn. She loved him most when he was this way, reckless, indomitable. At those moments of pure adrenaline, he was like a moth to her flame. His attention was total. Nothing was too good for her, no present too pricey. He would beg, borrow, or steal to please her, and she loved him for it. At home my grandmother used to shake her head, cooking up another one of her flavorless meals. Her disapproval became a permanent wrinkle across her brow, a puckering of her tight, white lips. She had never liked my father, never trusted him, but what could she do? Her own husband had been a cool and distant man, a mute, demanding provider who worked nights at the refinery and died of a heart attack at the age of fifty-one.

When my father was up, he was like a movie star, lit from the inside, exciting to be around, but when he fell, he fell hard, taking to his bed for days at a time. That summer he descended to new depths. He sequestered himself in their dark bedroom for days. He was the lump under the covers, the stain on the sheets. I remember sneaking in to stare at him. The silence of the room was so strong I could hear my own blood roaring in my ears. My movie star father lying on his back, eyes open but unseeing, lost in a quicksand of futility. I crept farther into the room and paused, letting my eyes adjust, then began moving closer to the bed. My mother was downstairs chopping vegetables, making a soup for him. A potion to bring him back to her. Lisa sat coloring at the table behind her, saying, "Mommy, look at this," but my mother was focused. The soup had to be perfect. She had to pour all her love into it. Otherwise he would know. Otherwise he would stay locked inside that fugue state, distant, unreachable. Otherwise he would abandon her for good.

I stepped up to the bed and looked at my father's face close up. His hair was tangled. His skin was shiny. He was wet around the mouth.

"Daddy?" I said.

Nothing.

"Daddy?"

His eyes were open, but he didn't respond. I reached out to touch him, moving slowly, spooked by his apathy, but needing to know, needing to feel. Behind me the door swung open. My mother was standing there, holding the soup she'd made him. Seeing me, she cried out. The bowl fell, crashing to the floor, breaking. I jumped.

"What are you doing?" she said. "Get away from him."

She ran to me and grabbed my arm, pulling me toward the door.

"Don't you know your father is very sick?" she said. "Very sick. He needs to rest."

Her face was tight, angry. She was holding my arm too hard, pulling me too hard. I was crying. She rushed me to the door, but in her haste she slipped and fell on the spilled soup, dragging me down. We tumbled to the floor together, landing hard. I lay there breathless. My mother's shirt was soaked. She got to her knees.

"Now look what you've done," she said, picking up the broken shards of the bowl. "Ruined everything."

"I'm sorry," I said, trying to catch my breath. "I'm sorry."

On the bed, my father was silent. If he'd heard us, he gave no indication. I climbed to my feet and stood there crying. I could see Lisa's face peering up from the bottom of the stairs, frightened. She was crying too. Crying because I was crying. On her knees, my mother tried to reconstruct the bowl, to scoop up all the shards, but it was no good, and she threw the pieces across the room. She got to her feet.

"Another bowl," she said, her mind already back down in the kitchen, already replacing the lost potion. She hurried past me down the stairs, moving past Lisa, not even seeing her, so focused was she on fetching medicine. So focused was she on resurrecting her fallen heart.

The next day my grandmother called the doctor, who came to the house, frowning and clucking. My father was admitted to the hospital the following morning. My mother never forgave her mother for that, for taking her husband away from her.

In the hospital, my sister and I emerged from the bathroom. We peered down a long hallway, looking for a sign, listening for the pitch of my mother's voice. Orderlies in white uniforms pushed carts from room to room. At the end of the hall was a gated elevator.

"I'm scared," Lisa said.

"It'll be okay," I told her. I looked left, looked right, closed my eyes and chose. *Eenie, meenie, minie . . .* I led Lisa down to the left, past offices, their doors open just a crack, past locked rooms, their windows dark. I tried to make a game out of it.

"It's like an adventure," I said.

Lisa nodded, face skeptical.

We came to the end of the hall, turned right. At every door we paused, and if I could, I peered inside. I saw nurses in white uniforms, orderlies in starched shirts with knotted forearms. Finally we came to a large window looking into a larger room. There were people seated at tables inside. Patients in blue uniforms, men and women gathered around them, children. The glass was crisscrossed with metal wire. I could barely see over the lower lip of the sill. Lisa was too short. I put my hands to the glass, peered inside.

"What?" said Lisa. "What is it?"

I searched the room and there, sitting at a table in the back corner was my mother, bent over, her head pressed against my father's head. She was holding him in her arms, rocking him back and forth. His eyes were open, staring straight ahead, unseeing.

"What do you see?" my sister wanted to know.

"I see Mommy," I told her. "And Daddy."

"Let me see," she said, struggling to pull herself up. But she couldn't reach.

My mother stroked my father's hair. The room was windowless, lit from above, dust motes whirling in the light. I have recreated this moment with actors, the falling blue beams, my parents' lowered heads. But I have never been able to capture the sadness.

"They're laughing," I told Lisa. "Daddy looks so handsome."

"Really?" she said, her face brightening.

"He has her in his arms and they're dancing," I told her.

Lisa's face broke out in a smile. She could see it in her mind, my parents dancing like they used to dance around the house, without music, my father humming, singing.

I watched my mother kiss my father's cheek. She was whispering to him, trying to call him back. And then she looked up. Our eyes met. A hot flush ran through me. My mother, younger than I am now, thirty-one, thirty-two. Her face was so sad. For a moment, it was as if I weren't there at all, as if she were looking backward in time at the girl she used to be. Then she seemed to focus, to see me, and she smiled, and looked away, turning her attention back to my father.

Later, when she came out of the hospital, she found Lisa and me sitting quietly in the car. She climbed in, humming. I waited for her to say something, to yell. But instead she just started the car.

"My good girls," she said. "So patient, waiting for me. What do you say we get some ice cream?"

Lisa started clapping her hands. As far as she knew, my father was getting better. He was dancing, singing. Next to her, I watched my mother's face in the rearview mirror.

"Is everything okay?" I asked her.

She turned, looking back. Then, reaching out, she touched my cheek. I flinched, expecting anything but warmth, gentleness, not because she was a violent woman, but because she gave her affection so rarely, especially in those last few weeks, when it seemed she didn't even know we were there. But sitting in the car, connected by skin, we shared another quiet moment I was too young to fully understand, and again she smiled. As far as she was concerned, I was on her side now, her ally. That's what our silent moment earlier had meant to her. I was a little girl who was finally learning what it was to be a woman, to need a man. She looked in my eyes in the backseat of our car and winked. From then on, I was my mother's confidante, her silent accomplice.

"Soon," she said.

Three months later my father came home, having been electrocuted out of his funk, cured for now, a happy, upbeat tenor, singing silly love songs, dancing my sister and me around the living room, wrapping himself around my mother and never letting go.

Six months later he was dead.

14

On Saturday I'm in the supermarket taking pictures of the Valentines, Nick and Clarice and their two kids, Bill and Jenny. Nick and Clarice were married ten years ago. I had photographed their wedding with a medium-format camera, peering down into the crystal viewfinder. Back then I thought wedding pictures could be avant-garde. I printed them with sloppy black borders, leaning toward shots that were just out of focus. Last week I tracked down Nick and Clarice, and asked if I could come over to take some pictures of their family, their life.

"Just the routine stuff. What it's like for you, married life."

Nick is a computer programmer who used to dream about being a rock star. Clarice was an actress who ended up in real estate.

"We're happy," she tells me as she pushes her cart up the frozen food aisle. Jenny sits in the basket, legs dangling. She's three. Bill, seven, runs ahead, looking for the kind of food that comes with prizes.

"It was tough giving up on music," says Nick, "but I had to be realistic. Bill was on the way, and we needed money. Some kind of security."

"I went and got my real estate certificate."

"And once Bill was born I never doubted for a second."

He takes a box of cereal off the shelf.

"Do I like this?"

"Get that one," she says, pointing. "You need the bran."

He puts the first box back, throws the second in the cart.

"I always say it's like finding your other half," he says. "When you're single, it's like a word on the tip of your tongue. Something you're forgetting. Someplace you were supposed to be. But then when you're married it's like, *Aha! Now it all makes sense.*"

She takes out her list, checks off the items in their cart. Jenny kicks her legs and reaches for things. Bright colors, pleasing shapes.

"You certainly never have to have that awful conversation ever again," says Clarice.

" 'Where is this relationship going?' " says Nick and laughs.

I float back and capture them in the middle of the aisle, surrounded by consumer goods. I shoot in color, hoping for deep saturation, the fluorescent glare of the meat counter down the aisle behind them, a blue-white light, like a glacier creeping slowly in the distance. Nick's hair is receding, and Clarice has put on weight. They've grown into their roles, and seem relaxed, like family life was always where they wanted to be, and being here it's exactly like they thought.

Shooting them, I tell myself I'm fine, happy. But it's been three days, and still he hasn't called. I tell myself I don't care. That it's for the best. I'm better off alone.

It's okay to lie to yourself, as long as you don't make a habit of it.

Bill comes running back with a bag of candy.

"This one has a race car," he says.

"No more candy," says Clarice.

She leans down to pick him up and I snap their picture. Later, when the film is developed, this shot will be the prize. The composition of it, the child's feet leaving the ground, the sense of motion, as Nick reaches up for a can of fruit on the top shelf, Jenny's wide eyes staring right into the camera, while in the distance frosted air rises from the packaged meat. Looking at them, I realize that the supermarket is their church. The place they go each week to remind themselves that everything is where it's supposed to be.

Nick wanders off to find some yogurt. I follow at a distance, snapping pictures, then run into Shelly in the produce aisle.

"Oh my God," she says.

It takes me a minute to place her. Nineteen-year-old Shelly, the bride-to-be.

"How are you?" I say.

"This must be fate," she tells me. She's wearing short-shorts and a halter top.

I watch Nick, the hunter-gatherer, returning to his family loaded down with dairy products.

"It's next month, right?" I say.

Shelly grabs my arm.

"Can we talk?"

"That's not what we're doing?"

"Really talk, I mean. Heart to heart."

"I'm here with some people," I tell her.

Her face screws up, tears forming in the corner of her eyes.

"Okay, okay," I say. "Just give me a second."

I say good-bye to Nick and Clarice and meet Shelly by the automatic doors. We walk next door to the coffee shop.

"I'm having doubts," she says once we're seated.

"That's normal."

"I kissed a boy. Another boy. On the Ferris wheel."

"Are you sure I'm the person you want to talk to about this?" I say. "Don't you have a best friend or a mother or something?"

"I just—How can you know? You know? What guarantee?"

"There's no guarantee. You have to want it."

"And I do. Sometimes. A lot. But maybe not every day. I mean, to think this is the last person, I mean, in bed. And I'm not sure I . . . well, let's just say Roger's a little quick, you know. Not exactly a long-distance runner."

"Shelly."

"And I know. *I know* that's not everything. I love him. I mean, sure I do. But maybe, I mean, more like a brother, you know?"

I don't say anything. This is not the role I wanted: marriage counselor, therapist. I'm the photographer. I don't get involved. I just take pictures.

"Shelly," I say. "I think you should talk to somebody who knows you better. Maybe this is just nerves, you know. Maybe you really are in love with him, and these are just, you know, doubts."

"But everyone's so excited. My momma just loves him. He's part of the family."

"That's not a reason to marry someone," I say. "Because your mother loves him."

She takes a piece of her hair and puts it between her lips, chews it. Nine years ago she was ten, a little girl who played house, who climbed trees, who thought boys were diseased, vulgar.

"How do you know?" she says. "How do you know when it's right? When someone's the one?"

I look out the window, all the families with their shopping carts, the mothers with strollers. The last thing I want to do is tell Shelly that you don't know. You can't know. That you can feel so positive about something one day, and then weeks, months, years later you realize it was a mirage. The last thing I want to do is tell this nineteen-year-old girl what it's like to be a thirty-six-year-old divorced woman.

"Maybe you should put it off," I say. "You're so young. Both of you. Maybe in a couple of years you'll have a better sense of your-self, what you want."

"But Roger wants to start a family," she says. "Right away."

"Are you ready for that?"

"He's such a sweet man. And he's got a good job."

"Shelly."

"I know."

"What about college?"

"Well, we talked about me going. Maybe in a year or so, after the first baby's born."

I stare at my coffee. I consider telling her that marriage is an idea that you both have to believe in. It's like that dream where you're flying and it's beautiful and liberating and anything seems possible. Just don't look down. Because the minute you realize that you're up there, that your place is on the ground, the minute you realize how impossible this is, that's the moment you start to fall. And when you get married, it's the same thing. You think this will last forever because you want it to, and your husband does too. At that moment and for all the days that come after, you exist in this state of grace because you believe. But then one day one of you looks down. One of you starts to doubt. And on that day, without even realizing it, you both start to fall.

I consider telling Shelly this, but I know she wouldn't under-stand. That at nineteen she can't know what it's like to get older, to compromise yourself, to lose faith. The ideas are incompatible with her young mind. All I would be doing would be offering her words, stories of how when I was a kid I used to walk ten miles to school through blizzards in my bare feet. When you're young, you can't hear the words that could save your life until you're ready. By then, it's usually too late.

"Shelly," I say. "You need to tell him. Talk to him. How you're feeling. Your fears."

She looks petrified. She doesn't realize how easy it is to do these things, to ruin everything. I remember myself at her age, an un-happy girl working a dead-end job in a dead-end town. I wanted to leave, to change, but it seemed so impossible. That I could actually pick up and go, quit my job, give notice to my landlord, break up with my boyfriend, tell my parents, my friends. It seemed over-whelming. And then one day, I did it and realized it's the easiest thing in the world. To pick up and go.

Easier than staying.

And then I hated myself for staying as long as I did, for treading water so long, when really what I needed was perched at the end of my legs the whole time. Those ruby slippers, heels clicked to-gether, a simple incantation.

I look at Shelly and want to tell her not to drive herself crazy over this. To tell her we fret for so long, live in turmoil, toss and turn in our beds, suffering late-night anxiety attacks so strong our bodies ache, and in the end, it's just a waste of time. In the end, the fine people in the marketing department of the Nike shoe com-pany were right. *Just do it.*

Not that I'm one to talk. A woman hiding in a tower built of disappointment and fear.

"Tell him," I say. "Otherwise you'll be living a lie. Are you willing to do that? Your whole life? Live a lie?"

But watching her eyes, I can tell that she's considering it.

15

In sleep, everyone is who they want to be. At night, after a few drinks, we sleep and dream and imagine ourselves whole, happy. Our lives are filled with adventure. We lie satisfied on beds of satiny down. In sleep, the world is a place of magic where the only nightmare is one of waking up. Of seeing things for how they really are.

Somewhere bells are ringing. I open my eyes. The room is dark. It's after midnight. I reach for the phone.

"What?" I say.

A man's voice.

"So that's it?"

I fumble around, trying to place the voice, heart beating fast. Is it him?

"Who is this?"

"You just throw a guy's shoes at him and don't call?"

Jerome. I lie back, close my eyes.

"Sweetie," I say. "It's late."

He coughs. Behind him I can hear a jukebox, people talking. He's in a bar.

"I thought I could come over," he says.

And fuck you, he means.

Come over and fuck you.

"I don't think so," I say.

"Oh, now you don't think so."

"You're drunk."

He snorts.

"That never bothered you before."

"I'm already in bed," I say.

"All the better," he says. "Just slip off your panties. Get yourself lubed up. I'll be there in ten minutes."

"Listen, Jerome."

"No way. No 'Listen Jerome.'"

"This isn't working out."

"I can't win with you, can I?" he says. "You keep changing the fucking rules."

"There aren't any rules."

"First I'm supposed to drop by the house," he says. "Then call, then take you home from work, and now what? Just disappear? You're making me fucking crazy."

I think about all those sweet nothings whispered by a man on a dance floor.

"I don't mean to," I tell him.

He starts to cry.

"I love you," he says.

"Don't say that."

"I can't sleep. I don't eat."

"Jerome, snap out of it."

"Oh, sure, 'snap out of it.' Why didn't I think of that?"

I sit up, reach for the light, but then think better of it. I couldn't deal with this in the light, all my ugly secrets, all my dysfunction.

"Jerome," I say. "Listen. You don't need me. I'm not good for you. I'm old and jaded, and you can do better. A lot better. You deserve to meet somebody young. Somebody bright-eyed and hopeful. A woman who'll love you for all your good qualities. Who you can love back without fear. I'm not that woman. I'm a minefield, and trust me, you wouldn't survive three weeks wandering around in a relationship with me. You'd be dead in six hours. I make *myself* crazy most of the time."

"No," he says. "No, you're special."

I lie back and put a pillow over my head, thinking maybe that's it. Maybe that's why this other man seems so appealing to me. This man who infiltrates other people's holidays, other people's memories. Because whatever my damage is, his may be just as great.

And then I think, *Is that crazy?* To want someone broken? To want someone who's been dented, scratched. Someone who won't judge. Someone like me. Because maybe somebody broken will understand all the things I can't bear to talk about without even having to ask. And yes, I know it's stupid to think he could be these things based on two minutes of conversation, based on a look, a dance, a smile, a collection of photographs.

But what else do I have?

"Jerome, listen," I say. "I'm not special. I'm just another broken old lady who doesn't trust anyone, who can't go a day without crying, who's always waiting for the other shoe to drop. You'd be better off marrying a houseplant. Believe me."

"I miss you," he says.

"That'll fade. Trust me. In three months you'll be thanking God for getting you away from me. You'll be the guy on the side of the road looking at the ten-car pileup and thinking, *Thank God that wasn't me.*"

I can hear him drinking. The song on the radio is Bruce Springsteen, musical memories of a long dead youth.

"I want to come over," he says. "I wanna fuck."

"Do me a favor," I say. "Look over at the bar. Is there a group of women there with matching handbags and fuck-me shoes? A clot of divorcées? If you really wanna fuck, just step up and buy one a drink. But be careful. Don't stick around in the morning or you might just find you're trapped."

He doesn't respond. I can hear his confusion on the other end of the line. The truth is, he never understood me, the cryptic things I say. It always made him think I was deep, when really I'm just obscure, self-referential. Jaded.

"Why are you always so fucking mean?" he says.

"I don't know," I tell him. "And I know you don't believe me, but I'm trying to figure it out.

16

photograph the home-wreckers at dusk. One by one, they come to my studio, furtively, hurrying up the front walk, looking over their shoulders, ringing the bell, as if lured by a police sting. I stand them in front of a blank white wall, tell them not to pose, not to smile unless they're happy, and so they don't. More than twenty-five people responded to my ad, and over the course of the next week I photograph five a night. There are more women than men, and the women tend to fall into two categories: Confused young girls in their twenties looking for father figures, and older women in their late thirties who are battling the odds that they'll never get married, never have children.

I tell them I want them to look at the camera the way they look at their men.

The way they would look at their men's wives.

I shoot them with a large-format camera on a tripod, pose them, focus, and then step aside and click the shutter with a remote line. This way I can look them in the eye, talk to them. This way they don't feel so naked.

Angela is twenty-four, a willowy, seductive girl with straight brown hair who works as a paralegal in a law firm.

"I started fucking my boss in January," she says. "We were on a business trip. We'd gone to lunches and things, you know, before. He's like forty-one or forty-two. Good-looking. Nice clothes."

She touches her face. I take her picture.

"In college I had a thing with one of my professors. I guess I like older men, but I never wanted to—I mean, it wasn't a goal of mine, fucking a married man."

I adjust the light so it falls more naturally on her face.

"He flirted with me from, like, day one," she says, pulling out a pack of cigarettes. "Is it all right if I smoke?"

I nod. She lights a cigarette.

Click.

"And I'm, you know, a flirty person. I like it, you know? The charge. Especially in that place, which was like old people central. So he comes on, and I'm giving back and thinking, cute guy, but then I see the ring and I reassess. Like I said, I'm not a slut. Although, I guess now I am, huh?"

She exhales, shakes the hair out of her eyes and glares at the camera, gives it her most seductive look.

"Is this what you're looking for?" she wants to know. "Get all us little sluts together and have us take it off for the camera."

She pushes her breasts together with her arms, bends forward, purses her lips.

I take her picture.

"If that's what you want," I say.

She shrugs, drops her arms, goes back to smoking.

"You don't remember me, do you?" she says.

I squint at her.

"No, sorry," I say. "Should I?"

"I worked with your husband."

I feel a sudden drop in pressure in my stomach, a tiny death.

"My husband," I say.

"Jimmy, right? Magnus?"

I nod. "We're not . . ." I say. "He's my ex now."

"Bummer," she says. "I was a paralegal in the office. A temp. I used to see you sometimes. At lunch."

I bump the camera, then fumble to refocus. She stands there smoking, watching me.

"So is that what happened?" she says. "Is that why you're doing this?"

"What?"

She drops the cigarette, grinds it out with her heel.

"Did he, like, fuck his secretary or something?"

"No," I say. "That's not . . . this is part of a larger . . ."

She looks at the camera defiantly.

"Because men are pigs," she says. "Pigs. Or maybe that's not nice to pigs. Maybe they're more like mushrooms. You know, the poisonous ones you dig up, 'cause you think they'd go good in a soup, and then you end up in the morgue."

I step back behind the camera, hiding, spying. That she knows Jim is like a noose to me, a sign that the world is shrinking, that there's no escape. I tell her to uncross her arms, to not be so defensive. She shoots me a look of judgment that resembles nothing more than anxiety, insecurity, fear.

"So do you still . . . see Jim?" I ask. "These days. Anymore."

She shakes her head.

"That was like three jobs ago. I mean, sometimes I see him downtown, you know, walking around in his shirtsleeves and a tie like all the other automatons. Why? Are you still, like, pining for him or something?"

I step out from behind the camera, change the CD, trying to keep moving, to cover how much she's thrown me. *Am I?* I wonder.

But no, that's not it. It's not so much about wanting him back as wanting back what I lost when he left. As if in packing to go, he took something I need.

Belief.

"He's cute," says Angela. "Kind of a dick, though."

I nod, take her picture.

"You don't know the half of it," I say.

Jane is thirty-nine and beautiful, but her eyes have deep lines around them and her upper lip is starting to get those vertical wrinkles. She poses for a half hour, then asks if she can take off her clothes.

"I feel like I'm hiding something," she says. "Like we're dancing around the real subject here."

I tell her whatever she wants to do. She unbuttons her blouse, slides out of her pants. Her breasts are large, her hips. She has a pale potbelly and a patch of pitch-black hair between her legs.

"I used to be skinny," she says. "A rail. That used to matter to me, how I looked."

I step back behind the camera and adjust the shot. I'm shooting in black-and-white, maybe because the issues are anything but. The way people feel, the things we do. Looking through the camera I notice that her nipples are inverted.

"Are you comfortable standing?" I ask.

She nods. The older women are better at rationalizing the choices they've made, the transgressions. They can maintain hope under the most grueling circumstances. They show up at my studio wearing too much makeup. It takes me a long time to convince them just to be themselves, natural. They can't afford to see themselves as they really are. I can identify with that.

"I think it's great," she says, "what you're doing."

"What am I doing?" I ask.

"Trying to understand. Love."

I don't say anything for a minute, then,

"Are you in love?"

She brushes the hair from her eyes.

"When I was younger, I used to fall in love every twenty minutes. Now I just worry about being alone."

"And yet a married man."

"This isn't science," she says. "Just because we can do math doesn't mean we are math."

"Meaning?"

"Meaning if love were so simple, don't you think we'd have figured it out by now? Meaning even though we act like there's such a thing as good love and bad love, it's all just a jumble. I mean, if we were only supposed to fall in love with good-hearted, healthy people, why is it so easy to fall in love with the lunatics, the assholes?"

I think about this, and wonder, not for the first time, how Jim talks about me. What he says to his girlfriends. Whether in his mind I was the loveless one, the harpy. Whether he thinks of me as dishonest, needy, cold. Whether he acts like the fly who's escaped a spiderweb, sits with his drinking buddies, licking his wounds, and says, *Hell, I'm just lucky to be alive.*

"I don't know," I tell her.

She turns to the side, stretching.

"I gave up trying to figure it out years ago," she says. "Now I'm just trying to be happy."

"And sleeping with a married man makes you happy?"

"Look," she says. "I don't want a man around me all the time. I like my privacy. I like that Charlie has to go home at night. I like that he treats me special, because I *am* special. Not the same old thing. And we have our stolen weekends, and that's great sometimes, but mostly I like that we can have dinner. I can come my brains out, and then have some time to myself. So, really, for me it's the perfect arrangement."

I take her picture as she talks. She seems completely comfortable standing there naked. Maybe what she says is true. Maybe this whole exercise of mine is about understanding love. Why we do what we do, feel what we feel? When you're young, you have this storybook ideal. You think there's this perfect person out there waiting for you. That fate will pull you in the right direction. You don't think about how your parents influence you. How if your dad was absent, you might be looking to replace him. How if your mom was domineering, you might replicate her. And then, from your first crush to your last, every experience you have molds you, narrows you. Every heartbreak. Until one day you wake up and realize that you have a pattern, a type. And instead of growing, you just keep repeating your mistakes over and over. Every crazy man you fall in love with, you tell yourself he's different. Every woman with a victim complex.

And then you realize that what you thought was going to be a matter of finding a round peg for a round hole is really about trying to find any peg that comes close to fitting inside a hole that's as jagged as a sawblade. And it becomes clear that only by giving up the idea of perfection can you begin to be happy, by throwing off the shackles of "should." By saying, *All right, I need a father figure. So what? What's wrong with that?* Or, *Yes, I like to be dominated by strong women. That's what I like. Is it healthy? Maybe not, but it's who I am, and I'd rather be me and feel complete most of the time, than deny myself the things I need and be miserable all of the time.*

The whole idea of broken is misplaced.

We're all broken.

And that makes us normal, because isn't normal all about the numbers? The majority? If it's mental illness to believe the earth is flat, it's only because today everybody knows it's round. But in the 1400s when everyone thought the earth was flat, those same people were considered sane. It was the people who said the earth was round who were thrown into asylums.

Night after night, I take pictures of people who've lost their way, but now I realize, they're not lost, because there's no such thing as found. You go out, and you fumble around and make mistakes and do the best you can. Anyone who tells you they know the way is a liar. And maybe that's why I take pictures. Because in that split second when the flash goes off, everything is illuminated. Later, I can sit with my magnifying glass and try to see things for what they really are. To see people, really see them, look in their eyes and find the thing that makes us human.

The things we have in common.

So I don't have to be alone.

17

He calls on the eleventh of October at 6:15 P.M. I'm in the living room editing. As I do every time the phone rings, I wait to answer it. I don't want to seem too eager. So I sit there, heart pounding, hand hovering over the receiver. One ring, two, three.

"It's me," he says.

"Me?" I say. "Oh right. The phantom. The thief."

"No. Just me. Gilligan."

"Gilligan? You're kidding, right?"

"No. Gilligan Ford the third. Now you can see why I don't throw my name around."

I sit back and look out the window thinking, *I'm obsessed with a man named Gilligan.*

"How'd the pictures come out?" he wants to know.

"Good. You and Ana look very happy. You can't even tell that you're insane."

"I want to see you," he says, interrupting, his voice frank, confident.

I feel warmth spreading through me. I try to control my breathing. *Then why did it take you so long to call?* I almost say. But I don't. I'm afraid if I push too hard he'll disappear. Melt like a snowflake on my tongue.

"I'm free Saturday," I tell him.

His voice on the phone is hoarse, intimate, the low tones vibrating in my ear, down my throat.

"Good," he says.

I think about all the things I could say, all the truths and warnings.

"I'll pick you up at eight," he says.

I call my sister, breathless.

"He called," I say.

"And?"

"And his name is Gilligan."

She starts laughing.

"His name is what?"

"Gilligan something the third. Ford. It's Ford."

"That is just about the best name I've ever heard," she says.

"Shut up."

"You'll have to change your name to Ginger."

"I said 'Shut up.' "

"I could *hang* up," she says.

"No," I say. "Don't. We're going out on Saturday. I need your help."

"Clothes, shoes, hair. Is that what we're talking about?"

"I was talking about therapy and emotional support, but I guess I could use some new shoes."

"Yes, you could," she says. "I've seen your closet."

We go to the mall on Friday. Wandering from store to store, I have a thousand nervous breakdowns. My head hurts, my mouth is dry.

"I can't do this," I tell her as we stand in the changing room. There is a pile of clothes on the floor, and I'm naked, my arms in the air, shimmying into another little black dress.

"You need a bigger size?" she asks.

"No. *This.* Dating. I'm thirty-six years old. I've been married. I thought I'd retired."

She zips up the dress, steps back. We stand there side-by-side, looking in the mirror. Lisa just turned thirty-four this year. She is everything I'm not: stylish, with great boobs.

"You don't get to retire," she says. "It's against the law. You have to slog it out with the rest of us. Go to trendy restaurants with strange men, order the lobster, drink too much wine, listen to him talk about himself, laugh at his jokes, all so you can find out if he's a good kisser or not."

"Why can't I just kiss him before dinner?"

"Because then he thinks you're a slut, and he takes you to Denny's, where it's breakfast twenty-four hours a day."

I study myself in the dress. It's the wrong length for my legs.

"Get this thing off me," I say.

We go to M.A.C. and let anorexic waifs slaughter us with mascara. While we're trying on shoes, I think about how everyone's had to do this. Everyone who's ever loved, who's ever gotten married. Winston Churchill dated, Teddy Roosevelt, Margaret Thatcher. Ronald dated Nancy. Mike Tyson dated Robin Givens, went to prison, got out, remarried. I think about all the women who've dated Alan Greenspan, who've gone to those trendy restaurants and sat across from him, ordered the lobster and listened as he droned on about lowering federal interest rates.

What was Henry VIII if not a love story? Deranged and predatory, but a love story nonetheless. Looking at the world this way helps keep it in perspective. To think of the Kennedy assassination as a tale of two marriages. Boy meets girl. Boy woos girl. Boy kills president. While directly opposite, playing itself out on the same world stage in the same time line, another boy meets another girl, woos her. Then the boy becomes president, has a dozen affairs, staves off the Cuban Missle Crisis, and the girl ends up in the back of a Lincoln convertible chasing the boy's brains out onto a Dallas roadway.

They say serial killers are incapable of having real relationships, but all the great dictators have wives. Even Hitler had romance in his life. I think about this as I try on a pair of four-hundred-dollar Prada mules.

"Yeah," says my sister when I tell her, "and Howard Hughes used to keep his semen in a jar next to his toenails, so consider yourself lucky that you're dating a guy who just crashes weddings."

I try on bras, pants, underwear. I model clothes in three-way mirrors, wanting to evaporate, disappear. Four more hours we shop, wearing ourselves down. At the end of the day, standing in my bathroom, I look in the mirror and see a new me staring back, hair styled, made up, new clothes. But as a photographer I know it's just a mask, that underneath is the same woman with the same problems. All we've done is dress them up, make them pretty.

Then again, sometimes that's the best you can do.

18

That night I pull out the photo album from my wedding. It's in a box buried under a pile of laundry in the back of my closet. I put it on the coffee table and then back away, spooked. It sits there like the book of the dead, offering up its wonders, its horrors, whispering to me to open it, to gaze with nostalgia and revulsion at the things inside. I go into the kitchen instead, pour myself a drink. *I'm fine*, I think. I have it all under control. I pour a finger of tequila into a glass, add some orange juice. I take a lime from the fridge, pull a knife from the drawer. I cut the lime, feeling its juicy kiss on my fingers, wet, acidic. I lift the knife to my lips, taste the citrus stain. I put my wrists on the cutting board, drag the tip of the knife along my arm lightly, just scratching the surface.

You want nothing, I tell myself. *You need nothing. Survival is all that matters.*

I take my drink into the living room, but the wedding album leers at me like a pederast from his car, so I go into my office and turn on my computer. I go to the classified section of the local newspaper and fill out another form.

WANTED: WIDOWS AND WIDOWERS FOR PHOTOGRAPHY PROJECT. CALL ANYTIME. DAY OR NIGHT.

I hold the tequila on my tongue, taste the sharp bite of salt. I think about his body, his smile. I'm overcome with a yearning so strong it makes me feel dizzy, weak. I want to take a match and burn out my eyes. Take a knife and cut out my heart. I don't remember these feelings when I was younger, don't remember ever feeling so much fear. The part of me that's been broken feels hard, like a knot of bone, and I tell myself I'm stronger now. But there is an angry red line running down my arm from where the knife has scratched away my reservation.

I go back into the living room, open the photo album.

If love stories are magical, entrancing, then there's something draining about stories of divorce. Something inevitable and overwhelming. Listening to them, we feel the same thrill we get from rubbernecking at the scene of an accident. They act as cautionary tales, titillating because they're happening to someone else. Scandalous because they contain all the juicy rot of sex and violence and cruelty we can appreciate in entertainment, but find so devastating when that entertainment becomes our lives.

Hearing divorce stories always makes me want to climb into bed and pull the covers over my head.

Because in the end, does it really matter why?

Does it matter the things he said, the things he did?

In the end can you bear the freefall feeling of everything I counted on crumbling beneath my feet? Or does the fact that it's *my* feet make it interesting?

Yes.

After all, living through it and hearing about it are two different things.

And in the end, don't other people's tragedies always make us feel better about our own lives?

I sit there and look at the pictures, and if you ask me why I would say I'm trying to stop myself. Stop myself from opening up again. Stop myself from daydreaming, from chasing a mirage.

I sit there and look at the pictures. After photographing eleven hundred weddings, they look like pictures of strangers. Who is that woman with the sparkle in her eye? That man with his hand on her hip, looking at her as if love is the tunnel of light that leads to heaven?

If I told you he said terrible things to me, would you believe it? If I told you this man, who has the kindest eyes, pushed me to the ground and screamed in my face, would you buy it?

I sit there and look at the pictures, and I think, *Are you gonna hide forever? Is that your new vow?*

I look into my own eyes and think, *How could you have been so blind?* But the truth is, he had no more sense on our wedding day that things would end the way they did than I. He didn't mislead me. He just wanted something else. He thought he wanted me, but he was wrong. He thought I was the one, but I wasn't. And he wasn't the one for me, because otherwise he would have stayed.

How sensible it sounds. How diplomatic. How Disney. To believe that we both woke up one day and realized it was over is to believe that people can agree to disagree. To believe that is to live in a world where violence occurs offscreen. Where everything always turns out for the best. Where people live happily every after.

I sit there and look at the pictures and I remember the little things. The way the bouquet smelled. How tight my shoes were. The heat of the sun. I remember the oranges lying on the ground, the sound of water rushing.

And I think, *I'm taking pictures of all these other people because I can't bring myself to look in my own eyes. I'm photographing other people's heartbreak, because I can't bear to think about my own.*

I go into the kitchen and make myself another drink. This time a little blood pops up from my wrist when I cut it. It burns as the lime juice seeps in.

I sip the tequila and then pour it down the sink. It tastes like drain cleaner. I go into the living room and take the photo album and throw it in the trash. I'm tired of pretending to be dead. Tired of hiding. I'm sick to death of feeling like a victim.

I fell in love. It didn't work out.

It's time to take the bandages off, to cut away the scar tissue.

It's time to stop punishing myself for somebody else's behavior.

I don't want to be numb anymore.

I don't want to be alone.

I take the bag with the photo album out to the corner and throw it into a Dumpster.

I do it before I can change my mind.

I do it and it makes a satisfying crash and I walk back into my house and open up all the windows and the doors.

And then I go into the bathroom and look myself in the eye. And the woman looking back at me is flushed and thrilled and terrified at the same time. Her eyes are wide, and she's smiling a toothy smile that makes me worry about her sanity.

For better or worse, I think.

For better or worse.

19

He picks me up at eight sharp. When the doorbell rings, I feel my soul leave my body and float up toward the ceiling. From high above, I watch myself stand and grab my purse. I watch myself smooth the front of my skirt and walk over to the door.

There I am, I think.

Nice shoes.

I wonder if I'll make it through dinner without passing out.

He is standing on the porch in a pair of slacks and a leather jacket.

I say, "Where's your suit?"

And he looks surprised, a little hurt, and says,

"Was I supposed to wear a suit?"

From the ceiling in the hall, I watch myself fumble around for the right words.

"I've only ever seen you in a suit," I say.

He nods.

"Do you think team mascots," he says, "that everywhere they go they wear those suits? The seal, the tiger, the dinosaur?"

"There's a dinosaur?"

"Dinger the Dinosaur. He mascots for the Colorado Rockies."

"Huh," I say.

We stand there for a minute, neither of us sure how we got so lost so quickly.

"Well," I say.

"Should we . . ." he says at the same time, and then we stand there for another minute trying to figure out who should go first.

"Go?" he finishes.

I look down the driveway at his car, black, foreboding, and feel panic bubble up inside me.

"Do you think . . ." I say. "Could we could just sit for a minute?"

I point to the porch swing.

"Sure."

So we sit in the dark and swing and watch the neighborhood kids play. We sit side-by-side, not touching, but I can feel his heat, his weight shifting, hear the sound of his breathing.

"Nice house," he says.

"Thanks."

"I like the swing."

"Yeah. Me too."

Silence. We sway back and forth.

"I think I should tell you," he says. "It's been a long time since I . . . since I went out on a date."

I brighten.

"Really?"

"The eighties."

I think about the eighties. High school, college. What a difference two decades make.

"Bush or Reagan?" I say.

"Bush."

The porch swing creaks every time we swing backward. For a few seconds there's just the sound of kids running and that oil-less creak.

"I feel like I should say something witty," I tell him, "but I can't think of anything."

He puts his hand on my arm.

"You're fine," he tells me.

I nod. In the dark I can see his profile, a black silhouette against the distant streetlights.

"Let's go," I say.

We listen to something jazzy in the car. The dashboard is space-age blue. I consider telling him it's been a long time for me too, but I don't. It's never a good idea for your baggage to show up before you do. So I tell him about the weddings I have this weekend. Three small ceremonies, two Episcopalian and one Greek Orthodox.

"The Greek Orthodox sounds interesting," he says. "What time on Sunday?"

"No," I tell him. "I won't be your wedding pimp."

He smiles.

"Did I tell you how beautiful you look?" he says.

I blush, grateful for the darkness, duck my head against the glare of oncoming headlights.

"No," I say. "Stop that. It's not fair."

He looks over at me.

"Why is telling you you're beautiful not fair?"

I roll down my window, let the wind blow over me, messing up my hundred dollar hairdo. He clicks his turn signal, changes lanes. We stop at a red light. I think about jumping from the car and running off, even go so far as to put my fingers on the handle, but then the light changes and we're moving again.

"Sorry," I say, "I'm not used to this. It's been a long time for me too."

He thinks about this.

"Good," he says finally.

"Good?"

"Why should I be the only one fumbling around in the dark."

We drive for a few minutes in silence. He heads east, pulls into the park, driving slowly down the tree-lined avenues. I watch the moon follow us through the sunroof. He makes a right, a left, and then we're pulling up in front of the aquarium, stopping. I stare at the light blue banners fluttering in the breeze.

"The aquarium," I say.

"You don't like aquariums?"

"I . . . I mean."

He puts his hand on mine.

"Trust me."

I don't dignify that with a response, but his hand is warm, and I let it linger. Outside, the aquarium windows are dark. The parking lot is empty except for a single car.

"It looks closed," I say.

He gets out of the car, comes around, opens my door. Overhead a cloud moves in front of the moon. I climb out, shivering. He takes my arm and leads me to the front door, knocks on the glass. After a minute a security guard comes over and opens the door.

"Thanks, Frank," says Gilligan.

Frank?

"You work here?" I ask as he leads me down a dimly lit hallway.

"No. I come here a lot though. The director is a client of mine."

We pass a cartoon banner for CREATURES OF THE DEEP, step onto an elevator. He presses two. The doors close.

"Client?" I say.

"I'm an accountant."

"Oh."

"I know what you're thinking, but accounting is dangerous again. Thanks to Enron."

"It was dangerous before?"

The doors open and we step into a large hall. Around us, the walls are glass, lit from behind and filled with water, multicolored coral, thousands of fish. They swim in patterns, pivoting, fish of all shapes and sizes, all colors, swaying, shivering, sparkling like glitter in the rippled light. The whole room is alive, and yet it has this pressurized silence, the sound of water pressing on your eardrums. In the center, a table has been set with candles. They glow white against the lapping blue light. I stand stunned, frozen in place. It's so beautiful I want to cry.

"Are you crying?" he asks me, startled.

Around us the fish move in schools, turning, darting in unison, and behind them bigger fish float in Technicolor. We are at the bottom of the ocean, floating in a deep blue sea.

"You must be some accountant," I manage.

He smiles, wipes a tear from my cheek.

"Is it too much?" he asks.

I look around. He's taking no chances. I think about the kind of date I would have planned. A booth in a diner near an open door, the car left running outside, pointed toward the on-ramp of a major highway.

"It's perfect."

He takes my arm, leads me to the table. We stand there looking down at our place settings, the beautiful white plates, a bottle of wine open, breathing. I look over at him, amazed, and he's backlit by blue water, fish swimming around the halo of his head and before I know what's happening I'm leaning in, kissing him, gently at first, then deeply, and his mouth is soft, lips parted. And I feel a different kind of disembodiment, as if this time my whole body is floating. As if I'm one of the fish suspended in liquid.

It feels so good it scares me.

I pull away, wipe the lipstick from his mouth with my finger.

"My sister said not to do that," I say.

"I never liked that woman."

The way he's looking at me makes me self-conscious.

"What?" I say, trying to hide, trying to disappear in plain sight.
He shakes his head.

"Everything," he says.

I pull out my chair, sit down, trying not to think about how many of my own rules I'm breaking.

"I need a drink," I say.

He smiles, pours me a glass of wine, sits. We watch a manta ray lift from the bottom of the tank and angle upward.

"What's for dinner?" I ask.

"Well, not fish," he says. "That would be wrong."

We eat our salads. I ask him about accounting. He tells me he's been doing it for twenty years.

"It has rules," he says. "I like that. I like that there's a book you can read that lays it all out, a series of laws. I like numbers. I like things that add up."

"There are things that add up?" I want to know.

He smiles.

"Remind me not to let you pay the check," he says.

"I have a woman who does my bookkeeping," I tell him. "She's Ukranian. Every month I hand her a shopping bag full of receipts. She says there's a special place in hell reserved for people like me."

"I do some corporate bookkeeping," he says, "some personal income tax work. I like things to be manageable, size-wise. I like knowing my clients personally. I think it's important not to surround yourself with strangers."

"And yet you go to weddings where you don't know anyone."
He smiles.

"Oh, I know them. They're the same at every wedding. The bride, the groom, the best man. Tell me you don't know just what I mean."

I poke at my food, eyes down. I can't look at him. He's like a light, a million brilliant watts just waiting to blow to my eyes out.

"Yeah," I say. "It's true. I can walk into a hall and in ten minutes tell you who's gonna be drunk by the end of the night, who's gonna sleep with who, who's secretly in love with the bride."

"Everyone likes to think they're unique," he says. "But really we just fit into a few wide categories."

I close my eyes and think about Jerome. About how much simpler that was, how finite. It's good to know your limits, not to over-reach. And yet here I am, underwater, out of my element.

"Are you married?" I say.

He stops. I stumble over my words.

"*Were,* I mean. Have you ever been?"

"I was," he says. "My wife died."

I think about this, about saying *I'm sorry,* but I don't. Instead I watch his face, the way his eyes fall, his head drops.

"So you go to weddings," I say.

He pops a tomato in his mouth, chews.

"It's better than going to funerals," he says.

I watch the sea life pulse and shift around us. The truth is, I've always been terrified of oceans, deep water. I have this recurring nightmare in which I find myself floating alone in the middle of the sea, surrounded by black water, not knowing what's under me, circling.

"How long since she . . . ?"

"Five years. She had cancer."

I consider telling him that despair is a kind of cancer—depression, anger, grief—but I don't.

"And how old are you?"

"Is this an interrogation?"

I try to smile.

"Sorry. I'm not good at small talk."

He nods, pushes his food around.

"I'm forty-two," he says. "And you're what, twenty-eight?"

"Yeah, right. My car is twenty-eight. I'm . . . you know, older than that."

He smiles, lifts the cover off a platter.

"I hope you like duck," he says.

Behind him a shark glides across my field of vision, its dead eyes staring. Seeing it, I shiver.

"Cold?" he says.

He lifts slices of duck onto my plate. I study his face, looking for clues, holes.

"My sister thinks you're a serial killer." I say.

"Really?"

"Or some other kind of criminal. Like an . . . arsonist."

"No."

I watch his eyes, knowing I'm ruining this, but I can't stop. I look away, watch the shark angle around the room.

"Were you married a long time?"

He sips his wine.

"Can't we just, you know, chitchat for a little while. I learned a new joke today. Do you wanna hear it?"

"I was married too," I tell him. "For a year."

"A guy comes home from church," he says. "And he's got a black eye. His wife says, 'What the hell happened to you?' "

The shark swims the length of the room, turns the corner. In a few seconds it will be behind me.

"We were married a little over a year," I tell him.

"The guy says, 'Well, I was sitting in a pew next to this big, fat woman, and when we stood up to sing, I noticed that her dress was caught between the cheeks of her ass.' "

I turn my head and watch the shark. It moves without effort, tail gliding from side to side, jagged teeth spilling out of its mouth at crazy angles.

"And it . . . didn't work out," I say. "I mean, we got divorced."

" 'So I reached over and pulled it out,' " says Gilligan, " 'and she socked me.' "

A school of pastel-colored fish scatter as the shark passes, the coral pulsing around them in glowing blues and greens.

"And I'm sure you're really nice and everything," I say.

"The next Sunday he comes home from church again, and his other eye is black."

"But I don't know if I'm ready for this. I think maybe this was a mistake."

"And his wife says, 'What the hell happened to you?' "

"Gilligan?"

"What?"

"I'm trying to tell you something."

"You don't want to hear the punchline?"

The shark is gone now. Only the smallest fish remain.

"Okay," I say. "Tell me the punchline."

"So the guy says, 'Well, I'm sitting in the pew next to that same woman again, and when we stand up to sing I look over and, sure enough, her dress is crammed between the cheeks of her ass. But I don't touch it, oh no. The guy on the other side though, he reaches over and pulls it out and she hits him. And then, because I know how much she likes it up there, I reach over and *shove it back in.*' "

He smiles and at that moment he's ten years old again, and I look at his little-boy face and think, *I'm so screwed.*

"What?" he says. "It's not funny."

"It's very funny."

"But you're not laughing."

"Shut up and kiss me," I say.

After dessert we wander down the hall and watch the penguins burble and cluster in their habitat.

"Did you know that emperor penguins are the largest of the seventeen species?" he says, taking my hand and holding it.

"Really?"

"They take turns moving to the inside of the group, where

they're protected from the icy cold temperatures and wind."

I look around.

"Are you reading this from somewhere?"

"No. Now pay attention. There'll be a quiz later."

I lean over and kiss him softly on the corner of his mouth. He puts his hand on the flat of my back.

"You're just sucking up to me so you can get a better grade," he says.

I watch the penguins jump into the water one by one.

"The women lay a single egg," he says, "then swim distances of up to fifty miles to find food, while the men stay home and warm the eggs with their feet."

"Their feet?"

"You know what I mean. At their feet. They sit on them."

I slide my arm through his.

"Now you're just making it up."

"I swear. I saw it on television, so it must be true."

When we get back to the main room, the table is gone.

"How are you doing this?" I say.

"I told you, the director is a friend of mine."

"You do his taxes. That doesn't get you a romantic dinner in the middle of the aquarium."

"I married his sister," he says.

"Oh."

He lifts my chin.

"Uh-uh," he says. "Don't do it. Don't make me tell you another joke."

"It's just so sad," I say.

"Yeah. But you know what I learned? It's no use waiting for happiness. Nothing's gonna turn bad memories into good memories. You just have to learn to live with them. To be happy anyway."

We're standing in the middle of the room, underwater, and the shark is circling us again. I take a deep breath and walk over to the glass. I put my hands against it and watch it swim, so close I swear

I can smell the water, that sea-green odor of salt and decay, so close I'm sure he'll turn and swallow me hole, gobble me up. My whole body's telling me to back up, run away, but I don't. Up close his eyes are spooky white. His teeth are crooked, serrated. I stare at them and in my mind I say:

I'm not afraid of you.

Bully.

You can't hurt me.

I am protected by glass.

But deep down I know that one day I'll have to break the glass if I ever want to be truly free. Swing the hammer, shoot the gun, burn the whole thing down. One day. But for now I stand there taunting the shark with my mind, while behind me Gilligan lifts my coat and helps me put it on.

20

I call my sister when I get home. After the endless good-bye on the front porch, the dizzying swirl of tongues, the heat of bodies pressed together. After my heart has swollen to twice its normal size. After we have said, "Okay, good night," like fifty-seven times and then just stood there staring into each other's eyes. After I've shoved him, literally *shoved him* toward the stairs, and still he won't go. Still he stands staring at me, as if by walking away he is saying good-bye forever. After we have moved to the porch swing and creakily made out for ten or twelve more minutes, his hands moving over my body, searching for the ache that stabs at me, needles me, makes me want to ask him in. After my lips are numb and I can't stop smiling. After he's finally made it to the bottom of the steps and I've opened the screen door and we are, for all intents and purposes, finished for the night, except if that's the case why is he suddenly on the porch again? Why am I back in his arms, swooning, tumbling? After he has gotten in his car and driven away and I've stood there on the porch for what feels like an hour staring at the moon, listening to the sounds of a neighborhood asleep, the wind in the trees, somebody's bicycle wheel spinning on a front lawn, the sound of a distant barking dog. After I've gone inside and thrown myself onto the couch feeling drunk and drained and alive, I pick up the phone and call my sister.

"Do you know what time it is?" she says.

"You said you were mad because I never called."

"I meant during regular business hours," she says. "Normal human hours. Whatever. I'm asleep."

I kick my shoes off, put my feet up on the sofa. I feel like an arctic explorer back from the pole, a mountain climber returning from twenty-thousand feet.

"I feel like Evel Knievel," I tell her.

"Who?"

"You know, the guy that jumped Snake River Canyon."

Through the phone I can hear her sitting up, fumbling for her cigarettes, a lighter clicking to flame.

"He landed like fifty feet short," she says. "Fell half a mile. Broke every bone in his body."

"All right, maybe that's a bad example. Neil Armstrong, then. I feel like Neil fucking Armstrong."

"Okay, Neil. So tell me."

"Amazing. He's amazing."

"Uh-oh."

"We went to the aquarium."

"The aquarium? What is he, six?"

"No, it was . . . we were all alone and there was a table. We ate dinner. And there were penguins."

"Uh-huh."

"It was amazing."

"You said that already."

"How about 'eek' did I say 'eek'?"

"What's his name again?"

"Gilligan Ford the third."

"That's still not a real name."

"Shut up. I love him."

"Did you order the lobster?"

"Duck. We had duck."

I go over to the end table, pick up his picture. A man in a suit sitting in a pew, smiling openly.

"Is he a good kisser?" my sister asks.

"It's like he invented it."

"Sounds like I need to come over and hose you down."

"I have this weird feeling in my chest."

"You're happy."

"That's it. You're right."

I throw myself onto the sofa, kick off my shoes.

"I'm so screwed."

"Tell me about it. Dave proposed to me tonight."

"Get out."

"He did. Down on one knee and everything."

"Oh my God. And?"

"And I said 'yes.' "

I start laughing.

"Shut up," she says. "It's not funny."

"It's so funny," I say. "In the best sense of the word, the I'm-so-happy-I-can't-stop-laughing-sense, the all-that-talk-about-not-loving-him, not-trusting-him-was-such-a-fucking-act sense."

"I know. I'm pathetic."

"You're great. I love you."

"Now I know you're drunk."

"Call me tomorrow," I say.

After we hang up, I go into the bathroom and take off my makeup. I think about Lisa getting married, that little girl who held my hand in the mental hospital. I want to get down on my knees and pray, light candles, sacrifice a goat. Anything to make her happy. To make it last. What's the point of being the older sister if I can't protect her from all the pain I've suffered, all the mistakes I've made? I wash my face and brush my teeth. On my left arm there is still the smallest hint of a red scratch, a fading line descending. I pull my hair back and look at myself in the mirror.

You had a date, I think.

You met a boy.

It's almost a love story.

And though I know that tomorrow I'll start freaking out, that my heart will race and my mind will churn, though I know that in the morning all the fear and doubt will return, tonight I let myself be happy.

21

The marriage counselor has a trim white beard. He sits in a padded chair with his legs crossed. His accent is pure Queens. His office is decorated with bamboo and dark wood furniture. Light streams in through the window behind the sofa, where Larry and Grace sit—a couple whose wedding I photographed in 1997. She wore an off-white dress with a ten-foot train. He had a mustache and a cummerbund. When I called Grace last week, she said things weren't going so well, but they were trying to work it out, seeing somebody. I asked, did she think I could come one time? She said she'd talk to Larry about it, but she didn't see why not. If it could help other people maybe avoid the mess they'd gotten into, she didn't see what harm a few pictures could do.

Larry is bigger than I remember, hulking. The mustache is gone, but he still works construction. Grace is heavier too. What was voluptuousness has turned to bulk. I float right, trying to stay out of their line of fire. There is a table lamp next to Grace, lighting her face. Larry is more of a silhouette, a jut of rock, lit from behind by light spilling in through the blinds. Across from them, the marriage counselor is segmented in slices of sun.

"Last week," he says, "we were talking about listening. Have you had any other thoughts on that?"

Grace fingers the sleeve of her shirt. From her body language, I can tell she's been looking forward to this all week, saving up for the one hour when her husband has to sit there and listen.

"I tried what you said," she says. "To be specific. So last Thursday when he forgot to take the trash out again I didn't say, 'How come you never do what I ask?' I said, 'It upsets me that you forgot to take the trash out tonight.'"

"Good," says the marriage counselor, then turns to Larry. "How did that make you feel?"

I watch Larry's jaw work. He's clearly uncomfortable, like a man forced to talk to a doctor about how his penis isn't working the way it should.

Click.

"It made me feel like why can't she take the garbage out instead of nagging me all the time? I mean, how hard is it? You pull out the bag, walk it out to the curb. Meanwhile, she's going on and on for like twenty minutes. It coulda been done ten times by now."

"Grace?" says the marriage counselor.

"Oh, so I'm supposed to do everything?" she says. "Cook *and* clean *and* do the laundry *and* take out the garbage. And what do you do then, Mister-I-sit-on-the-sofa-all-night? What do you do to make our home a better place?"

"I fucking work. Ever hear of it? Paying for things? That's me. I'm Mister-work-my-fucking-ass-off-all-day-long-so-you-can-buy-those-stupid-lawn-niggers."

The marriage counselor makes a note. Grace's hands start to flutter.

"He doesn't mean it," she tells us. "He's just angry."

"Don't say what I mean," says Larry.

"Remember," says the marriage counselor. "Don't fight. Listen."

I zoom in on Grace's face. On the phone, she'd started crying. She said she didn't know what happened. It's like she married a different person. Like one day he just turned into his father, a surly, lazy drunk, and she's still trying to retrace her steps, to track the change. She said, "I feel like one of those, what do you call it, forensic investigators, like on that show on TV. I've got fingerprints, a few hairs, a footprint, and I'm trying to reconstruct an entire marriage."

"I just don't know if I can take it anymore," she says.

"What's that supposed to mean?" says Larry.

"It means I don't know," she says. "It means what's the point?"

"Don't even think about walking out on me," says Larry.

"I'm just so tired," she says. "Tired of fighting, tired of always feeling . . . disappointed."

"Oh, believe me. We're both tired of that. Sick to death of it, Mrs. Disappointment, like who made you the fucking standard bearer against which all things get to be judged?"

"Larry," says the marriage counselor. "You're yelling."

Larry hunches over farther, his head drooping toward his knees like an avalanche. He is rocking slowly back and forth, fists clenched. Focusing on his face, I can see him mutter something under his breath.

"I'd like you to try an exercise this week," says the marriage counselor. "Try going out on a date. Pretend you're meeting for the first time. Take nothing for granted."

"That sounds good," says Grace.

Larry sits up. He stares at the marriage counselor as if he just grew another head.

"You want me to date my wife?" he says, and his tone indicates he's seriously thinking about coming over and clobbering this guy.

"As an exercise," says the marriage counselor. "It might help rekindle something."

"I'm not gonna date my wife. That's why I got married in the first place."

"Larry," says Grace.

"No, goddamnit. This is so fucking stupid, to sit here and pay this guy. To tell him all our fucking . . . I mean, what makes him so smart? What makes him qualified to say what's wrong with us? Nothing. And that's what's wrong with us too? Nothing. Nada. Everything's just fine."

"Are you crazy?" she says. "Look at us."

"What? You think marriage is supposed to be some bullshit like from those books you read, some fairy-tale la-di-da? Well, I got news for you, Miss-I'm-always-right-and-you're-always-wrong, it ain't that. It's about we work hard and make a nice home. It's about we have some kids, buy some comfortable chairs, a big screen TV, and I work my ass off and we get old, and when I die all that's left is an ass mark in the La-Z-Boy and hopefully the house is paid off."

"That's what marriage is to you? A comfortable chair?"

"It's I come home from work and you've got dinner ready and the kids are like, *Daddy, help me with my home work*, and I'm like, *Ask your mother*. And I have a few beers, watch some boob tube, and fucking pass out cause I'm so goddamn beat. That's what it was for my father and his father. It's I do all the heavy lifting and you make sure the house and stuff is taken care of."

She slumps under his onslaught.

"Maybe I want more than that," she says quietly.

"What? You think this is a fucking spa? You think we should be sitting around at night talking about current events and some painting what's hanging at the fucking museum? Maybe you forgot who we are. Where we came from. Maybe you forgot what I do for a living. I'm a fucking grunt. I carry lumber. I do drywall. I'm not some guy who listens to opera and wants to talk about books. And you knew that when you married me, so stop whining."

I move forward, take his picture, and he turns on me, slaps the camera out of my hands.

"Get that fucking thing outta my face. You think this is so fucking interesting? To watch my wife deprecate me?"

The camera sails across the room and crashes into the wall. My hands are stinging, my cheek already aching from where the corner of the camera body hit it. I stare at him, his ugly face, all the anger. And in my mind, I'm still taking pictures. In my mind I'm seeing the shots mounted on aluminum and hanging on a gallery wall.

Click, click, click.

From inches away we stare at each other, as his wife flutters around making apologies, hands dancing, as the marriage counselor jumps from his chair and retreats, stands back to the wall, fumbling for the right words. Larry glares at me, hands balled, breathing heavily, and I cock my head and study his face, his eyes, the angry slice of mouth. I think about all the men who've ever yelled at me, about Howard in college who called me a fucking cunt, and Dave who got so mad he couldn't talk, just kept walking around in circles punching the air, and Jim, his jaw tight, a vein throbbing in his forehead, who actually kicked down a door to get at me, and how he screamed, "There's just no winning with you, is there?"

I look in Larry's eyes, take his picture with my mind. And gradually, something in my gaze deflates him, something about the way I don't react, the way I just stare at him, and his shoulders slump and he looks away, sits back.

Grace has gone over and picked up my camera. She brings it over to me, apologizing. I take it from her, look at it. The lens is bent, the aperture ring broken.

"I think maybe that's all for this week," says the marriage counselor, taking his seat again, trying to regain his composure. "I think we should all take a time out and think about what just happened."

Larry looks at him, shakes his head like he can't believe he's still here listening to this, then stands and walks out. Grace watches him go.

"I'm so sorry," she says.

I put my hand to my cheek. Tomorrow there'll be a big bruise there, all purple and brown.

"It's not your fault," I say.

"I just don't understand him anymore," she says, stands tiredly for a minute, defeated, then follows her husband into the waiting room.

The marriage counselor goes into the bathroom, comes out with a wet cloth. I hold it to my face.

"How long were you married?" he wants to know.

"Who said I was married?"

"The way you looked at him," he says. "I just assumed."

I sit on the sofa and unhook the lens from my camera, examine it.

"A year," I say. "Maybe a little more."

"What happened?"

"You tell me."

He studies me, the light from the window behind me lighting his eyes, a slice of throat.

"He had an affair?"

I shake my head, put the broken lens in my camera bag, take out another, click it into place. The marriage counselor watches me.

"Did you?"

I stare at him for a moment, shake my head.

"I thought you were gonna be good at this," I say. "Like one of those television psychics. Help me talk to my dear departed husband."

He shrugs.

"I went to a community college," he says. "Half the time I'm just trying to keep people from beating each other senseless."

I lift the camera, take his picture. He looks like a man in jail. My cheek aches, a headache starting just above my eyes. A delayed sense of threat seeps into my blood, a sudden blossoming realization of the danger I was just in, as if some kind of shock is wearing off. The high of escape.

"What's the strangest relationship you ever saw?" I ask.

"Oh, I couldn't," he says.

I zoom in on his mouth, notice that the beard covers a small scar under his lip.

"Just between you, me, and the wall," I say and take his picture.

"Okay," he says. "There was a woman who wanted a divorce because her husband wouldn't let her put things in his ass."

"Things?"

"It's clear there was some kind of abuse in her past. But her husband, who was a college professor, was baffled. Why was this so important? What was it about the act of penetrating him that made her so irrational?"

"Things?" I say.

He shakes his head. I lean back, capture him in context, wondering if he picked out every piece of furniture in his office for its therapeutic value. Its soothing, nonconfrontational veneer.

"Then there was the husband who went to a party without his wife," he says. "Took off his wedding ring, put it on his key ring and promptly lost his keys. Even a guy who went to community college could see through that one."

I watch his eyes and wonder if he ever worries that he's doing more harm than good. I open my mouth, feeling heat from my cheek, pain.

"What do you think is gonna happen to Larry and Grace?" I ask.

He frowns.

"She has a decision to make," he says. "This is who he is. She had to have known it when she married him, but she was probably an optimist. Probably thought he was still growing. A young guy, just out of high school, working construction until he can save enough money for something better. But something better never comes, and one day he's turned into just another guy from the neighborhood, like his dad. And she has to either accept her role or leave him."

I lift the towel to my face.

"Does it hurt?" he wants to know.

I shrug.

"You should go to the emergency room," he says. "Have that checked out."

I stand and start packing my stuff.

"Are you married?" I ask him.

"I have a partner," he says and lets it hang there.

"Is it different?" I want to know. "Men with men? Women with women?"

"There are differences," he says. "But in the end jealousy is jealousy and insecurity is insecurity and people break up."

I put my bag over my shoulder. My cheek is throbbing.

"Sometimes I think that if aliens came down from space," I say, "they'd think we were all crazy. All this time and energy we waste on relationships, on love, when we could be out exploring space, forging world peace."

"It's only a waste of time if you think it is," he says.

22

At home I polish my lenses and check my supplies. I hang black velour against one wall of my studio, check the bulbs in my lamps, make sure I've laid in enough film. I load my cameras, set up my tripod. I do this all one-handed, with a bag of frozen peas pressed against my face. Outside the sun goes down, dissolving into a fiery orange stain. The sky turns bruise-blue, then black. I lie in the bathtub and run through all the other blows I've taken, physically, emotionally. I remember my father spanking me, throwing me down across his knee, saying how it was for my own good. I remember my mother slapping me—a whole flip book of high school smarminess revisited, pushing her to apoplexy, violence. I remember Dan Halloway punching me in the stomach in tenth grade, all the air going out of me, legs crumpling, sitting hard, one arm outstretched, fighting for air. I remember a college bar fight.

Girls from town ganging up on my friend Susie, and suddenly I've got someone's hair in my hand and I'm kicking someone else in the gut. And later my knuckles were scraped and we were running, panting, laughing, and coughing up details in a nonstop stream of words. Then Susie said, "Laurie, hold up. Your lip is bleeding." And I reached up and felt the split, tasted the blood. But I didn't care. I was high on adrenaline and violence.

I think about all the relationships I've ever had, and how sooner or later anger becomes a part of everything. Jealousy, insecurity, resentment. All the dangerous emotions. I think about Billy Mardel when I broke up with him, and how his face turned purple when he yelled. I think about the blind rage I felt when Oscar told me he'd been fucking another woman the whole time we were dating. The meat-eating frenzy that came over me, like a caveman with a knotted bone raised, howling.

I think about Larry's face in the marriage counselor's office. The undirected hatred, like a weapon of mass destruction.

I try not to think about Jim, about how diluted, fermented love can become hatred. How even the best medicines can become poisonous if taken in too large a dose.

My cheek throbs like a muscle, like a beating heart, and I think, *Love is like a superpower.* It can make you stronger than a thousand suns, faster than a speeding bullet, invulnerable. It can make you fly. But corrupted, misused, it can turn the reddest heart black. Spurn your lovers, abuse them, and they become arch-villains, everything positive turning acidic and cold. The stronger the love, the fiercer the hate when things fall apart.

I pull myself out of the bath, towel off, go to my computer and place another classified ad.

WANTED: VIOLENT HUSBANDS, BATTERED WIVES FOR CONFIDENTIAL PHOTOGRAPHY PROJECT. ALL PICTURES TAKEN SEPARATELY, UNLESS OTHERWISE DIRECTED.

Then back to the beginning, place another.

WANTED: STALKERS AND THEIR VICTIMS FOR PHOTOGRAPHY PROJ-
ECT. ALL NAMES WILL REMAIN CONFIDENTIAL.

I get dressed. My cheek is swollen, discolored.

At eight o'clock the doorbell rings. I answer it.

"Jesus," says Gilligan, "what happened to you?"

"Bug bite," I say.

I can tell from his expression he doesn't believe me, but he
doesn't say anything, just kisses me gently on the mouth. I take his
coat.

"I thought we'd have a quick drink, then get started," I say.

He nods, looking around. I've cleaned the surfaces, hiding anything incriminating in closets and drawers. All my secrets, all my
skeletons.

"Are you sure you're okay?" he says when I hand him a beer.

"It's nothing. A bruise."

He sits on the sofa. We don't know each other well enough for
him to press.

"So do you do a lot of this?" he says.

"Take pictures?"

"Of widowers."

I put my beer on the table, sit back.

"It's part of a series I'm doing," I tell him. "On love. What
happens."

"What happens *when*?"

"Well, for ten years I photographed weddings, and then one day
I wanted to know what happens. It's like if you build boats or cars.
Ten years later you wonder, are they still running?"

"All that time and effort," he says. "Was it worth it?"

"The census only tells you so much. Academic studies. We see
numbers, statistics. Fifty-percent divorce rate. But those numbers
have faces. Those faces have stories."

He crosses his legs. I wonder what his day was like, try to picture
him sitting in an office with an abacus, a ten-key calculator adding
up the numbers.

"Abandonment," he says, "affairs."

"Miscarriage."

I picture him talking on the phone in a professional tone of voice, scheduling appointments. I wonder if he looks at porn on the Internet. If he has movies and magazines at home. I picture him sitting on the end of his bed in a suit staring at the wall, aimless, listless, alone.

"And sometimes people die," he says.

We drink for a minute in silence.

"Do you remember Newt Gingrich?" he says. "Who divorced his wife while she was in the hospital dying of cancer?"

"What are you trying to tell me?" I say, wryly. And as soon as I do, I want to take it back. Even I know this isn't something to joke about: someone's dead wife.

"No," he says softly. "I was with her till the end."

I look at his face and my heart feels like a balloon expanding in my chest, stretching, ready to burst.

"Sorry. I didn't mean to . . ."

He meets my eyes, nods.

"Don't worry about it," he says, then touches his cheek. "So tell me."

I touch my face gingerly. It feels puffy and hot. I describe the marriage counselor's office, the argument, the blow.

"It's my fault, really," I say. "What did I expect? You don't go to a war zone without knowing you could get shot."

"Maybe next time a longer lens," he says.

"Telephoto. I can photograph from two states away."

We sit there looking at each other and there's a feeling in the air, a humidity of attraction. We look into each other's eyes and want, yearn, but decorum makes us keep our seats, decorum makes us look, not touch. There are rules about these things. Rules of behavior, rules of protecting ourselves, rules of not getting too carried away. And in the moments that follow I feel barbecued, microwaved, cooked from the inside out. To look in someone's eyes without talking, to pour your heart up through your face, shoot it across the room, to lose yourself in someone else's thoughts, it can make a person dizzy.

"Huh," I say.

He nods.

I hold out my hand.

"Come on."

He takes my hand and I lead him into my studio, nervous, wondering if taking him to bed would be easier, less intimate. I stand him in front of the black velour. From across the room he looks uncomfortable, as if only now does he realize what he's gotten himself into.

"Would you rather sit?" I ask him as I turn on the lights.

"No," he says. "This is fine."

I step closer, hold a light meter up to his face, taking readings.

"I don't think anyone's ever taken my picture before," he says. "Not like this."

"A virgin," I say.

"I'll be gentle." I say. "Just relax."

I put on some quiet music, something to drain the silence. He stands in an open-collar shirt, a pair of black slacks. I wonder what his body is like. Stepping behind the camera, I put my eye to the viewfinder. Things are easier to understand when you can crop them. When everything can be framed in a finite square or rectangle. The world makes more sense when you look at it one image at a time.

"Tell me about your wife," I say.

"She was tall," he says. "Taller than me. We used to joke about it. Say everyone's the same height lying down."

I frame him against the black, thinking about how his features will soften in the printing process. How the blacks of him, the shadows, will blend into the background. How those parts of him that are well lit will pop out. His face. His eyes.

"Did you like that?" I ask. "A tall woman. Does that appeal to you?"

He smiles.

"No. It's not a fetish. I just met her."

"Where?"

I watch him remember, take his picture.

"We met at a Halloween party. I was William Shatner. She was a dalmatian. A dog. I told her it was my mission to explore strange new universes and make out with all the women."

"Did you now?" I say.

He smiles.

"She told me she'd been spayed recently and the stitches were still healing."

I picture the room, smoky, filled with people in costumes, everyone pretending to be someone they're not.

"We dated for six months, then moved in together."

"What did she do?"

"She was a veterinarian."

"Of course."

He shifts his weight.

"Am I doing this right?" he says, looking at the camera.

"You're doing fine," I say and take his picture. "Just be natural, open."

He nods.

"Let me know if you want me to strip down," he says. "Maybe take some shots for the Men of Accounting wall calendar."

I smile, knowing he can't see, that I'm hidden behind the camera.

"So you lived together," I say.

"For about a year, then got married."

"Church?"

"Vineyard. Her family's from Napa."

"Do you still talk to them?"

I watch his face turn sad, as if weights have been attached to every muscle.

"Sometimes. Her mother calls me. It's terrible for them, you know? When you're a parent you always think you'll be the first to go."

I attach the remote cable, take a deep breath, step out from behind the camera. Suddenly, we're in the room together, face-to-face, separated by five feet of open floor.

"Were you happy?" I say.

He studies my face, nods.

"I mean, we had our fights. Buttons to push. She wanted kids. I wanted to wait."

He pauses, eyes down. I don't say anything.

"Maybe that wasn't such a good idea," he says, looks up.

Click.

"How long were you married before she got sick?" I say.

"Seven years. Then one day she started getting these headaches, nosebleeds. She ignored it for a few months before she went to the doctor. And they did some tests, CAT scan, X rays."

"She was so young."

"Thirty-four. I remember going to the doctor's office with her. I took the morning off work. She was wearing a yellow dress. It was summer. We sat in the waiting room. The air-conditioning was blasting and I looked over at her and she was shivering. The headaches were really bad by then, fuzzy vision. And she'd gotten really clumsy. Always breaking things, walking into furniture. When the nurse brought us in, we held hands. The doctor's office was a mess, really cluttered, books and files everywhere. He was a red-haired guy with a mustache. I remember his hands were small. Outside there was that sound, a truck backing up. You know, the beeping. And he said, 'There's a tumor the size of an orange in your head.' *An orange.* I don't think I've eaten an orange since then. Or had a glass of juice."

I think about the orange grove I got married in, all those oranges dangling from the trees, lying broken on the ground. Love for me. Death for him.

"He said they could operate, but it wouldn't do much good. Because of the tumor, where it was. So one minute we're sitting in the waiting room, happy, married, with a future, and the next minute she's dead. Sitting next to me, holding my hand. But dead just the same. And she was really good. Really strong about it. She's a doctor too, you know. A vet, but still she understands bodies, the things that can go wrong. And she says, 'How long?' And he looks at the desk, says 'Three months, maybe four.' "

He purses his lips, looks at me. Standing there, I can't believe the things people can live through.

"Quick," I say, "tell me the funniest thing she ever did."

He looks right, thinking, his face rearranging itself. Later I'll be able to see the transformation. To study the way the human face can change from despair to joy, the way everything you need to know about how a person is feeling is broadcast by the area between their hair and chin.

"She could write with her toes."

"Her toes."

"A lot of things. Not just write. Also play the piano. Not well, but still. She could put a fork between her toes, feed herself."

"Or you."

"Or me. Yeah, we did that once. She used to say, 'I wish I had a tail so I could swing from the trees like a monkey.' "

I stand there and watch him remember, and I wonder if it's possible that he could ever love anyone the way he loves her. Or if there'll always be a cap, a threshold he can never cross. And looking at his lonely face, I wonder if it would be so bad to be loved only that much if the person loving me was him.

"Take off your shirt," I say.

He smiles.

"Really?"

I nod.

He reaches for the top button, then hesitates.

"You first," he says.

I pull my T-shirt over my head. I'm wearing my best bra, the black one with the lace that makes my breasts look like they haven't yet succumbed to gravity. I drop my shirt on the floor, feeling the cool air on my skin. He looks at me, a different quality coming over his face. His eyes widening slightly, his breath quickening. I take his picture, wanting to remember the way desire looks on his face.

"If I'd known we were gonna take these kind of pictures," he says, "I would have shaved my back."

I unbutton my pants, watching his face, one hand still on the remote, lowering my zipper one tooth at a time. His face gets very still, blood rushing to his cheeks.

"Do you do this for all the widowers?" he says.

"Shh," I say.

He nods, licks his lips. I take his picture, then push my pants down over my hips. I want him to see me the way I've just seen him. Naked.

"I have a lot of stories to tell you," I say, "but I'm not ready."

He nods. I step out of my pants and stand there in my underwear, feeling his eyes on me.

"I just want to get to know you. Can we do that? Get to know each other?"

"Yes," he says, and has to clear his throat and try again.

I reach behind my back and unhook my bra.

"I have a lot of flaws," I tell him. "I'm mean. I don't have a lot of patience."

"That's—that's okay," he manages.

I lower my arms, exposing myself.

"I'm not that young anymore, and I'm insecure about it. I have a hard time trusting people. But I'm trying. I'm trying to like myself."

He's leaning forward now, without realizing, tilting his head, so that in the photos I take the top of his head will be just out of focus. I put my hands on my hips, slide my thumbs into the waistband of my underwear.

"People used to ask me what kind of animal I was," I say, "and I'd say a deer or a leopard. But now I think I'm a turtle."

I push my underwear down and they fall at my feet. I stand there naked, fighting the urge to run, to hide, wanting to do the opposite of everything that's been ingrained into me by years of tunneling downward, of covering up.

"At the first sign of trouble," I say, "there I go, into my shell."

He takes a step toward me, but I put up my hand and he stops.

"I just wanted you to see me," I say. "I'm tired of hiding. Tired of pretending I'm okay. I'm not okay, but I'm beginning to think that's just how it is. That this is as normal as I'm gonna get. And that scares me, that I'm never gonna be the person I was. Hopeful, trusting. I'm thirty-six years old and I've been married once and he left and I don't want to feel this way anymore. Like I can't be vulnerable. Can't relax. It's exhausting, always being on the defensive, keeping my guard up. I feel like Cuba."

He smiles and I take his picture and hear the auto-rewind kick in, and the sound of it is like a hypnotist clapping his hands. Suddenly, I'm aware of myself naked in this room. I see us for how we are, strangers. And me, this crazy woman with a giant bruise on her face who's turned her second date into a kind of freak show. And I think, *What am I doing? Why do I always have to screw things up?* I bend down and scoop up my clothes, moving slowly, trying to will myself invisible, knowing that any sudden movements might spook him. In my mind he's like this fragile animal and I'm a redneck in a recreational vehicle crashing through the woods, oblivious to the damage I've done. I straighten, but can't bring myself to look him in the eye.

"Don't move," I say.

And then, before he can speak, I run out of the room.

23

I stay in the bathroom until he leaves, ignoring him when he knocks, when he asks if I'm okay. I sit on the edge of the bathtub and listen as the front door opens and closes and then the house is empty and I listen to the sound of nothing, of the refrigerator motor clicking on in the kitchen, the distant sound of traffic. I stand up and put my clothes on. As I pull my shirt over my head, there's a knock on the bathroom window. I jump, let out a little yell, turn. He's standing at the window.

"Sorry," he says. "I just needed to make sure you were okay. I went to my car, but . . . I wouldn't sleep tonight if I didn't know."

I nod. He's dragged over a garbage can to stand on. I think about the neighbors, of Mrs. Davidson down the street calling the cops.

"You think I'm insane, don't you?" I say.

He shakes his head.

"You're just doing the best you can," he says. "I know how you feel. I mean, look at me. I go to strangers' weddings and cry at car commercials. I can't leave a building if there's a woman inside in any kind of trouble."

I won't look him in the eye.

"I've been teaching myself not to want," I tell him. "I lay on my back and imagine I'm made of rubber, metal."

"Sometimes I sit in the dark and listen to all her old answering machine messages," he tells me. " 'Hi, honey. I'll be home around eight.' 'Hi, sweetie. I'll be home around nine. I have to work late. I love you.' I sit there and imagine she's coming home any minute."

"I go to weddings and take pictures of married people, and sometimes I just wanna scream at them, tell them how stupid they are, how naive."

"If I see a dalmatian on the street, I have to find someplace to sit down, catch my breath."

I reach out and touch his face, thinking how cruel it will feel when he breaks my heart.

"You should come in," I say. "Before someone calls the cops."

He pulls himself up and over the ledge, loses his balance, falls onto the floor.

"I meant through the door," I say.

He lays there on the floor, a tangle of limbs, and I kneel next to him.

"Are you okay?" I ask him.

He reaches up, puts his hand on the back of my neck, pulls me down and then we're kissing and it feels like one of those under-water kisses where oxygen is passing through. The kiss of life.

"I'm scared," I tell him, when we separate.

"Then you're doing it right," he says.

24

Lisa lives with David in a two-bedroom apartment near the park. The three of us have dinner on Friday. David cooks a pork roast. He's six foot one with John Lennon glasses and he's wearing an apron that reads TOO HOT TO HANDLE.

"Any advice?" he says as he slices tomatoes for the salad.

"About the wedding?" I say.

Lisa is in the living room putting on music. David nods.

"Tell people you're having a bar mitzvah," I say. "They charge less. The minute you say 'wedding' everything's a minimum one grand."

He takes an avocado from the basket, cuts it open.

"Your sister," he says and leaves it hanging.

"You're telling me," I say.

"What about me?" says Lisa coming back.

"A ray of light," he says and kisses her.

She pushes him away.

"You smell like meat," she says.

I sip my wine. She's always been like this. Bossy, controlling. But I guess he likes it. *He better,* I think, *because she's not about to change.*

"Have you set a date?" I ask.

She makes a face.

"I'm still trying to get used to the idea," she says. "I mean, look how yours worked out."

"Ouch," says David.

I don't say anything.

David takes a cucumber from the fridge, lays it on the cutting board.

"I blame celebrities," he says.

"For my divorce?" I say.

"For divorce in general," he says.

"Why?"

"Don't encourage him" say Lisa, pulling herself up on the counter. "He thinks he's a philosopher."

"They have these three-week relationships," he says. "Meet on a film set, fall in love, get married, get divorced. They sell us the fairy tale and then one of them ends up in rehab or has an affair and within six months they're done. Finito. And I have to wonder, are these our role models?"

"When Gwyneth and Brad broke up," says Lisa. "I'm still getting over that one."

"They were perfect for each other," he says.

I open the refrigerator, hoping for something, looking for nothing.

"Self-help," I say.

"Exactly," says David. "For twenty years, they've been pushing this self-improvement crap on us, telling us the grass is always

greener, telling us not to settle, and then defining settling as anything less than money, power, celebrity."

"But you're immune," I say.

He opens the oven, peers inside.

"Nobody's immune," he says. "But I'm aware."

"Billy Bob and Angelina Jolie," says Lisa. "That one never inspired confidence."

"I bet the sex was great though," I say.

"Is that all you ever think about?" says Lisa.

"Slut."

"Tramp."

"Bitch."

Lisa jumps down from the counter.

"I think I'll get married in red," she says. She grabs her breasts.
"Topless. What do you think?"

David shakes his head, retreats to the bathroom.

"He's cheating," says Lisa once he's gone. "I know it."

"You," I say, "are insane."

"He's not?"

I shake my head.

"He worships you. Literally. Why do you think he asked you to
marry him?"

She pours herself another glass of wine.

"To throw me off the trail."

David comes back, puts a pot of water on the stove, covers it.

"We grow up on music videos," he says. "All these quick cuts.
Kids today, they have the attention span of a squirrel."

"Did you just say 'kids today'?" says Lisa.

David blushes. He opens the oven again, puts a thermometer
into the roast. Heat rises in waves, steaming his glasses, and he
straightens, takes them off, wipes them on his on apron.

"And advertisers," he says. "This instant gratification mantra.
Selling us this sense of entitlement, that we should always have

what we want, exactly when we want it. Like whatever happened to delayed gratification? To wanting something and working hard and then, when you get it, it's so much sweeter?"

"Like me," says Lisa.

"Exactly. It took me six months to get your phone number. Seeing you every day at work. At first, you wouldn't even give me the time of day."

"Get a watch," she says.

He chops celery, the knife clunking rhythmically against the cutting board.

"And then one day, a smile at the water cooler, a little look, and the rest of the day I can't concentrate. My mind is racing. I'm thinking, *Talk to her, ask her out.*"

Lisa pretends to yawn, but I can tell she's thrilled. To be coveted, chased. It's all she's ever really wanted.

"And finally we talk on the elevator coming back from lunch, but still you seem like this unattainable icon."

"Meanwhile, I'm thinking, just ask for my number already," says Lisa.

"And I did, finally."

"Finally."

"At the office Christmas party."

"If I remember correctly, it wasn't until after I pulled you into a supply closet and kissed you."

He sighs.

"What can I say? I'm not a big risk-taker."

We eat in the dining room, drinking two bottles of wine, devouring half a cheese cake.

"I just want to make it work," says David. "My parents got divorced when I was eleven. I don't want to go through that. I don't want to put my kids through that."

"We're having kids now?" says Lisa. "Why wasn't I informed?"

"Oh please. We talked about this."

"Sure. Right. Kids."

She looks at me.

"Can you imagine me with kids?"

I study her face. She and I are so different, and yet so alike. She has Dad's nose, Mom's hips. Her lips are fuller than mine, hair wavy. Unlike me, she's proud of her body, comfortable in it. She understands its power, isn't afraid to use it. I try to picture her children, but all I can see is us as kids, our fractured lives.

"Do I have to?" I say.

"At least they're making designer maternity clothes now," she says. "And kids' fashion has come, like, a million miles."

"Thank God you've got your priorities straight," I say.

I finish my wine, and, sitting there for a moment, I forget. Forget that this is David and Lisa's apartment. Forget that they're the happy couple and I'm the third wheel. I remember when the situation was reversed. When Lisa would come over for dinner, a wild twenty-seven-year-old girl, and Jim and I would feed her, put her to bed in the guest room. I remember standing in the doorway watching her sleep, my husband in the kitchen cleaning up, and feeling at peace. Feeling strong and grounded. Happy that I could do this for her, could give her a safe place to go, a place where whatever happened in her life she was always welcome. I remember at that moment, for the first time in my life, feeling like a grown-up. And thinking, *Oh, so this is what they mean.*

Lisa and David are talking about a trip they took to Spain last year. I watch them feeling a million miles away, the memory of another life so clear it feels like I've stepped into a time machine, like if I close my eyes it would be Jim's voice I hear, our dining room I'm sitting in, and soon we'll call it a night, tuck Lisa in, retreat to the bedroom, and he'll stand in front of the closet undressing, while I go into the bathroom and brush my teeth. And as I do, he'll be talking to me in that way he has of just thinking out loud. And I would pull my hair back with a scrunchie and wash my face. In the bedroom, he'd fold his pants, hang his shirt in the closet, still talking, and I'd sit on the toilet and pee with the door open, toilet paper folded in one hand, listening to him think. As I'd stand, as I'd flush, he'd come in wearing only his boxers, love handles cresting the waistband, and brush his teeth, turning away from me to spit, looking himself in the eye as he flosses. And I'd go into the bedroom and get undressed, slip under the covers, feeling the cool welcome of clean sheets on my skin, lying there with my eyes open, feeling like a woman with a family, a woman who knows that everything in her life was right where it should be.

"So?" says my sister after David clears the plates.

"So *what*?"

"How's Gilligan?"

I nod.

"Good. No thanks to me."

"Meaning?"

"Meaning I'm a freak."

"How about some specifics?"

I tell her.

"Naked?" she says.

I nod.

"You made him talk about his dead wife and then you took off all your clothes. I'm just trying to . . ."

"It sounds bad, I know."

"It sounds . . ."

"I feel better though. More relaxed. At least now he knows I'm a freak."

"Great."

"He didn't run."

"He was worried you were gonna hurt yourself."

"No, after that. We . . . talked, for a long time."

She shakes her head. In the kitchen we can hear David loading the dishwasher.

"Remind me never to get divorced," she says.

"Nice."

"You know what I mean."

"It wasn't my first choice."

She pours herself another glass of wine, shakes the last few drops from the bottle.

"Did you sleep with him?"

"Not yet."

"Second base?"

"He saw me naked."

"Well, sure. He *saw* but that doesn't mean . . ."

"We just kissed."

She looks at me skeptically.

"Maybe there was a little dry humping."

She smiles.

"I miss that," she says.

"Dry humping?"

"You know, that first kiss, getting to know someone. I mean, if I get married—"

"When."

"*When* I get married, I'll never have that again."

"That's true. But you'll also never have the insecurity, the rejection, the disappointment when things don't work out."

She purses her lips.

"I hope so. If I do this, I want it to last."

And looking at her I think, *That's exactly what I said.*

25

I drive home through the park, leaving the traffic behind, slipping down dark, tree-lined streets, windows down, feeling the air on my face. I steer by reflex. My mind is someplace else. A right, a left, and then there I am. I've zeroed in without realizing: the aquarium. I pull over and sit for a minute, watching the banners flutter in the breeze. I think about Gilligan, his gentle mouth, the feel of his body against mine. The air is cooler now, a ruffle of wind fluttering in my face. Right now just staying calm feels like the hardest thing in the world. After exposing myself, asking to be judged.

Inside, fish float silently in the eerie blue light. Outside, I roll up my window, start the car, and drive home.

Halfway there I slam on the brakes, pull over. There is a man standing on his front lawn yelling at his house. Upstairs a woman throws armfuls of clothes out the window. I grab my camera, step out onto the curb. It's too dark for handheld, and I don't have a tripod, so I rest it on the roof of the car, focus. Every room in the house is lit, a streetlight illuminating the man as he grabs his head, paces. I do the math in my head, set my exposure. Forty-five seconds. I pull the trigger. An avalanche of suits flies from the window and falls to the ground. The man runs over, picks them up. I advance the film, shoot again. The man stands there, looking up, his arms filled with clothes, while upstairs the woman screams something out the window.

"You bastard. You fucking bastard."

He looks at me. One side of his shirt is untucked. His hair is crazed.

"She won't listen," he says. "I tried to tell her. Explain."

A shoe flies past his head. The next one hits him. He flinches, rubs his chest where a black footprint has suddenly appeared.

"Maybe she just needs some time," I tell him.

He stares at me, as if seeing me for the first time, a stranger on his lawn wielding a camera.

"Who asked you?" he says and starts picking his things off the ground—shoes, shirts, pants—walking around in a kind of half-crouch, running out of arm space, as toiletries start raining from the sky. I step back, take a picture. Later, he will look like some strange primitive, hunched and burdened, surrounded by disposable razors frozen in midair.

When I get home there is a message from Gilligan. In my haste to call him, I misdial twice and end up talking to a man who wants to know, have I ever thought about phone sex?

"Hello?" mumbles Gilligan, when I finally reach him.

"Oh shit," I say. "Did I wake you? Sorry. I'm doing that a lot lately."

Mumbling. Sleepy.

"I just wanted to say goodnight."

"Hmmm," he says.

"You are asleep."

"Hmmm."

"If I make subliminal suggestions will you have to obey my every whim?"

"Mmm-mm."

"Or maybe you're not asleep at all. Maybe you're tied up. Maybe there's a piece of tape over your mouth, a gun to your head."

Nothing.

"Grunt once for 'yes.' Twice for 'no.' "

"Goodnight," he says.

"Goodnight."

I hang up, feeling fluttering, warm, and go into the kitchen. Just hearing his voice reassures me, picturing him calm in bed. Sleepy, untroubled. The phone rings. I pick it up thinking it's him.

"Miss me?" I say.

There is silence on the other end of the line.

"Hello?" I say.

A man's voice.

"Laurie?"

I pause.

"Who is this?"

"It's Jerome."

A sinking feeling.

"Hi. How are you?"

He doesn't say anything. I wait him out.

"I did what you wanted," he says.

"What did I want?"

"I found a woman my own age."

"That's great."

"I found about ten of them actually."

At the kitchen table I stack up my work prints, slide them into an envelope.

"You always were an overachiever," I tell him.

"I've gotten really good at picking up women in bars."

"You should write a book."

"Hah-hah, Laurie. Funny, funny."

"Look, Jerome . . ."

"Whatever. I'm just trying to figure it out. Why you don't want me."

"It's not that—"

"So you do?"

"No. That's not—"

"Well, what's wrong with me?"

"Nothing. You're a great guy. You're smart. You're funny."

"But you don't love me."

"No."

Silence.

"I think you do."

"Jerome."

"I think you love me, but you're scared."

I put my hand over my face.

"Jerome," I say. "We are not having this conversation."

"I've been drinking a lot."

"Don't do that."

"I see these women in bars and I sleep with them and I feel nothing."

"Maybe you should talk to someone. A therapist."

"I take them home and fuck them. I think it's gonna make me feel better, but it makes me feel worse. It doesn't mean anything."

I close my eyes and wonder if there's a balance in the world, a ratio that has to be kept—happiness versus misery—and when one person finds contentment, another has to fall into despair.

"Go easy on yourself," I tell him. "Give it some time. You'll feel better."

"The funny thing is, I wasn't that into you at first. I thought you were cute, sure, but kind of old, you know? A little sad. I mean, look at what you do for a living. This lonely woman taking pictures of other people's happiness. It's kind of pathetic, really."

I consider all the retorts I could make, all the snappy comebacks, but this isn't a competition. Maybe if I let him blow off steam, get it off his chest, he'll leave me alone.

"I never said I was anything special," I tell him.

"No," he says. "God forbid you should say something nice about yourself. God forbid you should show up."

"Jerome," I say. "I don't think you should call me anymore."

"You don't, huh?"

"No. I think you need to take some time and get some help. I'm sorry things didn't work out with us, but I never led you on."

"Oh no. Of course not. You were always really cold. That's your MO. Like love is some kind of factory, and one day you can just switch from making widgets to tires, or something."

"I'm hanging up now."

"Wait."

I stand there with the phone to my ear.

"What?" I say finally.

"I can change," he says.

I shake my head. I know what he's going through, the desperation. Hearing it in his voice makes my skin crawl. The memory of that tone in my own voice. I listen to it and worry that he's contagious. That his unhappiness will rub off on me.

"Good-bye, Jerome," I say.

I go into my studio. The black velour is still hanging from the wall. I load film into the camera, turn on the lights. I connect the remote cable and stand in front of the lens. It's one o'clock in the morning. I'm wide awake, mind racing. The world is a place of absolute silence. I look into the camera.

Click.

I take my picture because I don't trust mirrors. Mirrors lie. In the heat of the moment, in the midst of a crisis, they might as well be opaque. Photographs last. You can always study them later, after you've calmed down, once you're seeing clearly again. You can always go back and try to figure out what you were feeling, what it all meant. Photography is a way to create distance, detachment.

It's a way to catalogue all the things that seem inexplicable at the time. To document all the invisible specters. And yet photographing emotions is like trying to capture the images of ghosts inside a haunted house. You end up with something less than clear, a blur, the foggy traces of something moving, fleeting. A phenomenon attributable to changing heat patterns, to seismic activity or a sudden drop in barometric pressure.

I stare into the lens like I have nothing to hide. I think about Jerome and the way we look for completion in other people's lives. A billion single men and women drinking a billion drinks in a billion bars, looking for love. Searching each other's eyes for some kind of recognition, as if there can be no internal satisfaction without external validation.

The film advances. I stare into the open lens.

To try to capture emotion on the human face, to study it looking for insight, meaning, is like trying to name a thousand kinds of snow. You catch the flakes in your hand, rushing to save them in plastic bags, envelopes, as if they're evidence that needs to be taken to the lab. As if by preserving the impermanent, you can somehow stop time, stand in the frozen moment, and figure out what everything means.

But nothing is permanent. The world doesn't mean anything when you look at it one frame at a time. What good is one thought without the one that inspired it and the one that comes after? And emotion is worse. Where thoughts are solid, emotions are fluid. And trying to understand what a person is feeling by looking at one moment in time is like trying to understand water by writing the symbol "H_2O."

I think about my sister and her fiancé, about all the fiancés I've met. I take my picture again and again. I'm like a forensic technician blowing powder across a greasy fingerprint, though in this case the fingerprint is also me. I lean against the black velour and expose myself to film, over and over, hoping to catch a fleeting glimpse of something real. To gain some kind of insight into this crazy woman who's making my life so difficult. I stare at the lens, raise my eyes. I turn my face to the wall and take pictures of my back.

When I display the photographs I've taken this year, maybe I'll sneak my own picture into the mix. Maybe I'll print a tiny photo of me with the caption, HUSBAND LEFT HER, MARRIAGE ENDED, TRUST ISSUES. Maybe I'll take a hundred photos of myself and splice them together to create a huge portrait. My own face made up of smaller faces. Or maybe when I'm done with this roll, I'll rip it out of the camera and unspool the film onto the floor, letting it tumble, exposing my delicate image to the light, blinding everything, erasing myself. Like the picture of a UFO that suddenly fades, as if someone up there doesn't want you to see, as if the mysteries of the universe are better left unsolved.

26

We have dinner twice a week for three weeks. He pulls out my chair each time, opens every door. We hold hands in the car. The swing porch becomes our bedroom, the place I make my last stand, kissing, groping, fending off the inevitable. I don't invite him in again. I won't. I'm waiting for him to show himself, watching like a prison warden or high school principal. Sooner or later, he'll let down his guard, have one too many glasses of wine and then it'll all come out. How he's a wife-beating polygamist serving ten years to life in the witness protection program.

How he seduces small boys, has a thing for livestock.

How his mother dresses him in the mornings.

How he's just using me. How he has no intention of sticking around once I give it up.

When we kiss, I feel myself tumbling through space. Gravity is somebody else's problem. When we kiss, I would do anything he asked. Light a building on fire. Shoot a president. I go to sleep with his smell on my hands, the feel of him on my skin. When he touches me, places his hand over my heart, I can feel his warmth, like two pints of extra blood running through my veins. The porch swing creaks under our weight.

"I never thought I'd spend so much time making out outdoors," he says, face flushed, hair askew. "At least not after I turned forty."

I lean back, trying to collect myself, trying to keep my lips from parting, inviting him inside. Because once that happens, once he's inside the house, inside me, it's all over. Any sense of self-preservation I have will wither and die.

"I'm sorry," I tell him. "I'm just not ready."

He gets up, tucks his shirt back in, face flushed.

"That's okay," he says. "I'm not trying to—I don't mean to pressure you."

"No," I say. "You're not. I just . . . I feel bad."

"Don't feel bad," he says, and on and on we go, both of us apologizing for something that hasn't even happened.

He calls me from the car on the way home.

"I'm still kissing you," he says. "I know you think I left, but I haven't. I'm still there. With you. On the porch."

I close my eyes. "You're trying to kill me," I say. "This is attempted murder."

"You think I'm in my car, but the truth is, my hand is under your shirt. Your hair is in my mouth. I can feel your heart beating."

"I'm not doing this," I say.

"Oh, but you are."

We go out twice a week for three weeks. I tell him I can't see him any more than that, not that he asks, but this is who I've become, a woman who makes fleeting, random rules, who draws lines, and then crosses them recklessly, breathlessly.

At night, I lay in the bathtub exhausted, overwhelmed. I put my hands on my body and imagine they're his. This man is like a cult

I'm joining. A new religion based on self-denial. Based on blind devotion and night sweats. I'm like a Christian Scientist, and he's the medicine I'm trying desperately not to take.

We kiss on the porch. I feel his tongue enter my mouth, feel his breath on my face, and I inhale, breathing him in, wanting his soul inside me, dizzy, drunk, as if he doesn't exhale oxygen. As if his breath is some kind of drug, some airborne hallucinogen I just can't get enough of.

"You can't be real," I tell him.

"I am."

"No."

"Yes."

But I know in my heart that this is one of those dreams where, even if you pinch yourself, even if you feel the pain, you're still not awake. One of those dreams that makes you bolt upright in bed and say, *Thank God it was just a dream*, only to find it's not over, that this is just another twisted segment.

I kiss him out of doors, but don't let him in. It's the only thing that keeps me from dissipating, turning to ash, blowing away. I am the turtle girl, hidden, protected, just one quick contraction away from total hibernation. I kiss him out of doors and then send him home, and every time he comes back I'm stunned. Every time the phone rings and it's him and I realize that I haven't ruined everything, I feel this chain inside me slip a little bit more, this barbed wire surrounding my heart.

Every time he kisses me, I come that much closer to being exposed.

We kiss on the porch and the air is chilly. Our noses run. Our fingers shock each other with their temperature. We jump and flinch at the slightest touch.

"Sorry," he says.

"Sorry," I tell him.

It's deepest fall now, and we kiss surrounded by colors we can't see. Fiery browns and flaming yellows. One night after I've gone to bed, thinking he's left, he collects a pile of leaves outside my house and spends the night arranging them around the tree on my front lawn. When I emerge the next morning there is this blanket of red leaves woven together with a single yellow stripe running down one side. I stand there staring at it, transfixed, like a woman having a vision, a religious interlude, then I run inside and get my camera. The pattern is already starting to degrade. Over the course of the morning, the wind will kick up, and by the time I leave for work the leaves will be gone, scattered around the neighborhood.

I raise my camera and capture the moment. A sheet of colored leaves, arranged by hand, dovetailed, pruned. It is the sweetest thing anyone has ever done for me. The single most romantic act. I've had boyfriends who've written songs for me, poems, but this man has designed a flag. As if our relationship is a country. As if to say, *I belong here. If challenged I will defend it to the death.* As if to say, *I will be loyal forever.*

I stand on the lawn and study it with my camera, and as I do, a sudden burst of wind kicks up, and the leaves swirl and scatter around me like a virus, an airborne aphrodisiac infecting the neighborhood with its love.

27

On the fourth week he figures it out. He realizes that if he invites me to his house, we can kiss indoors. He calls me at home, tells me he wants to cook me dinner. I'm suspicious.

"It sounds like a trick," I say.

"How is dinner at my house a trick?"

"Don't change the subject."

"I thought you said your sister was the paranoid one."

"Don't suck up. What's the catch?"

He chuckles, as if my hang-ups are amusing to him, all my tortured neuroses. As if he can read them like invisible ink tattooed on my skin.

"There's no catch," he says. "I'm a good cook."

"Really? What can you make?"

"Just about anything," he says. "Fish, chicken, lasagna."

"Do you make soups?"

"Do you want soup?"

"No."

There's a pause. Looking up, I realize that I've put myself in a corner, taken the phone and retreated to the safest place in the room.

"You're not gonna make this easy for me, are you?" he says.

"Sorry."

"Should we say Friday at seven o'clock?" he says.

I look out the window. Mrs. Davidson is on her knees in her garden, planting bulbs. I think about our flag. The picture I took of it is hanging on the wall inside my bedroom closet. I go in there sometimes and close the door, look at it. I like having it there, like a secret. A rabbit's foot I can sneak out of my pocket and rub for luck.

"I suppose," I say.

"Good. I'm looking forward to it."

His voice gets in my head like a bullet sometimes. It ricochets around in there, making me feel all warm and shivery. Weak. I rest my head against the window glass.

"Me too," I say.

On Friday I dress in layers. I put on my most complicated bra, my weirdest belt. I wear a sweater, two shirts, and a camisole. My pants are cinched at the waist. This is called dressing defensively. My goal is to be attractive, but impregnable. I wear boots and tuck my pant legs inside.

Riding in the elevator, I feel like a cloud of gas, intangible, fleeting.

On the control panel there is a light with a plaque over it.

The plaque reads: HELP IS ON THE WAY.

The light is off.

I'm on my own.

He greets me at the door in jeans and a white, button-down shirt. There is a bottle of wine in one hand, a broken opener in the other.

"I'm having a little problem," he says and kisses me.

I step inside. This is the first time I've been to his place. It's small, spare, neutral, as if he's afraid to commit to a pattern, a color. The furniture is modern, but not excessively so. He has a triptych of paintings on the wall that look like a cold gray fog has settled on the canvas. Art as weather.

Across from them is a series of framed photographs. Vintage pictures of men and women gathered in semiformal settings. Men with hats posing together. Women in prints dresses serving food.

"Is that your family?" I ask him.

"The truth?" he says. "I got them at a flea market."

Instant ancestors, he calls them.

I hover near the sofa, aware of how comfortable I could be with him if I let myself. How lost I could get.

"Can I take your jacket?" he says.

I pull it tighter around myself.

"Why?" I say.

He looks at me.

"Well, for one thing, you're sweating."

I think about this.

"Okay, but no funny business."

He shakes his head, considers saying something, then thinks better of it. He reaches out. I take off my coat, hand it to him. He grabs it, but I'm not ready to let go yet, and we wrestle over it for a moment, me pulling one way, him the other, before I relent, before I let go and retreat to the other side of the room. I still have three layers left. The shell is intact.

He goes to the closet, hangs up my coat.

"I'm making trout," he says. "Do you like trout?"

I nod. I feel like a ten-year-old, churlish, pouty.

Why can't I just be normal? Why can't I just relax?

"You need help with that bottle?" I ask.

He looks at it, the cork immovable, the metal spiral of the opener sticking out like a cartoon mattress spring.

"I thought I might just smash it," he says.

"I'll find you a ship."

"What?"

"To smash the . . . Never mind."

He puts the bottle down, takes my hands, puts his face close to mine, looks me in the eye.

"How are you?" he wants to know.

I hold my breath. One whiff of him, his aftershave or shampoo, and I'm a goner.

"Good."

He looks at me skeptically. I think about going back to the elevator and pushing the emergency button, just so I can see that little light ignite.

Help is on the way.

"I'm a little spooked, actually," I tell him. "I don't know why."

"Well, come into the kitchen. Have a glass of wine."

He looks at the bottle.

"Or maybe a beer."

I stand in the kitchen and watch him cook. He moves from the sink to the fridge to the counter to the stove. It's not long before I figure out the pattern. He is always one step behind. As if the meal is cooking him. The water for the potatoes boils long before he's even peeled them. The fish is done before the salad is made.

"I'm better at math," he tells me, a squib of butter melting on the end of his nose.

"Less talking," I say. "More cooking. You have a reputation to live up to here."

At the dining table, we sit across from each other, separated by candlelight. After two beers I start telling him all my wedding horror stories.

"Food poisoning is pretty common," I say. "The Kentuckys had salmonella in the salmon. The Meyersons had E. coli in the tomato salad. I don't know what was in the couscous at that Lebanese wedding, but I almost died. Then there's fistfights. I've seen the groom crack open his best man's skull. I've seen two bridesmaids tear each other's dresses off, biting, scratching. I once saw the father of the bride get the father of the groom in a headlock and knee drop him, like in the WWE. I keep those pictures in a special file."

"I'd love to see them," he says. "Maybe next time I'm over you could bring them out onto the porch."

"Hah-ha."

He fills his glass, wipes a drop of beer from the mouth of the bottle.

"I remember one wedding I went to," he says. "Oh wait — it was mine. Where everything went wrong. It rained. My wife's parents got locked in their hotel bathroom. The priest got our names wrong. The best man forgot the rings. It was like a horror film. Afterwards, I had these T-shirts made. I SURVIVED THE FORD WEDDING."

I chew some cold trout, poke at my salad. Being near him makes it hard to eat, hard to swallow.

"My wedding was a blur," I tell him. "It was like I got up that morning and the next thing I new it was dark and I was in a car, driving. I felt like one of those alien abductees, who find themselves, you know, standing on the side of a highway, missing time."

He clears our plates, brings out a bottle of port.

"We're in luck," he says. "This one has a screw top."

He pours us each a glass. We go into the living room. Gilligan puts on some music. I have an overwhelming desire to take my boots off, but I know how dangerous that would be. The first step toward disaster. It's a slippery slope from bare feet to total nudity.

"Did you always live here?" I ask.

"No. We had a house, Michelle and me. I just couldn't stay there after. It was too awful. But now I like living in an apartment building. All these people stacked on top of each other, side by side. It's comforting somehow. You say 'hi' on the elevator. You get other people's mail. There's a guy on seven, we go for beers sometime. On Sundays I help Mrs. Anya down the hall do her grocery shopping."

I study his face, the eyebrows just starting to lengthen. The laugh lines around the lids. I picture him in the supermarket, pushing an old lady's cart, listening to her stories. Another goddamn boy scout. How can you not fall in love when they make themselves this perfect? When they're good-looking, they work hard, cook, and still find time for some local philanthropy? It's like a fucking Disney movie.

My Dinner with Gandhi.

"Tell me something awful," I say.

Before it's too late.

Before I fall too far.

"Something awful," he says.

"About you. What's the worst thing you ever did. Something mean and horrible."

He thinks about this.

"Worse than leaving the toilet seat up?"

I nod.

"How about parking in a white zone?"

"No. Something real. Something you hated yourself for afterwards. Something unsettling."

He sits quietly for a moment, trying to decide. I listen to the hollow sounds of classical music drifting through the apartment.

"Okay," he says. "When I was in high school I had a friend, Antoine Levay. He was a good-looking guy, smart. Antoine's mother was an alcoholic. She used to throw him out of the house about twice a week, and he'd come stay with me. I had a girlfriend at the time, Cindy, what was her last name? Stakowski. Antoine used to call her the ripest peach on the tree. Cindy Stacked. She was a voluptuous girl, flirtatious. I don't know what she was doing with me. This awkward kid who played the recorder. But this was freshman year. We were still young, one step away from childhood. Anyway, Antoine would stay at my house maybe two nights a week. He had his own set of keys. My parents loved him. We would lie awake at night talking about our futures. Antoine was going to be an architect. Or maybe a marine biologist. He and Cindy and I would go out on Saturday nights, trolling the suburbs in my father's Toyota. Antoine was the kind of boy all the girls went crazy for. Just the wrong side of handsome, brooding, thick-lipped. But Antoine, he didn't have a girlfriend. He wasn't gay. He was just distracted, as if the idea of a girlfriend had never occurred to him. We would drive around on Saturday nights and talk about everything, and Cindy, well, she liked him. She liked him so much that when I was at band practice she'd come over and fuck him in my parents' bed while they were still at work. Now, she wasn't having sex with me. In fact, I thought she was a virgin, but there she was, two days a week, banging Antoine on my father's side of the mattress. And I'd come home later with my books and my recorder and she'd be there, and she'd give me this sloppy kiss, all chatty. And I'm not stupid. She'd always say, 'Oh, I just got here,' but I knew something was going on. And one night I'm lying in bed and Antoine is lying on the floor and he says, 'Chief.' He called me Chief. 'Chief, that girl can't be trusted.' And I said, 'I know.'

"A few nights later I was out in my father's car. I was running an errand, and I see Antoine walking on the side of the road. I know it's him, because he always wore this ratty blue jacket. And he was walking toward his house, and I remember the inside of the car was really quiet. There was no music or anything, and I thought, *I should pull over, pick him up*, and I turned the wheel, just this little bit. I didn't speed up. I just turned the wheel and I hit him. I ran into him with my father's car. And he flew up over the hood and smashed into the windshield. Splintered it. And I must have hit the brakes too hard, because my head came forward and hit the steering wheel and the car ended up in a ditch. And for a few minutes, I think we were both unconscious, him lying on the ground and me slumped forward over the steering wheel."

Gilligan sits back, staring into space.

"The police had a lot of questions," he says. "Antoine's leg was broken, and he had a concussion. He ended up going deaf in one ear. I told them it was an accident. That I was slowing down to pick him up when I just lost control of the car. And Antoine, he never said anything. Never told them about Cindy or how I might be jealous. He hobbled around on his crutches, pretending he was just happy to be alive. Cindy broke up with me the next day. She started going out with the quarterback. And Antoine, he never slept over at my house again. We stopped saying 'hello' to each other in the halls at school. By senior year, we were strangers. He started doing all these drugs, skipping classes. He turned into this weird, long-haired kid with a limp. I don't know what happened to him after. Where he is now? I wonder sometimes."

The CD ends. We sit there in silence for a minute, then Gilligan leans forward, picks up his empty glass, puts it down.

"There was this moment," he says, "when I was heading toward him. He must have heard the car. Because he turned and looked at me, and for a second maybe we were looking at each other, eye-to-eye, and he . . . I swear, he smiled."

He pours himself another glass of port, leans back. I reach down and take my boots off, then put my hand on his shoulder, lean forward, kiss him on the neck, the ear.

I know now that the light is just for show. The plaque.

Help is never on the way.

You have to help yourself.

I kiss his face, his mouth, pull his shirt up from inside his pants, put my hands on his skin, feeling his hairy warmth. I know who he is now, a hit-and-run driver. And I'm his latest victim. Wide-eyed, expectant, watching the front grill grow. And something about knowing this, about seeing this other side of him relaxes me. To know that he isn't some kind of saint, the martyred widower. To know that he can be petty, scornful, filled with jealousy and the need for revenge. To know I'm not the only one who's given in to their basest emotions. The only monster. I take his face in my hands, open my mouth and quickly let him in.

28

Okay.

Now the biggest secret of all.

The thing I wish I could excise from my memory, pull like a rotten tooth.

It wasn't all my husband's fault. The separation. The divorce.

It was my fault too. Because I was weak, afraid. Because I felt abandoned, ignored. Because even though we had grown together, he started working late and I worked weekends, and suddenly it seemed like our marriage was just a shell. Because he wanted to make partner and that was more important to him than me. Because I felt taken for granted.

Because, because, because.

Excuses, excuses.

By the time our marriage was ten months old, we were fighting a lot. Bickering on the telephone, a pair of surly *Sesame Street* characters hurling insults from our battered garbage cans. Our marriage was starting to sound like a broken record. We talked less and less, and when we did, we had the same conversation. He thought I should be more supportive, think about his needs sometimes, put on the Laura Ashley dress and be the company wife. I wanted him home.

I wanted my husband back.

"We're still newlyweds," I said. "Technically. For the first year."

He kept promising. "Tomorrow," he'd say. "This weekend," he'd say, but then there'd be a phone call. His assistant, Clara.

"Jimmy wanted me to call you and tell you he got stuck in a meeting."

"Jimmy says he's sorry. He'll be home as soon as he can."

I got used to being alone again. Feeding myself. I got used to the sight of his stuff without him, a pair of shoes left out, his bathrobe hanging on the back of the door. Like a neutron bomb had gone off, killing all the men in town, leaving their clothes behind, their shoes and stereos. I started to feel like marriage for him was all about finding a convenient place to store his stuff.

I got lonely. I got bored.

I met another man.

My sister always used to say, "You should call the Better Business Bureau, report Jim for false advertising."

"He's just swamped," I'd say, sticking up for him. "He's up for partner this year."

And she would light a cigarette, spit smoke and say;

"I thought he was supposed to be *your* partner."

And me, quietly, the little mouse on the other end of the phone. "So did I."

Now I went to weddings and worried. I woke up in the middle of the night, my heart racing. This wasn't what I wanted. To be somebody's left-at-home wife. To talk to my husband more on the telephone than I ever did in person. I photographed the glowing brides around me, and I wanted to take them aside, probe them, give them a few words of warning. Tell them to look for certain dangerous patterns. Things that would explode later once the audition process was over, once the whole question of till-death-do-us-part had been resolved.

Late at night, I would watch Jim sleep and wonder: Was this satisfying to him? A wife he never saw, a house he came to just to sleep.

"Of course it isn't," he'd say when he was awake. This whole thing was frustrating, he told me, but it would only last a little while longer. Six months. A year. Couldn't I just be patient?

I couldn't.

That was my weakness. My shame. I was an impatient woman. A woman who was used to dealing with things head on. A woman who didn't want to need anyone, who couldn't stand hold music or waiting in line. A woman who saw red every time she went to the bank, the DMV. And he wanted me to wait six months for a sense of a wholeness, togetherness? When the point of getting married was that I was never supposed feel lonely again?

"I love you," he'd say. "Isn't that enough?"

It should have been, shouldn't it?

If I were stronger. If I were a better person. I should have waited, should have said *Yes, do what you have to do. I love you. I'll wait.*

We look back at our lives, and the truth is so bright it blinds us with its simplicity. But in the moment, everything is so murky.

My sister always used to say, "Uh-uh. No. You're right and he's wrong. This is like those Arab guys who marry American girls, take them back to the Middle East, and suddenly it's all *Put on the veil. Speak only when spoken to or my mother will set you on fire.*"

Today I think maybe she's right. Maybe it was his fault. I want to believe it more than anything. To absolve myself of guilt. Because in Jim's mind, I'm the evil one. The selfish bitch. Because I couldn't wait. Because I told him he was a bad husband.

Because I was unfaithful.

I tell myself I'm not to blame. That he drove me to it. This is how I live with myself. This is how I sleep at night. But the truth is, sometimes everybody's wrong. Sometimes both sides of the coin are scarred. Sometimes it's a question of degrees. There are no saints, only gradations of assholes.

So I went to weddings and photographed happy couples, and meanwhile I was miserable, lonely, adrift. And then one night, I'm in the camera store buying supplies and the guy behind the counter says, "What's wrong? You look so sad."

I should track him down, take his picture.

Alan Lewis.

My very own home-wrecker.

Alan Lewis, a little guy with a big smile. Twenty-eight years old. A landscape photographer. He gave me his number, said he had a large format camera he was trying to sell. He built them in his garage.

Did I want to come over and see?

This is the kind of line photo clerks give to their customers.

Should I tell you what he looked like naked? Or should I lie, pretend it only went so far? That I was just a lonely girl who flirted with infidelity, then walked away. It's awful, I know. I'm awful. And we should all strive to be better people. To be Mother Teresa. But sometimes it's hard. Sometimes you do things, and you don't know why. Sometimes there's this feeling in your chest and it feels like dying and you'll do anything to get it to go away.

Because there are no saints.

Only gradations of assholes.

So I closed my eyes. I looked the other way. I gave myself permission to fall off the moral map. I didn't choose to be bad. I chose not to choose. I let Alan Lewis do the choosing. The wanting. I let him take me home, show me his cameras. Not the first night. Not even the first month. But eventually. He was patient. We both knew it was inevitable. That's the way things feel sometimes, the bad things. They're inescapable. Meanwhile, the good things, the things you pray for, hope for, these things remain cloudy, uncertain. If Vladimir and Estragon had been waiting for ruin instead of salvation, the Devil instead of Godot, they would have been relaxed, cool as cucumbers, because thanks to gravity, falling is a piece of cake.

So I went to Alan's house. I let him take my picture. Let him take my face in his hands. Let him undress me. I was a brick, a cliff, a glacier. Numbers on a spreadsheet. Quadriplegics don't know the level of numbness I experienced. The loss of control.

I went to Alan's house, and when I left, I smelled of man sweat. My legs were tired. My vagina throbbed. My lips felt bruised. And I drove home in the rain, listening to static on the radio, flirting with the double yellow lines of the median. I went home and took a shower and never went back to that camera store again.

I went home and vowed to wait as long as it took. To be the perfect wife. For the next three months, I did everything he wanted. I made quiches for company potlucks. I washed my husband's underwear and folded it, balled his socks and scrubbed the rings from the toilet. I told myself I was lucky. I had a husband who loved me, a beautiful home. So what if I was the only one in it? We talked on the phone. He was the lump next to me in bed. When we had sex, which was almost never, I made him believe he was a miracle worker. I threw my legs in the air and pounded the mattress.

"Oh God," I said.

Oh God.

As if sex is really just another kind of prayer.

I was still numb inside, but I was committed to projecting all the emotions I knew I should be feeling.

But it just got worse and worse. Jim started sleeping at the office, folded up under his desk. He worked weekends. The firm was expanding. He told me we were going to be rich. I told him I didn't want to be rich. I wanted my husband back. He laughed. He thought it was a joke.

"Everyone wants to be rich," he said.

I would sit at the kitchen table on Sunday mornings alone and read the engagement announcements. I would look at the pictures. The grinning couples, fresh-faced explorers setting off in search of paradise. But then there were the other pictures. The women alone, smiling bravely. And I thought, honey, *If he can't even show up for the picture, what hope is there he's gonna stick around until death do you part?* I looked into the eyes of these women, the pixelated irises, the smudgy gray pupils, and I realized that unless I did something, said something soon, I was going to be this numb, rich widow for the rest of my life.

So that night when Jim came home, I said, "This can't go on."

And he shook his head and went into the bedroom to change his clothes. It was one o'clock in the morning. He had to get up in four hours and go back to the office. This was the last thing he needed. Another ambush by his nagging wife. I followed him, homing in like a divorce-seeking missile.

"I feel like I don't know you anymore," I said. "Like I don't recognize you. I should keep your picture up by the front door so I can check to make sure it's you when you come home once a month."

"Don't exaggerate," he said, taking off his shoes. "It's unbecoming."

In the last few weeks, he'd started handling me the way he handled crises at work. Like I was an unhappy client, a disgruntled judge. Humoring me. Patronizing me. Using the neutered language of conflict resolution.

"You said it would just be a few more months," I said, hating the sound of my voice, hating that I was doing this, hating him for forcing me to be the bad guy all the fucking time.

"It will be," he said, unbuttoning his shirt, hanging it up. His muscles had started to slacken from all the desk work and fast food he ate. Pretty soon they were going to pool around his ankles: his biceps, his deltoids, his lats.

As he changed his pants I catalogued all the broken promises he'd made, ticking off the dates on my fingers. I'd become a policeman with my list of infractions, my surveillance tapes, my incriminating evidence. When I spoke to my husband now I sounded like my sister.

"I should have stayed at the office," he said.

"What? What did you say?"

He turned away, wincing at the tone of my voice. I could tell he was calculating how long it would take to placate me. How long he'd have to do this before he could go to sleep.

"Could we do this some other time?" he said. "I'm exhausted."

And I looked at him, my husband, cornered in the closet, looked at myself, the inquisitor, the attack dog, and at that moment I hated us both. I tried to meet his eye, to find some sense of empathy, some hint that we were still in this thing together, but he wouldn't look at me.

"I had an affair," I said.

That got his attention. He looked at me, shocked, suddenly wide awake.

"What?"

I tried to stop myself, to shove my feelings back inside, but I just didn't care anymore. Anything had to be better than this.

"I slept with another man. In April. I just . . . got so tired of being alone. Unwanted."

He slapped me. His hand came up, and he hit me so hard my neck would hurt for three days afterward. My head rang. My eyes watered. My hand came up to my face. I stared at him in shock. His face was ugly with rage.

"Now you know how it feels," I said.

He raised his hand again and I flinched, but he didn't hit me. He looked at me the way you look at a pile of shit. And then he left the room, left the house. I heard his car start, heard him race away with a squeal of tires. And I stood there, my face aching, swallowed by the silence. Alone again.

Three days later, he served me with the papers.

Six months later, we were divorced.

I didn't fight it. I didn't ask for money. I didn't want anything from him. I didn't care that he was rich now, that half of that money was rightfully mine.

I was a divorced woman, and three months later it seemed like the whole thing had been a dream. We had been together so short a time, happy for such a small percentage. The good marriage was like a rainbow flickering between storms. The glimpse of heaven they give you just before they tell you to go to hell.

So you'll know what you're missing.

"He was always an asshole," my sister tells me.

In her mind, the affair was justified. An act of desperation. I tell her I'm an asshole too. Everybody is.

"Two wrongs don't make a right," I say.

"Sometimes they do," she says.

But when I ask her to tell me when, she just pretends to zip her lips and throw away the key.

29

I'm down to two shirts, a camisole, and my underwear when he leads me to the bedroom. He has his pants on, but his belt is undone. I feel dizzy, nervous, but so hungry I think I might just crack down the middle. If there were a team of experts monitoring me, working around the clock to protect me from myself, they'd be running around like headless chicken's right now. Sirens would be going off, red lights flashing. Men in moon suits would be turning steaming valves to relieve pressure. You'd hear their hysterical voices echoing from walkie-talkies across the perimeter. *Danger. We have a red light situation. Going to Defcon 4.*

Gilligan offers me his hand and I take it, following him wordlessly into the bedroom. We both know what's going to happen. We're like two chemicals combining, sparking, willing each other to explode. In the control room, the experts punch codes into their computers. They pull chains from around their necks, insert their keys, nodding, turning on the count of three. They can't believe I'm going to disregard the warnings on the side of the box. To mix sex and love. To risk light-headedness, dry mouth, nausea. To risk uncontrollable sobbing, feelings of euphoria and completion. To risk addiction. Gilligan kisses my eyes, my neck. He's like a heat wave washing over me. My face burns every place his lips have touched. I scratch at his chest, trying to dig out his heart, unearth his soul. He pushes me backward. My legs hit the edge of the bed, and then I'm falling, tumbling.

The mattress knocks the wind out of me, the sudden swirl of ceiling overhead. I pull my camisole over my head. Only two shirts left to go. Gilligan is on the bed now, on his knees, kissing my calves, my thighs. I grab him by the hair, pull him toward me.

"Ow," he says.

"Sorry."

I think about the pictures I have of him watching me undress. The desire on his face, like the kid brother of the desire I can see right now. The naive little sister. His eyes are glazed, hooded. He kisses me hard, resting his weight on his elbows. My hands are between us, fumbling at his zipper, pulling it down. And then I'm inside his pants. I take him in the palm of my hand. In the observation booth, the experts are preparing a strike team. They're reviewing their contingency plans, their worst-case scenarios. People are starting to panic. Gilligan pulls the last two shirts up and over my head in one swift motion. The only thing between us now is our underwear, my black satin bra.

Gas her, says one of the experts.

Too risky, says another, wiping his brow.

What about electric shock?

Gilligan reaches behind my back, wrestles with my bra. His earlobe is between my teeth. I can feel him grinding into me. The hunger has turned into famine, an overwhelming need for completion, insertion.

"I want you," I say.

And I do. More than anything. More than mental health. More than I want to survive.

In the control room, alarms are screaming. There are experts in moon suits running amok, clipboards flying. They've run drills before, sure, but nothing can truly prepare you for disaster when it comes. They flip switches, trying to shut down my central nervous system, to flush the hormones from my body. But the unthinkable has happened. All my defense systems have failed. The red lights have all turned green. The experts race down intestinal hallways, opening wall panels, switching to backup systems, overriding fail-safes, pushing their hardware to the limit.

I bend my leg, hook my toe into the band of Gilligan's underwear, pull them down. His hands are on my breasts and he's doing something unearthly to my neck with his tongue. There is a moaning sound filling the room now. A low keening. In a moment of clarity I realize it's coming from me.

Finally, one of the experts manages to flip a switch and suddenly I'm rolling Gilligan over, off me.

"Stop," I say.

We lay there panting.

"Really?" he says.

I can't feel anything above the neck. My insides are too big. They feel like they might burst loose. In the control room, the experts high-five each other, lift their bulletproof visors. I grab Gilligan's arm, roll over on top of him.

"No," I say.

Before they can stop me, before I can change my mind, I take him inside me. Heat and pressure. An act of clarity, focus, as if everything in the universe has been reduced to just one moment in time. One point in space. In the control room computer screens explode, panels burst into flame. People are thrown from their chairs. Gilligan reaches up and touches my face. His eyes are locked on mine, and this feeling between us, this power line jump-

ing across a rain-soaked highway, spitting sparks, this animal closure, is like a levee breaking, a dam, and the water tumbles
downhill, roaring, obliterating towns and villages. A beautiful storm
that leaves nothing but devastation in its path.

His eyes are wide open and he's smiling.

"You don't have to be afraid anymore," he whispers.

"Shut up and fuck me," I tell him.

30

For three months after my father came home from the hospital, he was his same old self. The hummer in the bathroom. The man who sang to houseplants. He had learned to macramé in the hospital, and when he couldn't sleep, he would make us little belts, little braided wallets. My mother doted on him, never leaving his side for more than a few minutes. And for the first time I can remember, my father lavished attention on Lisa. On me. He helped us with our homework, read to us. He stroked my hair as I lay slumbering, sang to me in his raspy voice. We were finally what I'd always wanted us to be: a happy family. Like the other kids, like TV. Then my grandmother had her stroke and was placed in a nursing home. And the bubble popped. Without her around the infrastructure broke down. My parents weren't good at the details, feeding us, getting us off to school on time. We started missing meals.

"Just see what's in the fridge," my mother would tell us when we said we were hungry.

Lisa and I got used to eating bread-and-butter sandwiches, condiments. We fended for ourselves. My parents started living off my grandmother's social security checks, which my mother used to cash down at the bank, smiling and saying of my grandmother, "Oh, she's fine. Just a little under the weather these days." Sensing our need, my parents retreated. My father went back to his poetry. His moodiness returned, those sullen, self-destructive tirades. I used to come home from school and find a trail of cigarette butts leading from the kitchen to his office. Every place he paused to have an idea, to write something down, there was an ash stain, a mangled butt. If there was no paper, he would write on his hand, or, more increasingly, the wall. Before long, our house was covered in unfinished couplets, skinny black hieroglyphics that snaked over doorjambs and along wainscoting. Like this one from outside the bathroom:

"Let down the hands of the ocean."

Or this from the phone nook:

"Promise tomorrow no more thunder."

It was as if once he started doing it, he preferred writing on the walls, preferred making his private declarations in public. He stopped bathing, stopped speaking more than a word or two at a time. He would lurk in the hallways watching us as we read the new words, studying our reactions. We were his family and his focus group.

"Tumble into oblivion."

"Follow Alice down that dirty hole."

I didn't know what most of it meant. Even today, they are phrases that seem mired in obscurity, there just to shock. Pieces of his complicated heart. He wasn't a good poet. His work was too personal, too heavy with private vendettas. After his death, my mother found stacks of rejection letters in the back of his closet, typewritten form letters offering no encouragement, no words of consolation.

"Bury me in my own mouth."

After my grandmother's stroke, he locked himself away again. Sensing his return to despondency, my mother panicked. She tried to smother him, like you would a man on fire. Feeling her neediness escalate, her insecurity, he fled deeper inside himself. As she tightened her grip on him, he turned to liquid, to dust, slipping through her fingers. He started going out in the morning, coming back after dark. He would drag old junk into the house, old pieces of engines, packing crates. He would be drunk or stoned. His clothes were increasingly messy, his hair unkempt. He stank of cigarettes and alcohol. My mother would fly into a rage.

"Where the hell were you?" she'd scream. "Are you trying to kill me? Your children? We thought you were dead."

"I am dead," he'd say.

Every morning he fled the house and every night he brought home more junk: pieces of discarded plastic and wood, old paint cans, tinfoil from someone else's leftovers. He piled the junk in his office, and late at night we could hear him assembling it, hammering, gluing. He had gone from being a poet who assembles random words to an artist who assembles random objects.

None of us were allowed inside to see what his madness had made. Not even my mother. When she wasn't watching, I'd sneak up to the door and peer through the keyhole. Sometimes Lisa would stand behind me, shielded, peering in over my shoulder.

"Let me see," she'd say, jamming her fist into my ribs.

My mother would be in the bathroom or downstairs smoking in the kitchen. Normally she stood watch over his office like a gargoyle, sitting on the landing, an ashtray by her hip, listening to the tear of nails, the staccato rhythm of the hammer.

"Your father's quite the artist," she'd tell us over and over. "He has such a brilliant mind."

She was lost without him, as if she were his shadow. And what good is a shadow without an object to block the sun? When he emerged to use the bathroom—and sometimes he didn't come out for days, he'd piss in bottles instead, crap in cans—my mother would be there, solicitous, seductive. She would grab for his arm and purr.

"Why don't you come downstairs and let me fix you something?" she'd say.

"Why don't you come to bed?"

She needed to see herself through his eyes to know she was real, needed to feel her skin touch his. But he would shake her off, would flee back into his room, slamming the door, piling furniture in front of it. And the hammering would begin again.

One night I awoke to find him standing over my bed. It was dark, the night-light having burned out long ago, only the slightest sprinkle of moonlight filtering through the blinds. Lisa was sleeping next to me, limbs splayed out as if she had fallen into bed from a great height. I looked up at his towering silhouette, breathless, the bedroom door open behind him, letting in cold air. After his death, I would confuse this memory, its timeline, and place it after his death, turning my living father into a ghost. For weeks afterward I waited night after night, one eye open, hoping to see him again.

"Daddy," I said, but quietly, not wanting to wake up Lisa, my mother, not wanting to share.

"You have to eat the olives," he said.

I nodded. I was ten.

"Remember," he said.

"Okay."

"Don't let the tire truck come. Don't enjoy the malty aftertaste. It's a lie."

Lisa stirred beside me. My father saw her, started to back from the room.

"Daddy," I said.

"Remember the lobby," he said.

And then he was gone, disappearing back into his room.

Just when it seemed we might never see him again, this manic phase ended, and one morning there he was, sitting at the kitchen table, clean shaven, having a cup of coffee, reading the paper.

"How are my beautiful girls?" he said and we ran to him, Lisa and I, racing to reach him before my mother squeezed us out and sent us packing.

For ten days he was focused, loving. He lavished us with attention. He doted on my mother, on us. He took us for walks, watched as we rode our bikes. My mother beamed under his eye, blossomed. In three short days, she became the ultimate housewife, cooking and cleaning, working herself to exhaustion trying to make sure he never disappeared again. But he was like a rainbow, a flash of colored light. Just as quickly as it had come, the switch flipped again, and he was gone, absent when we woke that Saturday. He left no note, just the front door hanging open. My mother, panicked once more, ran out to look for him, leaving Lisa and me alone for hours with a stern warning to stay indoors, stay away from the stove.

"Don't answer the phone," she said, grabbing her purse and rushing out.

We waited until she was at the end of the driveway, then ran upstairs to my father's office. We tried the door, but it was locked. We peered through the keyhole, but he had stuffed it up with something, This time all we saw was black. A padlock hung from the jam now, steely, impregnable. It was hours before my mother came home, downtrodden, empty-handed. She sat at the kitchen table as dinnertime came and went. I tried not to disturb her as I slipped into the pantry to find something for Lisa and me. I knew better than to ask "When's dinner?" Instead, I scavenged some peanut butter and crackers, took them to my room. Lisa and I sat on the windowsill, making crumbs and waiting, as day turned to night.

He came home long after dark, dragging a useless red wagon

and some cement blocks. He said nothing to any of us, just climbed the stairs and disappeared into his room. The next day he was out again, returning with a spool of wire, some orange cones, a block of wood. He had become a ghost again. The noise in the attic.

The next day he came home with a gun.

31

My sister calls me on Tuesday.

"Okay," she says. "I did some research and his story checks out."

"Whose?" I say.

"Gilligan. He *is* an accountant, registered with the state. He was married for seven years. His wife died of brain cancer."

"Lisa," I say. "No."

"He went to Brown for three years, then transferred to Stanford. I guess he wanted a bigger school."

"Please tell me you didn't call these schools."

"You want me to lie?"

"Lisa, God. You're gonna ruin everything."

"Calm down. I was careful. Most of this stuff you can get over the Internet."

I'm in my studio, editing, and I start pacing, mind racing, imagining all the ways this will come back to me.

"Listen to me," I say. "I want you to stop. Now. Today. Do you hear me?"

"I have a call in to his doctor. I want to make sure he doesn't have any STDs."

"Is there a language out there I can say 'no' in that would make you listen?"

"You can't be too careful," she tells me. "People these days are almost always lying about something. Half the CEOs in the country never did half the things on their résumés. My friend Sonya dated a guy for four years before she found out he had kids. Teenagers. Can you imagine?"

I lie on the floor, put my hand over my face. Happiness is like a radio station I can almost hear, bursts of static, quick jolts of music. I turn the dial back and forth delicately, like a safe cracker, but it's a frequency I can't seem to hold on to no matter how hard I try.

"Lisa," I say. "I'm never gonna talk to you again. I mean it."

I can hear her smoking on the other end of the line.

"Fine. I'll stop."

"Good. Thank you."

A long pause.

"So you don't want to know the secret?" she says.

"What secret?"

"His secret."

My heart starts pounding in my chest.

"I hate you as much as it's possible for one woman to hate another," I tell her.

"Don't hate *me*," she says. "It's not my secret."

"Lisa, no. You don't get to do this, to just wander in and destroy everything."

"I'm trying to help you."

"If you want to help me," I say, "worry about your own life. Stay out of mine."

I hang up the phone and lay there panting. Outside I hear the school bus grind to a halt, hear the kids jumping out. I listen as they run through leaf piles, kicking them apart, each kick a crackling explosion. I can picture their little faces, flushed from the cold, breath hanging in little clouds.

I pick up the phone, call her back.

"Yes?" she says.

"Okay. What is it?"

"What's what?"

"Lisa, I'm getting in my car and driving to your office. I'm bringing a knife."

"Oh, you mean the secret?"

"Yes," I say and close my eyes, squeeze them shut. I'm lying down again, because you can't fall off the floor. It's the lowest you can go without digging. I can hear my sister typing on the other end of the line.

"He's rich," she says.

I lie there for a minute waiting for the words to destroy me, then open my eyes.

"That's it?"

"His wife left him a fortune. She was some kind of heiress."

"Rich?"

"Yes."

I sit up. Outside the kids are yelling. I can hear a basketball bouncing on the asphalt. I am dizzy with relief.

"So what?" I say.

"Don't you think it's weird that he didn't tell you?"

"No. He probably wants to make sure I don't just like him for his money."

My sister opens a can of soda. I can hear it sizzle.

"I hadn't thought of that," she says.

"Not everyone is committing a crime," I tell her. "You should really seek professional psychiatric help."

"You first."

"Bite me."

"Go fuck yourself."

I stand up and peer through the blinds. There are knapsacks scattered in the street. Everything is red and gold. The trees are wooden skeletons, arms outstretched.

"How rich?" I say.

"Millions," she says. "Maybe a hundred."

I watch one kid take the basketball and shoot it at an imaginary basket. He dances around with his arms in the air.

"You didn't hear it from me though," says Lisa. "We never had this conversation."

I think about Gilligan in his car, a high school boy running down another boy, turning the steering wheel, the tires rumbling onto the shoulder. And then *thump*.

I think about Jim, about how he said we were going to be rich. Rich, as if it was a place you went where everything was perfect and everyone was happy. Outside a girl in a tartan skirt falls backward into a pile of leaves, arms outstretched. Overhead an airplane flashes orange in the setting sun. I go outside and sit on the porch swing.

My hands are shaking, not from the secret itself, but the idea of it. The idea that the other shoe is still out there, waiting to drop.

And not for the first time I think, *Get out now before it's too late. Before you care too much. Before you're just like your mother. Before there's no you without him.*

32

Everything has to be perfect. Months of planning, of dreaming, and bickering, and it all comes down to this. One day. After the hall has been rented. After the invitations have gone out. After the band has been chosen, the caterer hired, the flowers arranged. After the vows have been written, the guest list litigated, the best man elected. After the dress has been purchased and fitted, the brides-maids draped in satin. After all the sleepless nights, the minor traffic accidents due to fuzzy logic, due to trying to do too many things at once—stamp an envelope, call the caterer, make an illegal left turn. After the second thoughts and the third thoughts and the midnight panic attacks. After the bachelor party with its binge drinking, its laser tag and man-eating strippers. After the bachelor-ette party with its lingerie, its room temperature brie, and the "un-expected" arrival of the police officer with the breakaway pants.

After the relatives have flown in from out of town, stumbling off the plane, fumbling for their luggage. After the rehearsal and the rehearsal dinner, the chicken or salmon, red wine or white. After the parents have met and all the toasts have been made, words slurring, tears flowing. After the bill has been paid (wincingly, by the father of the groom) and the hotel rooms filled. After everyone has said goodnight and the lights are switched off, and minute by minute, hour by hour the last night of freedom runs out. After all this, there is no room for error.

Every Saturday morning, every Sunday, I wake up knowing that somewhere out there there's a bride who cannot sleep. A groom who spent the night eyes wide open. On my most mundane mornings, lying in bed, fantasizing about coffee, I recognize that there are thousands of people in the world staring their futures in the face, rehearsing the words "in sickness and health, for richer or poorer."

Till death do us part.

When I was a kid, I watched a mass wedding on TV. The reverend Sun Myung Moon had gathered hundreds of couples together in Yankee Stadium. The stands were filled with worshipers, family members. The brides stood in clusters, scattered like jacks across the loping green turf. They eyed their new mates with adoration, apprehension. The men were strangers, chosen by the reverend based on his own astrological projections, his hypnotic visions of their future. They stood on the outfield grass waiting for their new lives to begin. At a signal from the reverend, the hundreds of black-and-white pairs lined up like chess pieces under the yellow sun, holding hands. When I saw *Star Wars* for the first time, it reminded me of this scene. All the storm troopers dressed in white, lined up in rows, ready to marry the dark lord Vader, the universal groom who wandered among them, dressed in bottomless black.

This morning I wake before the alarm. I get up, take a shower, check my itinerary for the day. Two weddings. An afternoon and an evening. I'll have to run to make the second, ignore the speed limit, pray there's no traffic, riding the gas pedal, changing lanes, dabbing my damp armpits and reapplying mascara at red lights.

All week I'd waited for the call. I'd come home at night and check my messages, expectant, rewinding the machine, but nothing came. Wednesday, Thursday, Friday. The message never materialized. And every night before I slept I thought, *She's running out of time.* Shelly. Two more days till the wedding, one. Twelve more hours. Every time the phone rang I expected to hear her voice letting me know the wedding was off. But it never came. And so now, at ten A.M. on Saturday, I lint roll my dress, check my makeup. I pack my camera bags, check my supplies, finish my coffee, and head out to the car. It's a brilliant fall day, the air like a knife, a whisper of winter blowing on the wind. There's a feeling in the pit of my stomach, an unnamed dread. I wonder what Shelly is doing right now, Roger. Whether they slept together last night, holding each other the way you hold a life raft, the way you hold a hand.

I drive slowly, hugging the shoulder, thinking about the session I had yesterday. A woman who responded to my ad, who called me breathlessly, afraid to utter the words. "Wanted: Battered women." She came by last night to have her picture taken. Doris Goodwin. She was in her late forties, divorced five years. A curator for the Lexington Gallery in Chelsea, she told me. Her husband had hit her for thirteen years before she finally managed to get rid of him, before he found someone else to dominate. She posed for me in front of a blank white wall, showing off scars that had healed poorly, old bruises like onions budding just below the skin. Afterward, she asked to see my work. Nervous, I pulled out my prints.

"These are great," she told me, as she paged through my prints. "If you don't mind, I'd like to show them to Philly. He's the photography director."

I nodded, my tongue limp, and gestured, approximating sign language, approximating, *Yes, please. That'd be great.*

She sat in my living room drinking wine, talking about her ex-husband, about the change that would come over him, the punishment he dealt out, about the miscarriage he gave her.

"Most men just give flowers," she said, and smiled ruefully.

We talked about love for a long time. Doris said it was like a country, a place you can visit, where the language is strange, the vistas are breathtaking, the food is incredible, and more than anything you want to stay, but then your visa expires, your trip ends, and you are forced to go home and save your money in the hopes that one day you can go back. At home you pine, put posters on your wall, study language tapes, tonguing the words in your car. You collect the tchotchkes, stay up late poring over pictures of your trip. Nostalgia fills you with longing. You live in exile. Some people can't handle the distance: They adopt an accent, lie and say they're from there, that they live there still, when really they are just foreigners, outsiders. But they tell themselves it's true.

I live in a land of love.

Recently, Doris has been thinking more and more about rescuing the idea of love from the realm of romantic comedies, from the schlock of mainstream entertainment. She told me my work was an important step in that direction. I formed half sentences, stammered out sounds and syllables.

She took samples, told me she'd call to schedule a studio visit.

I didn't sleep at all that night.

Shelly and Roger are to be married in a church just outside town. The reception is at a restaurant a few blocks away. I show up an hour early, walk the perimeter. It's a familiar place; I've photographed over a hundred weddings here, I know all the best angles, the secret spots. Circling the church I have to keep pulling the hair from my eyes. The wind blows fresh lawn clippings across the grass. There is a hint of smoke in the air, the smell of suburban husbands doing their weekend groundskeeping; raking, shoveling, burning the brittle leaves that choke their perfect lawns. Inside, I use my light meter to set levels, thinking about Jerome and how I should probably start looking for a new assistant.

I meet Shelly's mother, her nervous father.

"We're just so thrilled," Shelly's mother keeps saying. "Thrilled."

I ask if Shelly is around. Her mother leads me back to the dressing room. Shelly is sitting on the windowsill in jeans and a T-shirt. She's smoking a cigarette.

"Shelly," says her mother, face sour.

"I'm nervous, okay?" says Shelly. She looks impossibly young. The vision of a perfect American girl, beautiful, self-possessed, innocent but not too innocent. As she exhales, I take her picture, capturing her youthful beauty, the cloud of smoke. Her mother starts making clucking sounds.

"Oh now," she says. "That's not the kind of . . ."

Shelly turns and stares at me. There is a defiant resolve in her eyes. The look of a woman who's made up her mind to jump into a volcano for the good of her tribe.

"This is it," she says.

I take her picture again, zooming in on her face, smoke wafting around her head.

"I'm going to go see if the Donnellys are here yet," her mother says. "You really should get dressed, honey. Henry says it'll take at least forty minutes to do your hair and makeup."

Shelly doesn't respond. Her mother throws me a pleading look, as if to say, *Reason with her*, then retreats, closing the door behind her.

I stand there for a minute watching Shelly smoke. The dress is on a hanger by the wall, wrapped in plastic, long white train spilling across the floor.

"So how you doing?" I ask.

Shelly touches her lips with her finger.

"I love him," she says.

"Good."

"I mean, what's not to love? He's smart, successful."

I watch her eyes, the way she turns and looks out the window, cataloguing escape routes.

"Shelly."

"And in just a minute I'm gonna get up and put on the dress. My mom hired someone to do my hair and makeup. Henry. So we'll do that."

"And you want to do your formal pictures after, right?"

"Whatever."

I pull out a chair and sit down, knowing I should duck out, knowing that no good can come from my being here, asking questions. It's none of my business. That's the first rule of wedding photography. You don't get involved. You just take pictures.

"You didn't talk to anyone, did you?" I say.

She shakes her head.

"You just pretended everything was fine. Because your mother loves him. Because he loves you."

She stubs out her cigarette, flicks the butt out the window.

"My friend Debbie is going to California," she says. "A bunch of my friends, driving. It sounds fun, doesn't it? I always wanted to see California."

"There's plenty of time to do all that. You're only nineteen."

She swings her legs down, stands.

"No," she says. "I'm gonna stay home, be a good wife. Pop out some kids."

She pulls up her shirt, touches her stomach. There isn't an ounce of fat on her.

"Roger says he can't wait for the first. He wants a boy."

I try to imagine her as a mother. Looking at her belly, I wonder if I'll ever be one. I'm thirty-six years old. Sometimes the need is so strong it feels like the marrow is being sucked right out of my bones.

"Shelly," I say. "It's not too late to call it off."

"Yes it is," she says. "Everyone's here."

I try to catch her eye, but she won't look at me.

"It's not. I've seen it done a dozen times. It's ugly and everything falls apart, but then it's over and you're free."

I stand and look her in the eye.

"It's always easier to destroy something than create it," I tell her.

She looks over her shoulder at the window.

"I could just . . . escape," she says. "Run away."

"No. If you really aren't sure, you need to deal with that. Face it."

She looks terrified at the idea, goes over to the makeup table, gets another cigarette.

"How . . ."

"Tell your mother. Tell Roger."

She lights the cigarette, hands shaking.

"They'll hate me."

"They won't hate you. It'll be hard for them, but they'll understand. You're so young. And if you do this and you don't want to, if you settle now, you'll be paying for it forever. You'll turn into the kind of person who settles, who lets other people make her choices for her, and then one day you'll realize that you don't know how to make up your mind anymore. You don't trust yourself. And then you'll be trapped. Because instead of being a nineteen-year-old girl with options, you'll be a thirty-year-old mother of three with nowhere to go."

She's crying now without a sound, just a few tears rolling down her face as she smokes. She's probably thinking about all the money her parents have spent, all the decisions they've made, the centerpieces, the honeymoon, the band. All for nothing. All that time and effort wasted.

"Just tell them the truth," I say. "You're not ready. You're not sure. This isn't your last chance, Shelly. You're nineteen years old. You have your whole life ahead of you. Decades to figure out what you want, to find a man you really love, to be someone yourself. To go to California."

She smiles.

"San Francisco," she says. "Or L.A. I could be an actress, drive a convertible."

"You can be whatever you want," I tell her.

Behind her, I can see cars pulling up in bunches, a long line of vehicles. People are arriving in their Sunday best, shoes polished, dresses pressed. All those distant cousins and southern aunts. The high school friends and band camp buddies. I think about the chaos to come if she backs out, the rumors and gossip. All the gifts to return. All the fallout, bridges burning.

"I can't get married," she says quietly. "I'm not ready."

"Do you want me to get your mother?"

She nods. I turn to go, but she grabs me, hugs me. At first I stand there stiffly, self-conscious. A few years younger and she could be my daughter. My girl. If I close my eyes, pretend. If I lose myself in the smell of her hair and let myself believe. I hold her tight and grieve for all the ways my life could have gone, all the unborn possibilities. What would it be like to be Shelly, young again, my whole future left to write? She squeezes hard, her face buried in my neck. I kiss the top of her head.

"It's gonna be okay," I tell her.

I find her mother outside, greeting guests, directing traffic.

"She wants to see you," I say.

"Good," she says. "I'll get Henry."

"No."

I put my hand on her arm.

"Alone," I say.

She nods, hurries inside. I stand there looking at all the faces; the family, friends, people who've traveled, who've driven all night, who've traipsed through international airports. I can picture the discovery on their face, the news. Faces falling, salacious looks of scandal and disgust. Another marriage down the crapper. Another wasted gift.

"Nice day," says someone behind me.

I turn. It's Gilligan. He's wearing a blue suit with a flower in his lapel.

"How do you find out about these things?" I ask him.

He takes a mint from his pocket, slips it into his mouth.

"I have my sources."

His eyes are bluer today, deeper My heart does that thing it always does when I look at him.

"What does that mean?" I ask him.

He shrugs.

"Nothing. I'm trying to be mysterious."

I watch the front door as Shelly's mother emerges, pale-faced, finds Roger standing with his family. She takes his hand, leads him inside.

"This isn't gonna be pretty," I say.

"What?"

I lift my camera, take his picture. He's had his hair cut recently. His face is smooth shaven.

"Are you rich?" I ask him.

He meets my eye.

"Define rich," he says.

"If you wanted to," I say, "could you never work again?"

He thinks about this.

"Work is an important part of my self-esteem," he says.

"Thank you, Tony Robbins. But you didn't answer my question."

He reaches out, touches my cheek. I flinch, pull my head back.

"You have an eyelash," he says.

He holds out his thumb. There is a tiny black crescent of hair on the end.

"Make a wish," he tells me.

From inside the church I hear a crash. I close my eyes.

Please, I think. *Let this thing be real.*

Eyes closed, I listen to the hum of voices, the rustle of wind in the trees. I smell smoke in the air. Somewhere, something's burning. I purse my lips, blow a kiss. A rumble has started moving through the crowd. I open my eyes. Gilligan smiles at me. Over his shoulder I see Roger emerge from the church, agitated, looking around.

"Get ready," I say.

He turns, puzzled, to look where I'm looking, and sees Roger pushing through the crowd, heading straight for us.

"You fucking bitch," says Roger as he reaches me. His face is the color of a sunburn, jaw muscles working overtime.

"Excuse me?" says Gilligan.

"You fucking bitch," repeats Roger, his face inches from mine.

"I'm sorry," I tell him.

"You told her to dump me," he spits.

I shake my head.

"No. I told her to listen to herself. She's not ready."

"Where do you fucking get off coming in here and messing things up?"

Gilligan puts a hand on Roger's shoulder.

"Hey, buddy," he says.

Roger pushes his arm away.

"Don't 'hey, buddy' me. This bitch ruined my wedding."

I raise my hand.

"Give her time, Roger. She's only nineteen. She's scared."

He shakes his head and looks at me with disgust. I try to imagine the humiliation he's feeling, the abandonment. It's not hard. You put yourself out there, make these giant proclamations, ready to declare your love in front of everyone, and then you find yourself having to backtrack, explain. You're like the astronaut who gets grounded after all the pomp and circumstance, the press conferences and photo opportunities, having to tell people, *Hey, who wants to go to the moon anyway? It's just a cold, lifeless rock.*

Roger's brothers have come over, his father the ragtime musician. Everyone is itching for a fight. News that the wedding is off has taken on a life of its own, circulating through the crowd. Looking over, I see Shelly peering from a second floor window. She holds my eye for a minute, then turns, vanishes.

"I'm gonna see that you never work in this town again," Roger's dad is telling me.

I tell him I could care less. That this isn't about me.

Meanwhile, Gilligan has gotten into a shoving match with Roger. There is too much emotion in the air, too many fractured dreams. I lift my camera and start taking pictures. I imagine what we must look like from above, this fluctuating ring of concentric circles, like a fist closing, and me at the center, fending off the inevitable with my camera.

Click, click, click.

"Back off," Gilligan is saying.

He shoves Roger. Roger staggers back, steps forward, punches Gilligan in the eye, knocking him down. Then Shelly's father emerges, pulling Roger away, trying to restore calm, but Roger's father, who's out twenty-five hundred dollars on the rehearsal dinner, grabs Shelly's father by the neck and then they're on the ground, wrestling. I get a photo of Roger's dad lying prostrate, pushing Shelly's dad's head back, trying to pop it off his neck. Then Gilligan jumps up, his lip bloody, and he punches Roger in the chest, staggering him. One of Roger's brother grabs Gilligan by the arms and they struggle, stumbling backward, as Roger's dad and Shelly's dad roll over and over on the ground, slamming into Gilligan's legs, knocking Gilligan over, knocking him into me, and the last thing I remember is falling, gravity pulling at my arms and legs, as overhead the clouds look like animals, like buildings and trains and tumbling landscapes. And then the sun winks. I see a steeple, a cross, a patch of blue.

And then black.

33

Gilligan drives me home, holding a handkerchief to his lip.

"I really think I should take you to the hospital," he says.

"It's nothing," I tell him, holding the back of my head. "Just a bump. I wasn't unconscious for more than a few seconds."

He shakes his head. Tomorrow his left eye will be swollen shut.

"God," he says. "I haven't been in a fight since high school."

"How'd it feel?"

"They make it look so sexy in the movies, but it's really just an ugly mess, isn't it? All that flailing around. I kept expecting to make those sounds, those flat, hard, meat-packing sounds with my fists."

He dabs blood from his mouth, folds the handkerchief, looking for a clean spot. I reach over and stroke his cheek.

"I'm sorry," I say.

"It's not your fault. That's what I get for crashing the wrong wedding."

I stroke his hair. My knight in shining armor. My big, strong man.

"That's right," I say. "I hope you learned your lesson."

"Next time I'll wear a helmet."

I smile.

"And knee pads."

He looks at me. For a moment there are only two people in the world, moving at high speed. Everything else is a blur.

"Who told you I was rich?" he says.

"Nobody. No one," I say. "I just wondered."

"My apartment isn't rich. My car. Just normal."

"No. I know. I just . . ."

"So why do you think I'm rich?"

I look out the window, not knowing what to say, feeling his eyes on me.

"Are you?" I say.

He focuses on the road and for a moment nobody says anything.

"My wife was rich," he says. "She left it all to me. I haven't touched a dime."

I slip my shoes off, put my feet on the dashboard, hug my legs. He changes lanes, accelerating through a yellow light.

"I mean, why should I profit?" he says. "What kind of trade off is that? Money? The executor keeps calling me. He wants me to make decisions, diversify. I tell him to give it all away. Cure cancer. He tells me he can do that, but there are papers I need to sign. He sends them in the mail. They sit there on my desk, unopened."

He is staring straight ahead, knuckles white.

"She died," he says. "And I don't want to feel good about it. I don't want anyone to feel good about it. Not the Red Cross or the victims of Nine Eleven or the fucking starving orphans in Somalia. I don't want anybody out there smiling, thankful, grateful that she's gone. Just send it all to me in cash I tell him. Let me burn it. But he won't do that. He thinks I'm just upset. That this phase will pass."

He pulls up in front of my house, stops, puts the car in park, turns to look at me.

"I mean, I've been reasonable," he says. "I get out of bed in the morning, go to work. I remember to eat most of the time, pay my bills. And everyone says, 'Oh, thank God. You seem so much better now.' Because I make jokes at the water cooler. Because I see movies and read books and act like a normal guy. Because I haven't fallen apart. But look, I just want to hold on to this one thing. Okay? Forever. Don't I owe her that much? To move on, sure, but not all the way. To leave one thing. Like you're in an accident and the wounds heal, but there's one scab you keep picking off, one cut you leave ugly to remind you, so you never forget. A scar you keep hidden under your clothes so that every time you look at yourself, every time you breathe, you remember."

I look at my house, the peeling paint. My head is starting to ache again.

"I might be in a gallery," I tell him.

He is staring out at the neighborhood, oblivious.

"What?" he says.

"I showed my work to a woman from the Lexington Gallery. She liked it. She wants to show the photography curator."

He comes back to me a little, takes my hand.

"That's great," he says.

"I feel like I've been hibernating," I tell him. "Hiding out in my safe little word with its padded corners. Its plastic guards in all the light sockets. But now everything's starting to happen at once — you, this — and there's no excuse anymore. No way to say *Woah, sorry* or *Slow down* or *Help*. It scares the hell out of me."

He watches the road, chews his lip.

"There was a whole year," he says, "where I walked around like a zombie, shut down. And if I saw a car I just thought, *Car*. If I saw a building, I just thought, *Building*. I had no imagination, no dreams. I sat in my office and added the numbers. I drove in circles. And then one day I was out driving and I saw this wedding party. The bride and groom coming out of the church, rice flying, and the car waiting downstairs, the limo, so I pulled into a parking space across the street and just sat there and watched. I watched those happy faces, the white dresses blowing in the breeze. And the next Saturday I went back and sat in my car and watched another couple leave the church, another bouquet tossed, and then a week later I showed up early in a suit and went inside. I was scared to death I'd get caught, but no one challenged me. I walked in with a dozen relatives, took the program they handed me, and sat in the back row. I sat and watched the bride walk down the aisle with her father. I watched the groom cry. And for the first time I could remember, I felt happy. *Good for you*, I thought. *People starving, war everywhere, poverty. Good for you. Show them we won't give in to despair. Show them that no matter how much death there is in the world we'll still fall in love. No matter how much pain and cancer and grief. Fuck you, with your weapons of mass destruction, your religious fanaticism. Fuck you, with your corporate greed and your smallpox bombs and your suburban snipers. Bring it on.* Every Sunday I sat there and watched these couples make their vows. In rainstorms and blizzards, on hundred-degree days. I sat there and when the groom kissed the bride I cried. For the first time since Michelle died, sitting there in my suit, surrounded by strangers. I cried, and they cried too. Everybody. Mothers, fathers, cousins, friends. We all cry at weddings, but they're tears of happiness. And there's something about that, about a room full of people crying for joy that saved my life. Because now I could let it go a little. I could look at all these happy people, these men and women making promises, and know that someone out there was carrying on. Like love is the Olympic torch and you run with it for as long as you can and then hand it off, and someone else takes it for a while. Like love never dies, it just moves on, reincarnated as someone else's marriage, someone else's baby."

A cloud moves in front of the sun. He reaches down and turns off the car. I touch his hand, lean over and kiss his cheek.

"That is just about the most beautiful thing I've ever heard," I tell him.

He looks at me, at my house. His left eye is already starting to close.

"So can I come in?" he asks me.

I grab his tie, pull him toward me.

"You better," I say.

34

And if this were a real love story that would be it. The end. Happily ever after. If this were a fairy tale, a movie. If life were a shining diamond. But it's not, it's a lump of coal, a mysterious crate lying forgotten at the bottom of a lake, and you don't know what's inside. Gold bars? Auto parts? A human head? Because in the end, none of the clichés apply. Every life is different. Like how they say it's always darkest before the dawn. But the opposite is also true: It's always, always brightest before the fall. The better to see what you've lost. A face frozen in the flare of headlights.

Smiling, waving good-bye.

Inside, I fix us a drink. The back of my head feels soft, circles of pain emanating outward like ripples on water. This is my second head injury in two months. I wonder if I should worry. Gilligan takes off his coat, puts it on the sofa. He studies the pictures I have hanging from clotheslines, my work in progress.

"I like this one," he says.

I hand him his drink. He's looking at a photograph of Angela, the home-wrecker. She is leaning into the lens. Her cleavage is exaggerated. Her expression is confrontational.

"It's a little out of focus," I say.

"When someone says they like something," he says, "you're supposed to say 'thank you.' "

"Thank you."

I drop onto the sofa, kick off my shoes. Sipping my drink, I watch him as he moves from shot to shot—Mrs. Anderson from divorce court, Harvey at the support group—studying his body, the angle of his head. And though he's not looking at me, I feel exposed.

"It's so good," he says coming over and sitting next to me. I don't know what to do with my hands, where to look.

"What do I say again?"

He kisses me, whispers it in my ear.

"Thank you," I repeat.

He leans back, sips his drink.

"Tell me about your family," he says. "I feel like I do all the talking around here."

I finger the mouth of my glass, running my knuckles in circles.

"My family," I say.

He puts his glass down, takes my hand.

"You have a sister, right?"

"Lisa," I say.

"How old?"

"She's thirty-four. Just got engaged."

"You like him? The guy."

"David? Yeah. If that matters."

"Why wouldn't it?"

I shrug. He reaches out, touches my cheek. This is the moment I should open up, tell him everything. This is the moment where I'm supposed to reveal myself. Back up the truck, dump it all out. Part of me wants to, more than anything. To confess, to spread my life out. But staring at the wide expanse of the past is like standing on a frozen lake, surrounded by patches of black, pockets of thin ice.

One false step, and I'll fall in.

"I don't know," I say.

"What about your parents?" he says.

"Dead," I tell him.

"I'm sorry."

"It was a long time ago."

He leans forward, kisses me on the lips. I try to hold on to him, to change the subject with my body, but he slips away, retreats. He opens his mouth to ask another question. I press my finger to his lips. For a moment, we just look into each other's eyes, and everything slows down. It's like I can read his mind, see what he's thinking, what he's going to say. Three simple words:

I love you.

It takes my breath away.

He doesn't say them, but looking into his eyes, I swear they're there.

Like the Loch Ness monster.

Like a hovering spacecraft.

The abominable snowman.

I look in his eyes, and I can hear them clear as day. The only three words that matter. They could throw out the rest of all human language for all I care, all the verbs and adjectives. The tired prepositions. Scrap all the useless business jargon and political rhetoric. Throw away all the descriptions of sunsets and war. Every noun and adverb, every tired suffix. Just give me those three small words hovering in the space between us.

Love you I.

A wave of energy moves through me, an electrical storm. I don't know what it means. It could be happiness. It could be fear. All I know is it's overwhelming. A fire storm of feeling crackling through my bones. All I know is sitting there I feel like I'm dying.

"Do you want," I say. "Do you want to see pictures?"

He blinks. The light fades from his eyes a little. He sits back, nods. I get to my feet, go over to the bookshelves. Even now I'm protecting myself. Even now I'm holding back. There are two photo albums standing side by side on the shelf. Photos of my family and photos of actors portraying my family. And maybe it's the head injury or the words in his eyes, or my own genetic reluctance, but I pick the latter, lifting the heavy leather book down from the shelf, and carrying it over to the table. I sit down next to him, mouth dry. He puts his hand on my shoulder. I risk another look, and I swear they're still there. Those words. Hovering, effervescent.

Like Santa Claus or the Tooth Fairy.

Seeing them is like being caught in a tractor beam. He opens his mouth, takes a breath. Feeling it coming, I'm dizzy, short of breath, because the words are inside me too, struggling, straining to get out. *I love you.* I open my mouth. My tongue flattens against my teeth. And now we're both sitting there staring, our mouths open. Wanting to say something, but paralyzed. Neither one of us speaks. His eyes are burying me, swallowing me whole. The moment hangs there, both of us swimming in a transparent bubble, wanting to say something. But it's too big, too monumental. The words, like nuclear bombs.

"So," he says, finally, looking away. "The pictures."

"Right," I say.

Looking down, I notice once more the book I've brought over. The copy. The fake. It's not too late to stand and get the other one. Not too late to say, *Oh, silly me.* But I don't. Instead, I sit frozen for another moment and then, in one smooth move, I crack the binding. I open the cover.

Behold the truth. The lie.

Me.

The first picture is of two actors lying on a horse blanket. Two characters from the sixties, with their long straight hair, their frozen expressions of glee. Mom. Dad.

"Hippies," says Gilligan.

"That was the time," I tell him. "What people wore."

We study the faded, yellowing photograph. If I were being honest, I'd explain how I used diluted chemicals to print these old pictures. How I scanned the negatives and doctored the color balances on my computer. How I tracked down date-expired paper on eBay and then left the prints in the sun for two weeks to make them fade. If I were being honest. But I'm not, so I say nothing. I go on letting him think this is real. My family. My past.

"You've got your mother's eyes," he says.

I turn the page quickly, feeling reckless, like I'm driving too fast on a winding road late at night when the rains come.

The next picture is of the whole family. Mom, Dad, Lisa, me. The girl playing me is three years old, a friend's daughter. She is a pretty little girl, dark-haired, brooding. She stands holding the baby, glaring at the camera, as nearby her parents sit side-by-side. The actress playing my mother is ignoring the children. Her back is to them, and she's gazing into her husband's eyes.

This is a theme that plays itself out in photograph after photograph. How the parents and the children seem to inhabit two different frames. Here we are at the circus, on the beach. The children look like an afterthought, smuggled into frame while the photographer's back was turned. They hover on the edges, sometimes just faces peering into frame. Sometimes reflected in mirrors. In the room, but not the photograph. There's us at the market. Us in the car. Pictures of a family in which no one is smiling.

At first, the images stay true to their originals, fading Kodak snapshots, but as the numbers mount they become more studied. The composition improves, the lighting. Black-and-white becomes the dominant medium. The depth of field evolves, becoming artful.

This is because I've started creating photographs from memories now. There is Laurie and Lisa, two little girls, holding hands, entering a foreboding brick building, swallowed by a revolving door. A shot where all that remains outside is the silhouette of Lisa's arm holding her doll. And then inside, the long shadows cast across the marble floor.

There is Laurie standing beside her father's bed. There is her mother in the doorway, a bowl of soup tumbling to the floor, her arm outstretched, hand pointing accusatorily. The father lies face up in bed, unmoving, unseeing.

"Who?" says Gilligan, starting to sense that something isn't right here. "Who took this one?"

I don't say anything. He studies the picture, turns the page, and sees a murky shot of a man's shoes, his legs. The foot of a bed. The man is lying on the floor. The shot is taken over someone's shoulder, low to the ground. A girl's shoulder. The angle is skewed, the floor tilting, and as if taken by gravity there is a thin red rivulet winding down by the man's ankle, rolling from the tip of his finger. And that's all you see, a fingertip, a leg, and down in the top left corner of the frame, the bottom of a full-length mirror, reflecting a slice of window, a blinding glare.

"Laurie," says Gilligan.

I sit there, afraid to look at him, afraid the words will be gone from his eyes.

"What is this?" he says.

I don't say a word. I just close the book, take it from him. I get up, go back to the shelf.

"I'm sorry," I say.

He stands, crosses over to me.

"That was . . . the wrong book," I say.

He looks puzzled, worried.

"The wrong . . ."

"Do you want another drink?" I ask.

He shakes his head, takes my hand.

"I want you to talk to me," he says.

"I can't."

"Why not?"

I am shrinking, disappearing. I don't know what to say.

"Because . . ." I say.

He puts his hands on my shoulders.

"Tell me," he says.

Standing there, I wish that I could take it back. That I had chosen the other album instead, the real one, with its fading snapshots, its posed tranquillity. I wish that we could return to the sofa, to the moment of impassioned declarations. But I know now that's impossible. I've ruined everything again.

"I took those pictures," I say. "Those were actors."

"I don't understand."

I go over to the window.

"It was an art project."

"But they're supposed to be your family?"

I nod.

"Laurie," he says, worrying now that I'm delusional, unbalanced, but wanting to give me the benefit of the doubt, to believe I'm just artistic, eccentric.

I take a step forward.

"I wanted to show you the way it really was. Not the cheerful little snapshots, not the public relations material."

"Okay," he says. "But why didn't you just tell me that? Why did you let me think it was real?"

"Because it is real." For a moment neither one of us speaks. I stand watching the trees blow in the breeze outside, the empty, motionless houses.

"Sometimes," I say. "There are pictures, images, you can't get out of your head."

He watches me, waiting.

"Everybody has them," I say. "You have them. I just had to get them out. Look at them in the light. So I could understand. Does that make sense? There's another book I could show you. Pictures of my mother in the hospital. On a respirator. Not my mother though, an actress. A model. A whole series of pictures. And all I'm trying to . . . I guess, this is . . . what I wanted you to see . . . the things I see when I close my eyes. The past. The truth. The things you can't convey with words. Or at least I can't. I don't know how."

He studies me. The twilight has faded and the house is dim now. It's like we're not really even here anymore. Like our moment is over and we're fading into the past, our relationship. Squinting, I search his face, his eyes, looking for the words, but they're shielded now. Opaque.

"I just don't understand why you couldn't tell me the truth," he says. "Why you had to trick me. Manipulate me."

"That's not . . . I didn't mean to . . ."

He takes his coat from the sofa. I move to intercept him, feeling panicked.

"You think I'm crazy," I say.

"I don't think you're crazy," he says. "I just think . . . I don't know. You don't trust me. And I've opened up and told you things, and all I get from you is . . . mystery."

"Gil, please."

"It's not fair," he says. "How am I supposed to trust you if you won't trust me?"

I reach for him, but his body language is all wrong. Arms crossed. He pulls away, and all I can think about is how I've seen the three words in his eyes.

The Jersey devil.

The Virgin Mary.

But now they're gone.

35

Later, when I call him, he's quiet, monosyllabic. When I ask him what's wrong, he says, "Nothing." He's just busy. He'll call me later. But he doesn't, and the next day I can't reach him at all. I try not to panic. I want to call my sister for reassurance, but then I remember that she isn't the reassuring type. That given the opportunity she will only make things worse, so I stew in silence, sitting in my darkroom, printing furiously. We haven't scheduled another date this week, and every day that passes without doing so makes me feel feverish, chilled. I tell myself not to worry. That he's probably just overworked, but still, in the bottom of my stomach, I know.

Everything is ruined.

A week later the photography curator for the Lexington Gallery comes by my studio. Doris brings him in her Volvo sedan. He is a tall man with gray hair, Philly Aldrich. I make coffee, pour some cookies out of the bag. He looks through my portfolio, flips through my prints. I stand nervously in the doorway. Doris explains how some prints are meant to be shown in groups: the before and after. Eric and Jeannine's wedding photo and then a shot of Eric in his kitchen, Jeannine in her car. Philly listens quietly, his face unreadable. After forty minutes he puts down the last print and takes a pipe out of his pocket.

"I'm going to put you in touch with Jasper Tully," he says, "who's putting together a group show for the spring."

I nod, feeling faint. He takes a tobacco pouch from his pocket, scoops tobacco into the pipe, tamps it down with his thumb, puts the pipe between his teeth.

"Are you finished?" he asks me. "With the series."

I clear my throat, tell him I still have some things I want to shoot. He nods.

"Well, it's very good."

"Thank you," I mumble, leading them to the door.

Outside, the sun has gone behind the trees. Philly pauses on the threshold, watching the kids on bikes, the hockey nets set up in the cul-de-sac.

"My wife left me in 1988," he says. "She said she didn't realize that marrying a starving artist meant literally starving. Six months later, she was engaged to a dentist. Now she clips coupons in Delaware, while I live in a beautiful loft, go to glamorous uptown dinners, travel the world collecting art. And I say, 'Don't get mad. Don't get even. Get ahead.' "

He buttons his coat, heads down the front walk. I watch them drive away, my heart in my throat. What just happened is so wonderful I'm certain that tomorrow I'll be hit by a train, that tonight I'll slip in the bathtub and split my skull open. I'm absolutely positive that before I can call the gallery, before I can show my work, a satellite is going to come crashing through the ionosphere and crush me in my sleep.

When opportunity knocks, they tell you, don't fuck it up.

I call Gilligan.

"I know you don't like me anymore," I say, "but something happened. Something wonderful, and I need to—"

"Why would you even say that?"

"What?"

"That I don't like you."

I fumble around for the words.

"I just . . . I wanted to tell you. I wanted you to know."

"What?" he says.

I look over both shoulders, take the phone into the bedroom closet. On the wall is the photo of our flag, one corner of lifting in the breeze, starting to disintegrate.

I speak quietly, tell him what happened, the curator, the gallery.

"That's great, Laurie," he says.

"I know. We should celebrate."

There's a pause. Then he says,

"I don't know."

"What?"

His voice is sad.

"I'm just not sure . . ."

"About what?"

"I worry about you. That's all. I want you to be happy, but I'm not sure you can be."

"I can," I say. "I am. You make me happy." My voice is pleading.

"Do I?"

"Yes."

"I thought I scared you to death."

"What's the matter with you? Why are you doing this?"

Silence, then,

"I have to go."

"No, wait. Talk to me. What's going on? If this is about the pictures, I'm sorry. I want to tell you now. Everything. Please. Let's just . . . we'll have dinner and I'll . . . spill my guts. Anything you want to know. I promise."

Silence. I can't stand it. Every second is like a knife strike.

"Are we okay?" I whisper, unable to get anymore volume.

Pause.

"Yes," he says.

"It doesn't feel like it. It feels like you're pulling back."

Silence. I'm clutching the phone so hard my knuckles are white.

"Maybe . . ." he says.

"What?"

"Maybe you're not the only one who's afraid of getting hurt," he says.

I feel some measure of relief coupled with panic. Panic at what he says, but relief because this is a language I can speak:

Fear, uncertainty.

"I'm not gonna hurt you," I tell him.

"You say that," he says, "but what if one day you just freak out, run away?"

"I won't," I say, feeling dizzy. "At least I don't think . . ."

"You're always so concerned with protecting yourself. Maybe I should protect myself too."

"No. You're the strong, silent type. I'm the basket case."

I listen to him breath. My yeti, my alien abduction experience. How bottomless the feeling when you realize the oasis was just a mirage.

"It's not funny, Laurie," he says quietly. "I want to be able to feel good about us, to relax a little. But I need to know it's safe."

Everything is spinning around me. I put my hand on the wall. He's having second thoughts. I'm too neurotic, too difficult. This is why I don't own rugs, because of how quickly they can be pulled out from under you. For ten days I've suffered his silence, wishing he would speak, tell me what's on his mind, but now that he is I would do anything to make him stop.

"It's not fair," I say. "This is the girl talk. I'm supposed to say these things."

"Sorry," he says. "Life's too short to keep it all inside."

I feel panic at the idea of losing him, panic that he will leave me. That I could drive him away just by being me.

"Please," I say. "Let's just celebrate. I'll put on a slutty black dress. We'll drink champagne and laugh at the world. Pick me up at eight."

"It's not that easy," he says, and his voice is sad.

I feel like paint that's been scraped off a wall.

"Yes, it is. Come on. We'll go out, have a good time."

"No. I need to think about some things."

"Is this because I asked you if you were rich?"

"What?"

"Because that was just a fluke. It doesn't mean anything."

"Listen," he says. "I'm really happy for you. Your work is beautiful. You deserve this, okay? You should be happy."

"How can I be happy if you're mad at me?"

"I'm not mad. I'm just . . . I need to figure some things out."

I feel like a small animal being crushed between two rocks. My voice is small, smothered.

"Please don't go," I say.

"I'm not going anywhere."

"I can't do this alone."

"You're not alone. But even if you were, you're stronger than you think."

"I don't want to lose you."

"You're not gonna lose me," he says.

But hanging up I'm not so sure.

36

Two days later, I'm crouching in the bushes taking pictures of Damien. It's five o'clock in the afternoon. Damien answered the ad I placed looking for stalkers. He's five foot six with greasy brown hair. For the last two years he's been obsessed with a former co-worker named Melissa. There is a shrine to her in his house, complete with a framed, poster-size portrait taken from the company directory, hair clippings, old office supplies (once handled by Melissa), and a wad of chewing gum, prechewed by Melissa's mouth.

"We have this connection," he tells me. "There's definitely love there. Synergy. She's just afraid to admit it."

He tells me that when Melissa moved out of her old apartment—mainly because Damien wouldn't leave her alone, wouldn't stop calling, ringing the bell—Damien went to see the landlord and rented the place himself. The day he got the keys, he walked

into the apartment he'd fought so long just to see, and stood en-
raptured in the living room. He said he could feel her presence,
her warmth. He wandered from room to room lying on the floor,
smelling the walls, eyes closed, feeling what she felt, seeing what
she saw. Then he went downstairs and unloaded the truck, and now
he sleeps where she once slept, bathes where she once bathed.

"She was in such a hurry," he says. "She left a lot of stuff behind."

By digging behind radiators and other appliances, looking under
floorboards, he found toenail clippings, old mail, a sock. Lying
prostrate under the bathtub he was able to scoop up three used Q-
tips, a dirty cotton swab covered with mascara, the cap to a tube
of depilatory cream. And like everything else of hers, he added these
items to the shrine.

I ask him to show me where Melissa lives now. I tell him I want
to shoot him in action. He says he'll drive me over, but I tell him
I'd rather drive myself. The truth is, I don't want to be that close
to him, shut up in his dirty vehicle, breathing his nutty air. So we
go in two cars, him leading, me following at a safe distance, wondering if this might not be the end for me, if he isn't leading me
to some secluded spot where he can rape and dismember me. I
wish I'd told someone where I was going.

Damien pulls over on a quiet street, parks. I pull in behind him.
He steps out of the car, wearing a sweatshirt and stocking cap. I
grab my camera bag, take a deep breath, and join him on the
sidewalk.

"Which one's hers?" I ask.

He ignores me, turns and starts walking, focused, like a dog
that's got a scent. I follow, ask him to tell me how they met.

"We both worked in accounts payable," he says over his shoulder. "But really I think I've been dreaming about her my whole
life."

He's wearing a pair of dirty jeans, and he has no ass. Just this
flat flap of denim hanging down from his waist.

"Did you ever date?" I ask him.

He doesn't answer. The street we're on is lined with small apartment buildings. It's rained recently, and the gutter is filled with soggy leaves. The asphalt shines like a dirty mirror. He slows as we approach a light blue building, seven stories tall.

"I'm not supposed to get too close," he tells me.

Later, studying the court records, I'll learn that Melissa has taken out three successive restraining orders against him, and each time the court has forced him to keep a greater distance. Step by step, block by block, they are slowly litigating him out of visual range.

He crouches down behind a row of mailboxes, peers up at the building. I take out my camera, frame him against the black wrought-iron fence.

"We used to talk all the time," he says. "At work. She was so pretty I couldn't think. I used to lie in bed at night and pretend she was there next to me, and I'd watch her sleep. How peaceful she could be."

I ask him to tell me which window is hers. He points to the fifth floor. The lights are on inside. I reach into my camera bag and pull out my longest telephoto lens. Standing close to Damien, I can smell the salami he had for lunch.

"We love each other," he says. "She's just afraid of our power. That much love. I call her sometimes and talk to her machine. I can tell from the messages she leaves that she misses me. The way she says 'I'm not here right now,' Like she's really sorry she missed me, my call."

I crouch down behind a bush and aim my camera up at the fifth floor. I want to see Melissa the way he sees her. A princess locked in a tower. The lights are on in the kitchen, the living room. I watch for a minute until she comes into frame, wearing a sweater, her hair pulled back. She's thinner than she is in Damien's directory photo. Her cheekbones are more pronounced. I photograph her as she leans down to pick up her mail.

"Can I get a copy of those?" Damien asks me.

"No," I tell him.

He takes a pair of minibinoculars from his jacket pocket. The way he looks at me I wonder if he thinks we're on a date. Like this is a rational thing to do, take the new girlfriend over to spy on the old. He smiles at me. His teeth are yellow.

"You're pretty," he says.

"Don't even think about it," I tell him.

He asks me if I've ever been in love, really in love. "So bad you can't eat, can't sleep." I consider telling him how little I've slept the last two days since Gilligan told me he needed time to think. I could let him in on how hard it is to eat. The fear that gnaws at me. Fear that I've fucked things up, ruined everything. Fear I'm not good enough. Not smart enough. Not pretty. I think about my first boyfriend in high school, Evan, who broke my heart and left me hollow and desperate, who got into my head like a virus, had me driving by his house, calling his mother. I was so overwrought I didn't recognize myself. So lost I couldn't find my way out for six months. But that was high school, and he was my first boyfriend. I was sixteen, still getting used to all these new emotions. I think about Jim. The night I passed him on the street in my car, saw him walking arm-in-arm with another woman, and how I followed him three blocks to a restaurant. How I sat outside and watched them order, and when he reached out and held her hand, I pitched forward, hit the horn with my head, then drove off in a panic.

I tell myself it's not the same. We're not the same, Damien and me. That he's a crazy man, and I'm just a regular girl with a healthy sense of perspective. But seeing us here together, I'm not so sure.

"Look," he says. "She's dancing."

I look through the viewfinder. Melissa has put on some music and she's dancing around the apartment, swaying in time to an invisible beat.

"I love it when she dances," says Damien. "She has such a good body."

He makes a sound in his throat, and I feel like running, like ringing the bell and warning her, telling her to close her blinds. Instead I take her picture, zooming in, recording her shut-eyed gaze, the smallest smile on her lips.

Click.

My cell phone rings. I take it out of my bag, answer.

"Has he called?" my sister asks.

"No," I say, looking through the viewfinder, aware of a change in Damien's breathing beside me. A quickening.

"You didn't call him, did you?" she asks.

"No. I don't want to crowd him. He told me he needed time to think."

"Shake it," mutters Damien. I'm afraid to look at him. I take the other camera from around my neck, snap his picture, shooting from the hip. Later, I will see that he's lying on his stomach, groin to the ground. He has his eyes to the binoculars, and he's pretending to kiss her.

"Well, I think it's a little weird," says Lisa. "To turn around so quickly. Maybe he's seeing someone else."

My heart stumbles, misses a beat. I haven't told her about the photo album, about my inability to communicate. I couldn't face her judgment, her diagnosis.

"You think?" I say.

"It wouldn't surprise me. A good-looking guy, rich. I bet women throw themselves at him all the time."

Melissa stops dancing, goes into the kitchen. I photograph her getting a soda from the refrigerator.

"Have I told you lately how much I hate you?" I ask Lisa.

"Just yesterday, in fact," says Lisa.

Damien gets to his knees. He wipes his mouth on the back of his sleeve.

"If you want," he tells me. "I can give you some pointers."

"Who's that?" my sister wants to know.

"Nobody. I'm working."

"Like, when you go home," says Damien, "get out a measuring

tape and measure out a hundred feet. It's farther than you think."

"Stop talking," I tell him.

"Who is that?" says Lisa.

"Or, you know, make sure you call him from public phones. They're harder to trace. You have to think in terms of records. Because when you go to court they can produce all that stuff. And then you have to go home and measure out five hundred feet, which is a lot farther than most measuring tapes will go."

I take his picture, hands raised a few feet apart, like he's a fisherman talking about the one that got away.

"Who the hell are you talking to?" my sister asks me.

I stand and walk a few paces away.

"Nobody. Just—I'm shooting a stalker."

"You're what?"

"We're outside this girl's apartment. He's spying on her with binoculars."

My sister lights a cigarette. I keep telling her to quit, but she says it's my fault.

"You're killing me, you know that? Your crazy life."

I listen to her rant for a minute, just noise in my ear, watching Damien crawl forward on his stomach like a soldier. I wonder if the restraining order applies to vertical feet. He stands, puts his hands on the bars, looks up. I take his picture, and later when I get them back, it will be like we're in jail together. The photographer and her subject.

"It's for my project," I tell her. "Love. I'm meeting with that gallery director next week."

My sister inhales, coughs.

"You didn't give the stalker your phone number, did you?" she asks.

"Post office box," I tell her. "And I'm driving a rental car."

Damien comes over, pulls an apple out of his pocket, takes a bite.

"Can I talk?" he says, reaching for the phone. I turn away.

"Listen," I tell my sister. "I'm not sleeping. I feel really spooked. What if he's dumping me?"

"He's not dumping you," she says. "But you should take this opportunity to figure out what you want from him."

I put my hand on my forehead, worried I'm coming down with something, worried I feel clammy. Hot.

"Maybe he just needs some space," says Damien. I stare at him. He smiles weakly.

"The stalker's right," Lisa tells me. "You don't want to come on too strong."

"Who's side are you on?" I ask.

"Mine," she says.

I give the phone to Damien. He puts the half-eaten apple back in his pocket, lifts the phone to his ear.

"Hey, what are you wearing?" he wants to know.

I walk over to Melissa's front gate, look up at her window. There are two cameras hanging around my neck and the weight is like an anvil dragging me down. I don't want to be so negative all the time. To live in a state of constant pessimism. And goddamnit, I feel like I've gotten so much better. I can be happy. Why couldn't I be happy? I want to call Gilligan and tell him he should have seen me six months ago. A year. Back then black wasn't a dark enough color. I was like a broken engine, metal shrieking against metal, smoke rising darkly.

I turn around. Damien is still talking to my sister.

"Fillings," he says: "A few caps. The dentist says I don't brush as much as I should."

I take the phone from him.

"Having fun?" I ask her.

"I told him my name was Stephanie. She's this girl at the office I hate. Stephanie and Damien have a date for Saturday night."

"You're a terrible person," I tell her.

"Everybody needs a hobby," she says.

"Oh shit," says Damien.

I turn. There is a police cruiser pulling up, lights flashing. Two cops jump out, guns drawn.

"Uh, Lisa," I say, lifting the camera with the wide angle lens and shooting wildly. "I think I'm getting arrested."

Damien walks in circles, cornered.

"I'm not resisting," he yells. "I'm not resisting."

The cops grab Damien, throw him to the ground, cuff him. He's still yelling. I take five pictures in quick succession. Another police cruiser screeches to a halt. Two officers, a woman and a man, jump out. They rush me, arms outstretched. I backtrack, trying to get as many pictures in as possible before I'm caught.

"Look," I tell them. "I'm not with him. I'm just a photographer."

They grab my arms, throw me up against the car, cuff me. One of the officers takes my cameras. The other two officers have Damien on his feet and they're dragging him over to the cruiser.

"Melissa," he yells. "I love you. I LOVE YOU!"

They put him in the car, making no effort to protect his head as they shove him inside. I take his picture with my mind, zooming in. Then my officers are turning me sideways, none too gently, and inserting me into their vehicle. I fall in awkwardly, without the use of my arms. The handcuffs are biting into my wrists. Already my fingers are getting numb. This is a first for me. To be captured, restrained. What a month I'm having. First knocked unconscious by an angry mob, now on my way to jail. There's an argument to be made that I may be hitting bottom here. Crapping out. Around me the police car smells of ammonia and sweat. The backseat is covered in plastic for easy cleaning.

I look out the window. Blue and red lights flicker on the sidewalk. A squirrel darts across the weed-covered lawn. I wonder if they'll take my picture at the station, what kind of camera they'll use. The last thing I see as we drive away is Melissa, standing in her front doorway, arms crossed across her chest, staring out at me from behind bars.

37

I'm in jail for six hours. The police question me in a room without windows. I tell them I'm a photographer, that I'm doing a series on what happens when love turns bad. They keep asking what newspaper I work for. They can't understand that a sane individual would take pictures of lunatics for the pure art of it.

"You're not too bright, are you?" the detective wants to know. She's a heavyset woman in her midforties. "This guy could have raped you, killed you."

I sit there rubbing my wrists. The fluorescent light makes everyone look strung out, like a roomful of junkies.

"I could charge you with aiding and abetting," she tells me. "Put you in jail for three to five."

"I'm sorry," I say. "I never meant to hurt anyone."

I tell her this and think about Jim, Gilligan, myself. How easy it is to damage the things you love. You don't even have to try.

She shakes her head. "You know how many times this guy's been arrested? Five. Now he'll probably get jail time. You should see the poor girl he's been stalking. Jumpiest person I ever met. You can't even sneeze without sending her into hysterics."

Sitting across from the detective, I wonder what it's like to feel watched all the time. To know that someone is out there plotting, fantasizing. The corrupt stepbrother of the thing we all desire: to be loved unconditionally. To feel safe, watched over, cared for. This is the catch-22 of love. It only works if the feeling is mutual. It's only beautiful if the obsession goes both ways. To tell someone you would die for them, that you can't live without them, is a declaration of true romance if that someone is your lover, your wife. But if they're not, if that someone is a total stranger, a coworker, an ex, then the imagery of death becomes terrifying, the threat implied. To love someone who won't return the favor, someone who actively dislikes you, detests you, someone who lives in fear of you, is an act of leprosy. It is beauty turned on its ear, and it mocks the thing we want the most. Because now the ultimate intimacy has turned into the ultimate exclusion. Unrequited love, like the last desperate act of the true outsider.

When we were at his house, Damien told me that sometimes he just can't take it. All the feelings. They make him dizzy. He can't open his mouth wide enough to let them out. He knows that if Melissa would just talk to him, look in his eyes, she would see her destiny.

He is the one for her.

"Why can't she see that?" he asked me. "No one will ever love her the way I do. No one would protect her, provide for her, worship her, the way I do."

I think about Melissa, poor Melissa, jumping every time somebody sneezes. I wonder what this ordeal has done to her ability to carry on normal relationships. To trust men. When you realize what kind of darkness can lurk in their hearts. When every boy she dates starts getting phone calls in the middle of the night. When you have to get to know everyone you meet under a state of constant siege.

I sit under fluorescent lights and tell the detective I'm sorry. I wasn't thinking clearly. Which, more often then not in my case, is true.

They let me go with a warning. The police return my cameras, my film, after I promise I won't share the pictures with Damien. After I convince them he doesn't even know my name, much less how to contact me. My sister is waiting for me among the thugs and ruffians, a pretty young thing with a Kate Spade handbag surrounded by men with scars, women with black eyes.

"You're making me old before my time," she tells me as we climb into her car.

"Sorry," I say.

She drives me back to my car. I consider asking her to stop in front of Melissa's house, consider telling Lisa I just want to ring the bell, apologize. But I don't, I know what she'd say:

Haven't you done enough damage for one day?

I drop off the rental car, drive home smelling like ammonia. I run inside, pulling my clothes off as I go, leaving them strewn like a trail of bread crumbs all the way to the bathroom. Inside, I take a hot shower, scraping at my skin with a loofah. I close my eyes, feel the water on my face, in my mouth.

Don't think.

Just feel.

And yet I can't stop asking myself, *Why hasn't he called? What is he doing?*

I stand on the bathroom floor, dripping. The air around me is cloudy with steam. I tell myself to let it go. Not to be a hypochondriac where love is concerned. Photographing stalkers doesn't make me one. Just because I'm vulnerable, just because sometimes I feel desperate, lonely, doesn't make me the kind of person who builds shrines. Just because I have pictures of Gilligan in my studio. Just because there is a photograph of the flag he made me in my closet. That's not a shrine, is it? One photograph? So what if it's in the closet? I'm a photographer. This is what I do. It doesn't mean I'm obsessed, doesn't mean I'm a crazy woman who doesn't deserve love. At least I've dated the man I want. At least we've lain together. So what if I sweat uncontrollably in the middle of the night? It doesn't make me a danger to myself and others.

I'm just a woman who's having troubles with her boyfriend.

Is he my boyfriend? Can I call him my boyfriend?

I stand there dripping, wondering, trying to fight off the panic that closes around me like a mouth.

At that moment I don't know if I'm more like my mother or my father.

I tell myself that this time is different. This man. This man who took me in his arms and told me I didn't have to be afraid anymore.

And more than anything I want it to be true.

I stand there dripping, and not for the first time I think how much simpler life would be without words. Without dialogue. How much simpler if we only had pictures to communicate, a language of shapes and color. Where a smile meant happy, and a frown meant sad. Where there was nothing more to making someone love you than to point to your and heart and theirs. Nothing more to cheering someone up then to open your mouth and laugh.

Like pictograms on a dark cave wall.

Open arms. Open hands. A heart with an arrow through it.

Me. You.

Together.

What more could anyone need?

38

Gilligan works in an anonymous office in midtown Manhattan. I go to see him Thursday morning. It's been six days, and still he hasn't called. I get the address from the phone book, change my clothes six or seven times. How do you dress to do something you know you shouldn't? What do you wear to confront a man who, when it comes right down to it, owes you nothing, but a man you think you could love? I want to look provocative, but not desperate, independent, but not aloof. The whole pants-skirt debate takes an hour in and of itself. Eventually, I settle on slacks and a sweater, then spend a half hour applying and washing off my makeup, thinking about how ridiculous I must look, a woman speeding around the house, shedding her skin, racing back and forth to the bathroom.

The building is a slate-gray tower. His office is on the tenth floor, room 1040. I stand in a long empty hallway staring at the number, trying to decide if this is some kind of joke. An accountant in room 1040, like a dentist with hairy hands and a cartoon tie. I feel dizzy, reckless, but then when do I not? It's probably dietary. This whole thing I think is me struggling under some great emotional weight could probably be cleared up with a little more calcium in my diet. A one pound Prozac tablet.

I knock quietly, put my ear to the door. Nothing. I close my eyes, straining to hear. The door opens. I stumble back, trying to recover, to look natural, nonchalant.

"Laurie."

"Hey, hi," I say, recovering my balance, putting a hand against the far wall.

He's wearing a gray suit, a brown tie and glasses.

"Glasses?" I say.

"I have an astigmatism," he tells me. "I usually wear contacts."

I smile stupidly for way too long, a thousand butterflies in my bloodstream.

"I don't have an appointment," I say.

"That's okay," he says. "I was just gonna get some lunch. Do you want to join me?"

I try not think too much about the invitation, if it's genuine. My brain is like a perpetual motion machine at this point, spinning on and on, worrying every little thing down to the bone.

I nod, "yes." He tells me to come inside while he gets his things. I follow him in. The office is modern, cozy, with potted plants and a sofa. The walls are covered with photographs of other people's relatives. There's a toy basketball hoop set up on the wall across from his desk, with a trash can underneath. Balls of paper line the floor around it.

"You need to work on your jump shot," I say.

"Story of my life," he tells me.

There is a framed photograph on his desk. Michelle, the dead

wife. I pick it up, look it over. She's a pretty redhead, caught turning, the light behind her throwing a halo, like a Vermeer painting.

"I'm sorry I haven't called," says Gilligan. "I've been really busy.
The end of Q-four and all that."

Standing there, it occurs to me that I'm never going to marry
my high school sweetheart. All those storybook romances, the simple purity of young love, have passed me by.

"I want to be your friend," I tell him.

"Oh," he says quietly and looks at his shoes.

"That's not *all* I want," I tell him, "but it is a pivotal part. That
we can talk to each other. About anything."

"I had a lot of filings."

"You said that. I didn't come to put you on the spot."

"Why did you come?"

"I missed you."

He nods. He looks so sad. I take his hand.

"My family," I say, "I don't have a lot of happy memories."

"I'm sorry," he says.

"No, I'm sorry," I tell him. "I just . . . you asked about them, and
I didn't know what to say. Most of the time I don't know what to
say."

He doesn't speak, just sits quietly, looking out the window.

"I think about having children sometimes," he says. "Do you
ever think about that?"

"You having children?"

He shakes his head.

"You're impossible," he says.

I watch his face, trying to decide if he's just bantering, or if he's
already given up on me. I can't tell, so I put his dead wife's picture
down, go over to the window. Looking down I see traffic patterns,
the shrunken figures of pedestrians. When we were kids, my sister
and I used to stand on the sidewalk in the middle of a crowd and

look for true love. We'd study the faces passing by and say "Him. That's my husband." Or if we saw a really fat man or one with a goiter we'd point and say, "He's your lover."

"I like kids," I tell him.

He rubs his eyes.

"Sometimes I think it's too late," he says. "I never wanted to be an old father. One of those creaky, geriatric dads who's too arthritic to toss a football. Even if I start tomorrow, I'll be fifty-five when my kid turns thirteen."

"I got arrested last week," I tell him.

"What?"

"It's a long story."

He stares at me for a long time.

"You are the queen of the non sequitur," he says.

I sit on the edge of the desk.

"What do you want me to say? I'm thirty-six. My body's like an angry mob ordering me to reproduce. Sometimes my ovaries hurt. They actually *hurt*."

"I see kids on the street and I feel like stealing them."

"Watch it," I say, "or you'll be the one getting arrested."

He moves some files, perches on the edge of his desk.

"Did you come all the way down here just to be flip?"

I shake my head.

"Because you could have called," he says.

"You're not happy to see me?"

He looks at me. I look back. My hands are shaking. He nods.

"I am," he says.

"Me too."

"I guess I'm a masochist."

"Hey."

We go to a Vietnamese restaurant, sit in a booth by the window.

"I think you're great," he says.

"But?"

"Why does there have to be a 'but'?"

I try to keep my voice light. I don't want to push too hard, scare him off. At the same time, I refuse to pretend everything's all right when I know it's not.

"Because," I say, "you said you had to think, and then you didn't call for a week."

"I've been . . ."

"Busy. I know."

Silence. He stares at his hands.

"I just don't know if I'm ready," he tells me. "I thought I was."

And at that moment, I understand why people ask you if you're sitting down when they deliver bad news. I feel everything falling away, like the world is tilting, turning, trying to shake me loose.

"Ready for what?" I say. "What are we doing here?"

He shakes his head, looks out the window.

"No," I say. "You started this."

"I know. I'm sorry."

I take my napkin, put it on the table, appetite now just a distant memory, something that happens to other people.

"She's not coming back, you know," I say.

He stares at the table.

"I didn't mean it like that," I tell him. "I'm just upset."

"I don't want you to be upset. I'm not saying anything here, doing anything. I just wanted you to know . . . I'm having . . . doubts."

"But . . ."

"You're so different."

From her. His wife.

"It's not a contest," I say.

But of course it is.

"From me," he says. "You're so different from me. The way we communicate."

"Or don't."

"The way we look at things. I don't know what else to say."

I watch people pass outside the window, men in suits, women in skirts. They work for companies with policies against falling in love. Companies that think they can regulate the power out of the relationships we have with men.

"Don't apologize," I tell him. "If you're breaking up with me, just do it."

"No," he says. "That's not . . . This is why I wanted to wait. I need to figure things out. For me. Myself."

I stand up, grab my purse. Clearly I've worn the wrong outfit. It must be the pants. These must be my break-up pants. Maybe if I'd worn the skirt, he would have stayed. If I'd left the eyeliner on, accessorized better. He looks up at me like a puppy, a lost little boy.

"You know where I live," I say.

He reaches out to me.

"Laurie," he says, "wait."

But I don't. I turn my head and walk out. This way he can't see I'm crying.

39

I walk for an hour, turning randomly. Midtown is a maze of bodies, bike messengers cutting corners, racing between double-parked cars. I walk quickly, half-running, like I'm chasing something, following someone, but I just keep falling behind. There is a sensation in my chest, a deep cavity ache, the certainty that whatever it was I was waiting for has passed me by.

There are no saints.

Only gradations of assholes.

I step out into traffic, crossing against the light, not even looking to see if cars are coming. A bike messenger breezes by, so close I can feel his long hair on my face. The city is alive, pulsing, too many bodies, too many sounds, too many smells. If I were a turtle I'd be inside my shell by now, getting small, getting quiet.

Time passes. I stop on a busy corner, look up. Slowly everything comes into focus. There is a revolving door in front of me, a familiar entrance. A doorway from a previous life. I look up at the building, the gleaming glass panels.

Of course, I think.

I would be here.

Outside this building.

I think about backing up, lying down in the middle of the street and letting traffic roll right over me.

I'm so bored with my own emotions I could scream.

I go inside, climb on an elevator and push fifteen. I ride up surrounded by frat boys in suits ribbing each other, talking trash. I catch one of them checking me out, my breasts, my legs. I kick him in the shin.

"Ow," he says.

"Eyes on the road, Jack," I say.

He steps off on ten, throwing me a nasty look. I feel reckless, a bomb about to go off. The elevator doors close, then open again on fifteen. I step into the reception area. I have no idea what I'm doing here, but I'm not about to turn back now.

I walk up to the receptionist.

"Jimmy Magnus," I say.

"Laurie?"

I turn. Jimmy is standing there with an armful of files. My ex-husband, looking trim and fit. Handsome.

"You lost weight," I say.

He nods.

"What are you doing here?"

I shrug. I don't know what to tell him.

"I need a drink."

He thinks about this.

"Come on," he says.

I follow him to his office. He closes the door, tells me to have a seat. His office is on the corner now, all window.

"I guess you made partner," I say.

He goes to the credenza, pulls out a bottle of scotch, two glasses.
"Last year," he says.

"Congratulations," I tell him. He hands me a drink. I raise it. He clinks my glass with his.

"How are you?" he wants to know.

"How do I look?"

"Good," he says. "But you always looked good."

"I think I'm broken," I tell him.

He doesn't say anything.

"I think you broke me."

"Laurie."

"Do you remember dropping me? Or putting me through the dishwasher?"

"I remember you sleeping around. Is that what you're talking about?"

"I didn't sleep around. I slept with one guy one time."

"Oh sorry. I thought it was something major."

I watch the moving clouds reflected in the glass of a nearby building.

"I don't want to fight with you," I say. "That's not why I came here."

"What do you want?"

"I don't know. Some kind of closure."

"I'm not still mad at you, if that's what you mean."

I press my hands to the glass and remember the shark swimming, its dead eyes. I remember what it felt like to be surrounded by water and not be wet, to feel submerged, weightless.

"You're not?" I say.

He shakes his head.

"We both made mistakes. I had no business getting married when I did. It wasn't fair to you."

I finish my scotch, get up, get myself another glass.

"I feel like I'm trying to follow my own footsteps in the snow," I tell him, "find my way back to something, somewhere."

"I'm getting married again," he says.

I start laughing. I can't help it. He joins me for a minute, chuckling, then looks worried when I don't stop, when I start to look deranged.

"That's . . . that's the best thing I've heard all day," I say.

"Her name is Julie. She's an investment banker. We met in Bali."

I sit on the sofa, kick off my shoes.

"Do you love her?"

"Yes."

"How do you know?"

"Because whenever anything happens to me I feel like I have to call her. And when nothing happens I feel like I have to call her. And at the end of every day I can't wait to see her."

"Did you love me?"

He nods.

"Doesn't that bother you?" I say. "That you could love two people? That love can feel so real and then end?"

He sits behind his desk, loosens his tie.

"I think when you get older you have to rethink all the basic principles," he says. "That you can find true love. That it lasts forever. You realize that every relationship you've ever had has ended, but that doesn't make them all failures. Who says a relationship is only good if it ends in marriage? I've dated women for three months and then split up because we weren't right for each other, but now I look back on those months fondly. The time we spent with each other. It was enough. That was how long those relationships were meant to last. And I think we do ourselves a disservice by demanding that everything has to last forty years in order to be real. It makes people stay in relationships longer than they should, makes them feel like failures when things don't work out."

I look at him, thinking, I used to kiss those lips. I used to stroke that hair and now . . .

"So you don't think our marriage was a failure?" I say.

"I'm not saying that. I felt really devastated for a long time. Really hurt. But I'm on the other side of it now."

"You are?"

He nods. I sip my scotch, feeling grounded by the throaty burn.

"What's it like over there?" I ask him. "The weather?"

"Mostly sunny," he says. "The occasional scattered cloud."

We sit in silence, drinking, looking out at the world.

"I hated you for a long time," I tell him.

"I hated you too."

I lie back on the sofa, look at the ceiling.

"What else can you do with all that love?" I say.

He takes a picture from his desk, hands it to me. It's Julie, blond, perky. I think about all the offices in town, all the pictures on all the desks, and not one of me.

"She's cute," I say.

"She's twenty-eight, ready to quit her job, settle down."

"How nice for you."

He shrugs.

"I'm old fashioned. I realize that now. And I'm not gonna fight it."

"Does it bother her that you're divorced?"

He puts the picture back on his desk.

"Sometimes. She thinks it's unromantic. In her head she wanted the prince on the white horse, uncorrupted, virginal. I tell her the second time's the charm."

He looks at me.

"How about you? Anyone special?"

I finish my drink. An airplane is rising high above us. I wish I were on it.

"He's an accountant," I say. "His name's Gilligan."

"His name is what?"
"He's madly in love with me, but he's scared."
"Love can be scary," says Jim.
I slip my shoes on, stand.
"You're telling me," I say.

40

The gun my father brought home was a Smith & Wesson .38 caliber revolver. It had a muted, oily sheen. It was patched with rust. Where he got it I'll never know. He brought it home one evening with a box of lightbulbs and a bag of half-eaten dinner rolls. My sister and I were already in bed. We could hear my mother downstairs watching television, a game show at high volume. Then the front door opened, closed. We scrambled out of bed and over to the doorway, where we could hear the muted rumble of my parents' argument. We crouched in the dark of our room and strained to make out the words. The stairway was fifteen feet away, fifteen feet of old wooden boards that were slowly spitting their nails back into the open air, nails that caught on socks, that bloodied toes. Moonlight fell through the half-cocked bathroom door between us and the landing, lighting dust motes blue. On the other side of the hall, lamplight rose from the downstairs, bright white rays setting the ceiling on fire.

"None of your business," my father said, his voice rising, breaking the rumble.

"Don't you walk away from me," my mother yelled.

There was the sound of a struggle, the sound of heavy footsteps on the stairs, and then lighter footsteps rushing after. Lisa grabbed my hand. The whites of her eyes were enormous. Down the hall I saw the top of my father's head appear, then stop.

"Let go," he said.

"Please," said my mother. "Just tell me what I did. What's wrong?"

He shrugged her off, climbed to the landing. She came after him.

"If you don't stop and talk to me right now," she said. "I swear I'm leaving."

He fumbled in his pocket. In one arm he held a cardboard box, open at the top. The other hand pulled out a set of keys.

"Good," he said.

My mother stood in her nightgown, her face in shadows.

"I mean it," she said. "I hate you."

She grabbed for him. He shoved her, and she staggered back, gripping instead the cardboard box, which flew from his arm and fell, crashing onto the landing, then tumbling down stair after stair, lightbulbs flying free, popping as they fell. My mother saved herself from following them down by grabbing the newel at the top of the landing. She swayed dangerously, regained her balance. Meanwhile my father was struggling with the padlock. My mother lunged for him. He pushed her away again, and this time she fell to the floor. And then I was out of my room and running. My father had the padlock off now. He was opening the door. My mother was lying on the floor panting. I ran past her. My father stepped into the room. He turned to close the door. Still running, I felt a sharp bite on the bottom of my foot, and then I squeezed through the closing door, like an arrow, slipping past him before he even knew I was there. Inside the room I tripped over something almost immediately and fell. And then the door closed behind me, and we were in darkness.

I lay there panting, feeling different kinds of pain shooting up my right leg. Stubbed-toe pain. Skinned-knee pain. And something else. Something sharper, deeper, coming from the bottom of my foot. On the other side of the door, my mother was pounding, calling my father names, ordering him to open up, begging. He stood silently in the dark. Around him I could make out shapes. The room had changed dimension from when I'd seen it last. It was no longer square. It smelled of rancid milk and scorched metal, a smell I would later come to associate with burning brake pads, so that whenever I heard the screech of tires on asphalt, I thought of my father in that room.

"Daddy," I said quietly.

He reached over and turned on the light, blinding me. He bent over. His silhouette was enormous, looming as he peered down. He squinted as if unsure who I was, as if I must be some kind of omen. Around him the room seemed to spin, hanging frozen in zero gravity. The furniture had been nailed to the walls, the ceiling. He had fastened cardboard so that it obscured the borders where floor met wall and wall met ceiling, turning the room into something unnatural, seamless. Wire and mesh were woven into mounds of plaster. And everywhere there was writing. Sometimes words, sometimes phrases, sometimes only letters. My father stood over me, haloed by a single naked bulb hanging overhead.

"What do you want?" he said.

"I ate the olives?" I told him. My heart was beating fast. Blood was leaking from my foot. The pain was bright, startling.

My father nodded. He looked me over, noticed the way I was holding my foot, the blood. He bent down, then stopped, impeded by something. He reached behind him and pulled a gun from his waistband, placed it on the floor. Then he crouched and grabbed my foot.

"Don't cry," he said.

He examined the sole of my foot, the ball. He used the tail of his shirt to wipe away the blood, then pulled a piece of curved glass the size of marble from my skin. He studied it for a minute, then stood and went over to the window, where he took a tube of glue from the sill and proceeded to glue the bloody glass to the wall.

"Perfect," he said.

I sat there holding my foot, looking at the gun. It was huge, like a cannon, its empty black barrel unblinking. I was afraid to move, afraid to touch it. My father came over, picked up the gun, put it back into his pants. My mother, who had been quiet for a moment, listening, renewed her pounding. My father went over, put his back to the door. His body shook with the force of her blows.

Over his head was written these words:

Just Married.

He looked at me.

"What's your name again?"

"Laurie," I said.

He nodded.

"I went to the dump," he said. "There were people there. We stood around waiting for something to happen. The nurse came around and gave us pills. We swallowed them without water. And we stood, waiting. My feet got itchy. What would happen? When? A dog came by and waited. The sky was yellow. There were so many people there. Why did I feel so alone?"

I thought about Lisa, alone in our room, hiding, crying. About my mother on the other side of the door. There was a clock over my head, dangling from a chain. There were cigarette butts glued to the wall in patterns.

"Daddy, I'm scared," I told him, my father, who was supposed to protect me from these things, who was supposed to love and nurture me.

"Me too," he said, then raised the gun and shot himself.

41

I've never been good at writing things down. Putting them into words. I have a hard enough time talking, telling people what's on my mind. Give me a typewriter, a pencil, and I freeze, turn to stone. I wonder, why is it a blank piece of paper can be so inviting in the dark room and so oppressive in the living room? But the truth is, sometimes in life you have to do the things you hate. Which is why, tonight, I sit down and write it all out. The story of me. Of my mother and father and what happened. Things I've never told anyone. Not even Jimmy. I take a ballpoint pen and a pad of paper and write until my hand cramps, and then I send it to Gilligan, with a return address and a stamp. I don't include the photographs I've made. I don't focus on the gory details. The last thing I ever wanted was anybody's pity. I just give him the facts. I want him to know I trust him. That it was never about telling lies.

It was never about manipulation. It's just that some things are harder to say than others. Some stories are harder to tell. That's why I chose to show him pictures. I was opening the door, leaving clues, giving him the opportunity to come in if he wanted. To go deeper if he chose. Some memories you don't want to relive over and over. Some stories get worse every time you tell them. Gilligan has his own grief to contend with. He should understand. The real stories, the stories that make you who you are, are precious. They're worth being miserly with, worth protecting. If you tell everyone you meet your most private thoughts, your most painful memories, it cheapens them. Turns them into anecdotes. And worse, if you open up, if you tell those stories to someone, and they reject you, then aren't they rejecting your stories, your experiences, saying your suffering isn't good enough? The things you've lived through are unremarkable, unimpressive?

I write down what happened and send it to Gilligan, and then I try to put it out of my mind. I try not to think about him going to his mailbox, opening the letter, reading it. I try not to think of him judging my life on a literary basis, try not to picture him reading stone-faced, unmoved not by the circumstances, but the words I chose to relate them. This is the other way in which pictures are superior to words. It is harder to dismiss an image based on the quality of the craft, because images pass unfiltered into our brains. Because we see them and we react immediately. They do not accrue in our heads like words, building on each other, never delivering their full weight until the last period is in place.

I write a letter to Gilligan and I say, I wasn't trying to keep secrets. I was just trying to tell you the story in my own way, to use my own images. But because you didn't understand, here is the translation. Here is what happened.

We are both the product of loss, I say.

Let us find ourselves together.

42

On Monday, the phone calls start. A dozen blue-blood mothers calling to let me know they won't be needing my services anymore for their daughter's wedding. It seems that news of my intervention at Shelly's wedding has gotten around. The gossip mill has been working overtime, bending truths, casting stones. I'm bad luck now, a meddler. Hire me and you might as well wear black to the wedding, might as well pray for rain.

"We just can't take the risk," says Mrs. Harrison, Kimberly's mom.

"I'm not anti-wedding," I tell her. "This was one girl."

She hems and haws. I can hear the ice tinkle in her glass, an afternoon boilermaker to make the day go faster.

"I just don't think it's your place, do you?" she says. "To come in, knowing nothing, and give these girls, these impressionable girls, frightened, to give them advice."

"I know," I say. "And I'm telling you, it won't happen again."

Silence. Her mind was made up before she even called.

"I don't expect my deposit back," she says.

That afternoon Mrs. Moody calls, Mr. Douglas. They all say the same thing. They can't take the risk. There's too much at stake. *Would you hire a midwife with a murder conviction?* one mother asks me. I tell them I understand. Part of me feels panicked by what I'm losing, the work, the money. But another part feels relief.

I call my connections at each of the wedding halls, looking for sympathy, insight.

"Just lay low for a while," they tell me. "People are angry. They don't like to be reminded how easy it is to call the whole thing off."

I take out my calendar, scratch off each canceled job. The rest of the year is suddenly wide open. I feel strangely buoyant, like a prisoner who's just been granted parole. I call my sister, take her to lunch. We order salads and wine.

"I think this may be it," I tell her. "I think I'm getting out of the wedding game altogether."

She nods, sips her wine.

"Are you okay?" I ask her.

She shrugs. I tell her about blacklist. She doesn't even get upset.

"Don't you want to ridicule me?" I say. "Tell me I'm being irresponsible."

"You're the older sister," she says. "You're the one who's supposed to have it all together."

"I know."

She finishes her wine, orders another glass.

"You're supposed to be the role model, the one I go to when everything falls apart."

"What are you talking about? What's falling apart?"

She shakes her head.

"Lisa," I say.

"We're postponing the wedding."

"What? Why?"

She screws up her face, and for a minute it looks like she's going to break down, cry, but she doesn't. I've never her seen her like this, hesitant, vulnerable.

"He thinks I'm a control freak. That I have power issues."

I don't say anything.

"I tell him it's not true. I just know better than he does. He's indecisive."

I poke at my salad, appetite gone. Another meal I don't feel like eating. I should write a book. The Heartbreak Diet.

What are we doing here? I wonder. Why can't anybody just be happy with what they have?

"I talked to this one couple," I tell her. "They made a deal. He was always right, but it was always his fault."

"What if he doesn't love me?" she says. "What if he's just afraid of me? Like I'm the army. A trap."

"He loves you. He just doesn't want to feel like your employee."

The waiter comes by to see if everything is satisfactory. I consider giving him a long list of grievances, mostly having to do with the infuriating nature of men.

"Do I really treat him like an employee?" she asks.

"Last week you had him redo the laundry because the pillow cases were yellow."

"He didn't bleach the whites."

I stare at her.

"Why would you bother to separate if you're not gonna bleach the whites?" she asks. "What? I'm not a control freak. I'm just . . . particular."

"You're a nightmare. When we were kids, you never let me play the way I wanted. Remember the Barbies? How I wanted Malibu Barbie to join the Peace Corps and follow Jungle Ken to Africa?

But you said no, Malibu Barbie didn't have all her shots. She had to stay home and marry boring old Businessman Ken?"

"I'm sure I never did anything like that."

"Oh, bullshit. You've been bossing people around your whole life. What are you so afraid of? That someone else is gonna make a decision you don't like? So what? You have to learn to compromise."

She winces.

"Don't use that word."

"It's not a joke, Lisa. You're just impossible sometimes. Bottom line: You can be a real bitch."

"Look who's talking."

"I know," I say. "I am too. I'm not saying . . . All I'm . . . I know I have a problem. And I'm trying to work on it. Not to be so uptight. So demanding."

"So negative."

"Yes. And you should consider . . . working a little bit, too. On you."

She doesn't answer, just pokes at her salad for a minute.

"Mom did a real number on us, didn't she?" she says.

"Hey, Dad was no picnic either."

She takes out a cigarette, lights it. For a moment my parents' marriage looms over us like a rain cloud, black, foreboding. We don't talk about it. We haven't for years. The subject is too spooky; to return to that age, to relive the feelings of powerlessness and fear. We know we're damaged. What's left to say?

But this time Lisa surprises me.

"What happened in that room?" she asks.

I swallow. The old me would dodge the question, change the subject, but sitting there, I realize I'm tired of running from my life every time things get difficult. The rules I've made to protect myself aren't working. So maybe I need to change them. Throw them out.

"He said he was lonely," I tell her. "And then he shot himself."

She thinks about this.

"How could he be lonely? We were all right there. Mom especially."

I poke at my food, push my plate away.

"He was mentally ill," I say, but even as I say it, I know it's just an excuse, a convenient rationalization. Because don't I feel lonely too sometimes, even when I'm surrounded by other people?

"You're not him," I tell her. "And I'm not him either."

"Are we her?" she wants to know. She finishes her wine, orders another. "I've spent my whole life trying not to be her."

I shake my head.

"We're not her either," I say. "You're just you, and I'm just me."

Lisa wipes her eyes. She looks haunted, uncomfortable, like she can't figure out where she is or how she got here. Like she thought she had everything under control, but now it's all going to hell.

"I love David," she says.

"I know you do."

"He understands me."

"He puts up with you."

She purses her lips, pushes out smoke.

"He wanted a jazz trio at the reception. I said, *What are we, sixty?* He got so upset. I've never seen him so upset. He said, *Why do you always get to choose everything?* I told him 'cause I was the sensible one."

"It's his wedding, too."

"But people are gonna come and see things and it reflects on me. I don't want to look stupid."

I wave the smoke from my face.

"Do you make faces during sex?" I ask her.

"What do you mean?"

"When you're having sex, do you make faces? Do you say things?"

"What kind of things?"

"If you watched a videotape of yourself having sex I bet you'd think you look stupid. But you know what? It doesn't matter. Because you love him. You make those faces, because it feels so good to love him, you don't care how you look."

"Yeah, but we're not doing it in front of Aunt Jackie and a hundred of my closest friends."

"What do you care? This isn't about them. It's about you. You think it matters what Aunt Jackie thinks of your wedding? I guarantee you, you won't even remember seeing her at your wedding. She'll be a blur, just like the rest of them. All that matters is that you're happy, that David is happy. I mean, it's your fucking wedding day. Don't you want David to be happy?

"Okay, I get it."

"To feel like he gets to be an equal partner?"

"I said I get it."

"Because the truth is, we don't control anything anyway. That's just an illusion."

"Laurie."

I sit back, pick up my wine glass.

"Now do me," I say.

"What?"

"Do me. Tell me what's wrong with me."

She smiles.

"You know what's wrong with you."

"I know. But I need to hear it. I need it tattooed on my arms, so I don't forget. So I don't go back to thinking I'm normal."

"You are normal. For you."

I take one of her cigarettes from the pack, light it.

"When did life become a self-help book?" I want to know. "When did it all get so complicated?"

"It was always complicated."

"No. People used to get married young and stay that way until they died. It wasn't all about personal growth and chronic dissatisfaction."

"And all the housewives were on Valium, and all the husbands had affairs," says Lisa. "Don't get nostalgic. Things were always hard. We just used to repress it more."

I stub out the cigarette.

"I just worry that one day we're gonna reach the point where no one's willing to put themselves out for anyone else. We'll be this race of selfish animals, dying out because we can't be bothered to connect."

Laurie puts her silverware on her plate. Neither of us has eaten more than two bites.

"I guess it's just about taking the risk," she says. "Putting yourself out there, without armor, without conditions."

"A human target."

I think about my shell. The turtle. What if I don't retreat? What if I refuse to cover up, to protect myself? What if I simply open my arms and close my eyes and say, whatever happens, happens? What if I told Gilligan that I love him and I want him, and I'll be here when he's ready?

The thought of it overwhelms me. The simplicity. The risk. Like jumping off a mountain top and hoping for an updraft.

Lisa sighs smoke, puts her cigarettes back in her bag.

"All right," she says. "I'm going home to grovel."

"Good."

She stands, puts on her jacket. My little bitch of a sister. I don't know what I would do without her.

"You're beautiful," I tell her.

"Don't ever change," she says.

But I am.

43

Jasper Tully is in his mid-fifties, a white-haired man with tiny glasses. I meet with him the following Tuesday, take the train into the city, lugging a portfolio full of pictures. I ride downtown in the back of a yellow cab, assaulted by brightness and noise, surrounded by bodies at rest and in motion, dwarfed by skyscrapers and history. I think about all the artists who've lived and died here. Succeeded and failed. All the photographers who've clawed their way into the limelight and the ones who've vanished into obscurity. Outside the gallery I stand on the sidewalk. A truck rattles down the cobblestone street behind me. I think about myself at twenty-four, how hungry I was for recognition, how this moment would have been a dream come true. And then ten years of wedding photographs, fifteen, and all the childhood dreams have been tempered. All the irrational fantasies of instant stardom, instant wealth.

I'm wearing black. I'm wearing Prada. I'm trying to look hip. Two days ago I got a postcard from Shelly. There was a picture of the Pacific Ocean on the front. I pinned it to my wall. Until recently I would have been envious of her escape, her take-life-as-it-comes attitude, but now the idea of an open-ended future seems irresponsible to me. What I want in my life is more grounding, not less.

I haven't talked to Gilligan since lunch last week. And yet, I feel strangely calm. After leaving Jimmy, after having lunch with Lisa, I thought I would go home and build a bomb shelter, retreat to a safe distance deep under the earth's crust, but I didn't. I had work to do, prints to make. I felt as if I'd reached the end of something. Like I had two choices: to collapse completely or just get on with my life. No matter what I did, how much I worried, something would happen. No matter how upset I got, how desperate. If I was happy, sad. Gilligan would come around or he wouldn't.

I am learning to let go.

I hoist my portfolio, walk inside, and show Jasper my work. He speaks with what he tells me is a Flemish accent. His hands are small, precise, like the hands of a jeweler.

"I see a lot of photographs," he tells me.

"I bet."

He turns the pages, spreading photos out on a long white table.

"You have a good eye for composition," he says.

"Thank you."

He looks through the stalker pictures. Damien on his knees, binoculars pointed up toward the sky. Melissa dancing, her eyes closed. The cops arriving, guns drawn.

"I love these," he says.

Heat washes through me, a feeling of levitation. For the last week I've felt like an ocean after a storm, everything slowly returning to normal, smoothing.

I stand, knees locked, swaying slightly. Jasper looks at the photos of battered women and their husbands, the bruised faces, the scraped knuckles; shuffles through the portraits of divorce.

"What do you think about blowing some of these up?" he asks me. "Showing them in light boxes?"

"I think that sounds great."

He looks at the photos of Nick and Clarice in the supermarket; Eric in his kitchen; Julia, the homewrecker, naked, arms akimbo. Looking over his shoulder, I think, *everyone I've photographed is just a different part of me.* A different face. Jasper holds a picture of Shelly up to the light. She's smoking a cigarette on the windowsill, her wedding dress glowing in the foreground.

"I've been married eighteen years," he tells me.

"Happy?"

He nods. He's wearing white cotton gloves. He reaches up, pushes his glasses up the bridge of his nose.

"I like the mix of black and white and color," he says.

The last picture in my portfolio is a wide-angle shot of Jimmy in his corner office, the city spread out behind him. He is smiling. His fiancé's picture is angled toward the camera. This man who loved me, who promised me everything. He has everything he wants now. And the truth is, I'm happy for him. I never wanted him to be miserable. I just didn't want to be miserable alone. He sits smiling at the camera, looking confident, relaxed. In the window behind him there is a ghostly shadow, a hint of the photographer frozen in the glare of the flash.

Me.

"I'm thinking April," says Jasper. "Does that give you enough time to print these?"

I nod, breathlessly.

"I can put you in touch with a good lab. They'll help you with the large prints, the light boxes."

"Great," I say. "Thank you."

"No. I'm excited. Philly was right. Your work is exceptional."

Outside, I stand in the middle of the street and smile at the sun. I am thirty-six years old and this is my new beginning. My moment of arrival. The city throbs around me, elevates me. Clouds are moving in from the west, bringing the first snow of the year. Soon everything will be blanketed in white. Soon I'll lie in my backyard and make snow angels with the neighborhood kids. Thanksgiving will come, and then Christmas. I will stand in my darkroom making prints for the world to see.

I'm a real photographer now.

Nothing has been wasted.

All the broken pieces have been salvaged and turned into something strong.

Real.

I stand on a New York City street corner and think,

I can do anything I put my mind to.

I will never doubt myself again.

44

When I get home later, there is a man sitting on my front porch, swinging in the shadows. My heart skips a beat. I find myself walking faster, clutching my grocery bag to my chest. But when I reach the stairs I see that it's just Jerome.

"What are you doing here?" I ask.

He stands, brushes at his pants.

"I wanted to apologize," he says.

"For what?"

"The way I've been acting."

I shift the groceries onto my hip. We haven't talked in three weeks. I can't imagine what he means.

"Forget it," I tell him.

"Here, let me help you with that," he says, and takes the bag from me.

I take out my keys, open the front door. He follows me in, puts the groceries on the kitchen counter.

"I've been doing a lot of thinking," he says. "And I realize I was projecting a lot of stuff on you."

I put my purse down, check my answering machine. There are three messages. I want Jerome to leave so I can listen, but I owe him some kind of resolution. I feel generous now. Good humored. I've found a part of myself I thought was gone forever.

Poise.

"Listen," I say. "I just want you to be happy."

"I know," he says. "And I know you've been through a lot of really hard stuff. With your husband and all. And I came to tell you I'll wait as long as it takes."

I stare at him.

"What?"

"You just take your time, work through it. I'll be here when you're done."

I go to the fridge, get a beer. He's like an echo, spitting back my own words, my own thoughts.

"Jerome," I say. "No."

"I love you, Laurie. And I know you love me. You're just too hurt to admit it."

I study him, thinking of Gilligan. Who am I to say my love is real and Jerome's isn't? What if Gilligan feels the same way about me the way I feel about Jerome? Apathetic, slightly repulsed. Maybe I'm fooling myself. Maybe Jerome is the best I can hope for. Two heartbroken losers standing around in an empty kitchen.

Maybe we've both seen too many movies where everything works out in the end.

I feel this wave of doubt, and I muscle it down. It's not the same thing at all. And if you ask me how I know, I'd say I just know. I'm not going to waste any more time asking unanswerable questions. For better or worse, from now on I'm going to have to take things on faith.

"Jerome," I say. "I'm in love with someone else."

He blinks at me, dumbfounded. A blush comes to his face, heat rising in waves. This isn't a scenario he had considered.

"What?" he says.

"I met a man," I tell him. "We've been going out for a few months. And . . . I love him."

He's shaking his head, as if trying to stop the ringing in his ears.

"No," he says. "That's not . . . I know you. The way you are."

In Jerome's mind, I'm a woman in need of rescuing. He is the noble knight, a romantic martyr. He will take whatever abuse I have to give, because he thinks he's stronger than me, that he can take it. He wants to be my faith healer, laying on hands, absorbing my pain. I study his face, the blush still in his cheeks. He's so young. I wonder what his mother was like. How needy she must have been. How demanding. Or maybe there has been a whole series of girlfriends who all made him dance like some drunken cowboy, bullets ricocheting around his feet.

"What we had was never about love," I tell him. "You knew that. I was always clear. We were just keeping each other company, blowing off steam."

"I know you said that, but I knew . . ."

"Jerome," I tell him. "Listen. Never try to read a woman's mind."

He opens his mouth to retort. I can tell he's been practicing this speech for weeks, going over and over it in his mind. Before he can get a word out the doorbell rings.

"Hold that thought," I tell him.

I go into the hall, open the door. Gilligan is standing there.

"I got your letter," he says.

His face is haggard. He looks like he hasn't slept in days. Seeing him, I feel panic. I want to grab him, but I also want to run. He knows my secrets now. My failures. There's so much I should say, but, caught by surprise, I worry I'll swallow the words, that they'll come out wrong. That nothing I say will make him stay.

"Hi," I say. "Good. I mean, come in. I just . . . there's someone here, but I really want to talk to you."

Jerome comes into the hall behind me.

"Is this him?"

Gilligan looks at Jerome. Jerome looks at me. I don't know where to look. We stand there for a moment, the three of us, everyone doing the math in their head. If I could, I'd crack open my suicide tooth, swallow the poison within. I'd fake a seizure, fall to the floor, spasming. I'd point toward the street and say, *Holy shit! What's that?* Then run and never stop.

"Okay," I say. "This isn't what you think."

"What's going on?" says Gilligan.

"I really wish you'd called," I tell him.

"I love her," says Jerome.

"Jerome," I snap. "Be quiet."

The look on Gilligan's face is like seasickness. It's road rage and outrage and zero gravity all at once.

"Jerome is an ex-boyfriend," I tell him. "Not even a boyfriend. We just . . . slept together. Before you met me. Before we ever talked."

"I see," says Gilligan, and from his tone it's clear he's only sticking around to be polite. That whatever doubts he had about me have now cemented. Not only am I a black hole of despair; I'm also, apparently, a cheap slut who bangs men half her age.

"I gotta go," he says, and turns, heading for the stairs.

"Wait," I say.

Jerome grabs my arm.

"Let him go. You don't need him."

"Jerome," I say. "If you don't let go of me, I'm gonna put you in fucking traction."

He releases me. I run after Gilligan, catch him at his car.

"Wait, please," I say.

He takes out his keys, fumbles with the lock.

"I love you," I tell him.

He stops, turns. His face is flushed, angry.

"You're a drama queen," he says.

"I'm not. I'm sick of drama. Sick and tired."

"You're self-destructive."

"No."

"You sabotage yourself. Maybe without realizing."

"I used to, but I don't anymore. Not with you."

His face is pink, eyes narrow. His hands are little fists. He looks like I feel, scared to death.

"You just can't let yourself be happy," he tells me.

I look him in the eye, feeling clear, unbreakable.

"I am happy. You make me happy."

He looks at me skeptically. I take a step forward, trying to coax him back to me like a frightened pony.

"I think maybe you're the one who's afraid of being happy," I tell him.

He stands quietly, face unreadable.

"I think you're doing everything you can to convince yourself that I'm not the right woman for you. But I am."

He backs away, looking for distance, perspective.

"I don't trust you," he says.

"I don't trust you either, but I'm trying. And you should try too, because it's worth it. We're worth it."

He kicks at the ground. I can see the breath leave his mouth, tiny white clouds dissipating. I take another step forward, slowly, not wanting to spook him.

"Look at me," I say.

He lifts his eyes, hesitating, meets mine. I smile at him. With my mind I tell him:

I will be clear for both of us.

My strength will be the strength of a hundred women.

"It's okay," I say. "I'm here. I'm not going anywhere."

He looks away. I can see his struggle. He had it all worked out in his head, but now he's not so sure. Nothing is what it's supposed to be.

"You make me crazy," he says.

"Good. You make me crazy, too."

He smiles, then just as quickly the smile passes. Sadness returns. The wind kicks up around us, blowing cold, making my cheeks sting. I'm standing out here with no coat, in just a T-shirt, but I don't notice. I put everything I have into reaching him, breaking through.

"I don't want to be alone," he says. "I'm tired of being alone."

"You're not alone."

He shakes his head. I want to put him in a headlock and drag him back into the house, throw him down on the bed, make him understand with my body.

"We can do this," I tell him.

We stand there for a minute making little clouds, like thought bubbles in comic books, except ours are empty.

"I loved my wife," he says. "And she died."

"I'm not gonna die," I tell him. "I'm too mean."

He doesn't say anything. I take another step closer, and now we are almost touching, almost connected.

"It just seems so implausible," he says. "Like we're trying to walk around the outside of a skyscraper on the tips of our toes."

"Don't look down," I tell him.

"Too late."

I put my hand on his shoulder. He doesn't pull away. I take that as a sign of progress.

"You want it to be easy," I say. "Foolproof. I do, too, but it's not. It's messy and terrifying and sometimes you wonder, what's the point? Because if it's this hard just to make a connection, it must be impossible to make it last."

He looks over my shoulder at the house.

"Jerome is watching us," he says.

"Fuck Jerome. Jerome is well on his way to his first restraining order. The point is, don't panic. Don't write me off just because I'm difficult. I know I'm difficult, but believe me, I'm worth the effort."

He looks me in the eye. The ground tilts under my feet. I think about New York. The show. I think about what Jim said, about being on the other side.

Around us the first snowflake falls, then another.

"That's the first nice thing I've ever heard you say about yourself," he says.

I stand up straight, looking at him through the ivory flurries.

"You make me like myself," I say.

He smiles. It's snowing harder now, the whole world speckled with white. I'm looking at his face. We're so close, the fog of our breath combines between us and floats up into the sky like a cloud. There is a look in his eye, a rawness, vulnerability.

I see three words.

The Loch Ness Monster.

Big Foot.

"I love you," he says quietly, and at first I think I've hallucinated it. It comes and goes so quickly, but then I look in his eyes and see that it's true. He said it. He means it.

And what happens next is scientifically impossible. Impossible because scientists are still trying to figure out what caused the Big Bang. What came before it. If inertia is a documentable phenomenon . . . if an object in motion tends to stay in motion . . . if energy begets motion, then where does energy come from in the first place? What happens to start the ball rolling?

One moment Gilligan and I are standing face to face. We are stationary, our eyes locked. The next moment he is leaning forward, his face coming together with mine. Where once there was nothing, now there is a kiss. Energy. An object in motion. He kisses me, and I am ten thousand fish swimming, turning as one. I am a flock of birds falling into a perfect V. He kisses me, puts his arms around me, and I am a herd of antelope racing across the savannah. I am every bee in every hive, every ant in every hill. With Jerome watching from the house, Gilligan takes me in his arms and puts his mouth on mine, and I am a snow cloud pouring its heart out on an open field.

And this is just what love is.

Impossible.

Scientifically, mathematically unproveable.

And yet here we are.

45

Lisa and David get married in April. She wears a red dress. A ship's captain in a white uniform with epaulets performs the ceremony. He talks about the beauty of the sea. The whole time Lisa is beaming, laughing. It's as if, after dragging her feet for years, she has discovered the slaughterhouse is really a waterslide. Relief lights her face. David looks stunned. He's wearing a kilt the traditional way, and every time there's a breeze he flushes and starts batting down the hem. I am the maid of honor. "My wedding slut," Lisa calls me, though thankfully she doesn't try to dress me. I wear a simple blue sheath, my hair curled and piled atop my head. My nails are shiny and white, and I try not to bite them. Before the ceremony Lisa and I sit in matching chairs having our hair and makeup done. We pass a bottle of wine back and forth between us.

"Worst kisser," says Lisa, sipping Zinfandel through a straw.

"Barry Egan, eleventh grade."

"With the harelip?"

"It was like kissing a sandwich."

Lisa puts her glass down, checks her lipstick. Her left hand is gripping the arm of the chair the way you clutch the armrest of a car that's going too fast into a turn.

"David was so cute last night," she says. "He couldn't find his lucky underwear. Ransacked the whole apartment. I said, baby, at this point our luck is set. For better or worse. A pair of underwear isn't gonna help."

J.T. uses a curler on her hair. He is a short man with bleach-blond hair.

"You have fabulous breasts," he tells her.

"Thank you, darling."

I look at J.T. in the mirror.

"What about me?" I say.

He looks at me, shrugs.

"Eh," he says.

Lisa starts laughing.

"Do you go tonight?" I ask her. "The honeymoon."

"Tomorrow," she says. "I can't wait. After three months planning the you know, all I can think about is having an umbrella drink on an empty beach. I just have to survive the next two hours."

"Try not to vomit," I say.

She sticks her tongue out at me. I study our reflections. We're two sides of a coin. Without her I never would have made it. I would have self-destructed in eighth grade, in high school, after my divorce. We're sisters. We hang onto each other. That's what survivors do, the vow they make. Even in the midst of all her wedding-planning chaos, Lisa brought me coffee late at night, pulling up in her Volvo, letting herself in. Even at her craziest she was looking out for me, making sure I was all right. I've been in the darkroom for weeks now, printing and reprinting. My gallery show is in five days. Tomorrow we hang. I'm so nervous I can't think, so excited I can't sleep.

"Relax," Lisa tells me. "You're gonna be fabulous."

But I can't help myself. At night I lay there second-guessing everything. Border or no border? Should I have gone with the platinum prints? I've studied the images so much they are burned in my brain. Shelly smoking. The support group. Mrs. Anderson. They've replaced my memories, my subconscious. I think in still images now. Black and white. Color. Every night Gilligan has to pull me from the darkroom and drag me to bed, often in a fireman's carry. Thrown over his shoulder, I watch the darkroom recede, protesting, wanting to get back to work.

But today I'm trying to put it aside. Today I'm thinking about Lisa. About marriage. This is the first wedding I've been to in six months, the first in ten years without a camera in my hand. I keep catching moments that would make great pictures, but I try to let it go. To let the world be fluid, a human experience instead of a series of frozen expressions. More than once I offered to shoot the ceremony, but Lisa said no.

"I want you to enjoy yourself," she said. "For once. For me. Will you do that?"

Now, sitting side by side, I reach over and grab her hand. She looks at me.

"Still tough," she says.

"Still tough," I tell her. "But now with more tender."

When my hair and makeup are done I wander outside to get some air. It is a beautiful spring day. The daffodils are just starting to bloom. Gilligan is waiting down by the water. He is wearing a pinstripe suit and shiny shoes.

He says, "It feels weird."

"What?"

"Being here. Invited."

I take his hand, watch the river.

"You could go back out," I tell him. "Climb a fence. Put on a fake mustache. Sneak past the ushers speaking a foreign accent."

He kisses my cheek.

"Very funny."

I love his smell. The way he tastes. I like to bury my face in his neck and open my eyes, so close I can't see anything but the blur of his hair. I like to be eclipsed by him, to press my nose to his nose, too close to focus. He makes me feel calm, because, finally, nothing is missing. We've become inseparable. Sometimes I look at him and I can't believe he's mine. That he wants me and only me. He moved in with me in February, squeezed his life into my tiny, one-bathroom house, a temporary fix until we could find something bigger. Now we drive around on the weekends, clomping through kitchens and sun porches, haggling over real estate, measuring. He has become my shadow. My closets are filled with his clothes. My shelves are filled with his books. Sometimes I trip over his shoes and can't believe my good luck. He drinks milk out of the carton and I can't stop smiling. He leaves the toilet seat up and I'm ecstatic. Because isn't this what everybody wants, a second chance?

I put my arms around him. The air is filled with the smell of freshly mowed grass.

"Everything is so good," I say. "I keep waiting for the other shoe to drop."

He straightens his tie.

"Why do people say that?" he asks me. "The other shoe. Like one shoe dropping is good."

I bite his shoulder.

"Work with me here," I tell him.

The ceremony starts. Music, the processional. Lisa is a glittering ruby. David can't take his eyes off her. He is smiling and crying at the same time. The moment is bigger than he can comprehend. The ship's captain prays for clear skies and smooth sailing. I hold the bouquet and watch Gilligan in the front row. He is listening to every word, his face serious. What will our future be? I wonder. I think about it all the time, but I am not afraid. I think about the fights we'll have, the stupid things we'll argue about. But I am not afraid. I imagine all the ways he'll get under my skin, all the ways I will confound him just by being myself. But I am not afraid. We will yell. We will struggle. We will stick. It is the choice you make. He meets my eye, and for a minute we stare at each other, and it is all there. Everything I need.

I look at my sister, focused, beaming, holding David's hand, and I understand why weddings are so important, why people don't just shake hands in private spaces and promise to stick together: Because making it public makes it real. Because turning the promise into an event is like carving it in stone. It's a celebration, sure, but also a dare. Say it out loud, sign the license, make it legal. This is how important it should be. So important that it takes a judge to break the covenant. So important that breaking the covenant ruins your life. Because when you're in love, when you're getting married, you don't want divorce to be easy. If it's going to happen you want to be destroyed, devastated, because next to love the only thing with any meaning is suffering.

But there is no suffering here today. No sorrow. Today we cry because we're happy. We watch the bride and groom in all their grace and beauty, and we picture ourselves up there, repeating the vows, making the promises. Their joy is our joy. We are together, wishing for a happy ending. I study my man. His eyes are wet, lips quivering. I love that he cries at weddings. That he is not ashamed. At night we lie in the dark and whisper. We say all the things we are afraid to say out loud.

"I don't want to lose you," I tell him.

"You won't," he says.

"Promise when we're old you'll open all the jars."

"I promise."

"And I'll remember everything. Where you put your glasses. Which pills you have to take on what days."

He slips his arm under my neck. His nose is in my hair, lips pressed against my skull.

"What about kids?" he says. "Will I be the good cop or the bad cop?"

"What do you want?"

"I don't like to sit backwards in chairs," he says. "It makes me nervous."

"Then you'll be the good cop. And I'll be the heavy, the leg-breaker."

He rolls over onto his back.

"Sometimes I get this incredible feeling of déjà vu," he says, and before the words have even left his mouth I know just what he means. Her. The dead wife. It hangs in the darkness, the words repeating in my head.

"Me too," I say. "Like I've been here before, in this car, driving to the supermarket, but then I look over and see you."

He adjusts the pillow under his head. I lean over and kiss him, just as I do at Lisa's wedding. After the ceremony, after the crying and the singing. After the ship's captain has blessed their union and they've kissed under a cloudless sky, and now it's time to party, to eat and dance and make drunken toasts. We walk toward the reception hall, animated, laughing. Lisa and David move ahead, greeting well-wishers. I try to catch up to them, but Gilligan grabs my arm, pulls me back. He puts his arms around me, puts his lips to mine. We are skin-to-skin, tooth-to-tooth, our breaths mingling. And I remember everything. Our first dance, the aquarium, the way everything's aged. But then I forget it all, because being here now feels so much better than living in the past.

When we part there is a photographer standing there, a young woman with cat's-eye glasses. She levels her Nikon at us and asks, can she take our picture. When we say yes, her assistant raises the bounce, throwing diffused, golden light onto our faces. And in that moment I am aware of all the things that cannot be captured on film: the smell of sod in the air, the sound of birds, of children chasing each other in the distance, the context of who we are, where we've been and where we're going. And I look at Gilligan and he looks at me, and there are no words to express anything. Just feelings. And these too, can't be captured on film, any more than they can be captured in words. The moment hangs there, on the verge of forever. Soon we will be a photograph, a frozen image of two people arm-in-arm, in love. A picture to be framed, to be slipped into the family album. A picture our children will look at after we're dead, that our great-grandchildren will see one day and wonder, *Who were these well-dressed, grinning people? These strangers.* A picture that will end up in a box in an attic somewhere or sold at an estate sale for twenty-five cents along with hundreds of other photographs of people who are no longer around. Because in the end images are disposable, but life—what it means to you when you're in the chaotic, voluptuous thick of it—is not.

The photographer adjusts the shutter speed, frames us against a backdrop of willow trees. Gilligan squeezes my hand. My lips are still tingling. The sun is so bright I feel translucent.

"Smile," she says.

And we do.

. . . And they all lived happily ever after.

Acknowledgments

Thanks to everyone who helped me when I needed it. You're the best. That includes, but is not limited to, anyone who fed me when I was hungry, anyone who gave me a ride when I was stuck, and anyone who watched my dog when I was out of town. Thanks to all the women I've ever kissed. Truly, those were the best moments of my life. Thanks to my agents and editors, and to the CEOs of all the giant conglomerates that publish and produce my work. Bottom line be damned—I know you're all about the love. Thanks to my family, especially Violet and Zander, the best kids in the world. May you never experience any of the things that happen in this book. Thanks to my dog, Ella. If you can read this, baby, you can have all the treats you want. And most of all, thanks to everyone who has ever fallen in love and stayed together. You're my heroes. And to those of you out there trying to make those relationships work, I say, *Keep trying. It's worth it.* Lastly, thanks to the Grotto. You know who you are. And to those of you who just got in my way and didn't help at all, I say, *Get out of the way next time!*